DEBRIDEMENT

Mike,

Enjoy! Just remember, this is a book of fiction — right??

Sean
2/5/2014

DEBRIDEMENT

A NOVEL BY

SEAN DOW

TWO HARBORS PRESS

Two Harbors Press
322 First Avenue N, 5th floor
Minneapolis, MN 55401
612.455.2293
www.TwoHarborsPress.com

ISBN-13: 978-1-62652-492-7
LCCN: 2013919292

Distributed by Itasca Books

Printed in the United States of America

For my mother,

who couldn't believe her sweet son

could think such things.

For my father,

whose relentless pursuit of right and wrong

has always been an inspiration.

I love you both.

———

CHAPTER ONE

My name is Jack Hastings. A few months ago, most people would have responded with an unremarkable "Yeah, and the sky is blue, what's for dinner?" Now, I'm the source of water-cooler conversations, the most famous physician in the country. My fan club outpaces that of many actors, and there even are rumors of statues—wish I could go see one.

I didn't graduate from one of the beautiful Ivy League schools with those vying to run our country's future. I don't treat (or kill) the famous stars of the entertainment world. Presidents don't come to my door, and I don't have a syndicated TV show from which to dispense advice for the ill or lovelorn.

Mine used to be a satisfying but relatively boring medical life, doing what all the others in my field do—wake up, save a life or two, go to bed, and then get up and do it again the next day. I loved what I did and could imagine nothing I'd rather be doing. New challenges and problems were faced every day, and I commonly had the chance to help people through some of the most difficult times in their lives. (It's probably best if I leave out the part about the nurses.)

I had no outrageous ambitions; no dreams of accomplishing anything more than the personal satisfaction of a life well lived. If I could make it through to the end, a comfortable retirement would be nice, but I'd be just as happy working until my time came.

Fate, it turned out, had an entirely different plan.

CHAPTER TWO

———◆———

I work at Intermountain Regional Medical Center, referral center for a large portion of the Pacific Northwest, as a specialist in pulmonary and critical care medicine. We are the redheaded stepchildren of the medical community. Nobody really pays us much mind until the sky falls, which usually happens around o-dark-thirty. Something changes after midnight and we somehow become caped heroes.

The typical call would come at 2:30 on a snowy January morning. "Jack, I've got this really fascinating patient in the ER. I don't know what it is, but something is wrong. Suppose you could go see him? If he's doing better in the morning, I could always take over, but I'd feel a lot better if someone like you could take a look at him for now."

Most days, by the time things settled down enough to allow me to venture home, I would feel like I'd been run over by a Mack truck. (Sometimes it's more like a Yugo, but I always know I've put in a full day.) Hippocrates' famous truism, uttered more than two thousand years ago, remains true: "Life is short, but the art is long."

CHAPTER THREE

Fall 2010

Another day in the can. One more Mack truck disappearing into the distance, multi-tread tracks firmly impressed across my battered torso. It was dinnertime or what often passed for it. A time to relax, catch up on the mail and drain the swelling out of my ankles. If she hadn't already hit the sack, I'd spend a few minutes talking the day over with my lovely wife.

I often look at this life I chose and wonder. High-stress hours stretched endlessly forward into my future, along with pointless meetings run by self-important hospital administrators, every one of them worth less than the close-door button in an elevator. They recently started speaking 'corporate' after a management retreat at a winery on the shores of the Columbia River. Hospital life has been a new version of hell ever since.

The highly paid consultants at the conference turned the

doctors into 'physician partners' and 'thought leaders,' and taught the upper echelons of management to "think outside the box." If the person who started that phrase is ever identified, his life expectancy will be seriously affected. It's one of the most annoying and pointless phrases ever created.

The hospital's capable managers excelled at keeping the employees in a state of perpetual fear, afraid to speak their minds, and they learned to perfect the glad hand technique as effectively as any aspiring politician.

"Jack, we'd *really* like your opinion on this," which translates loosely into "we'll pretend to listen and then do whatever the hell we want, and oh, by the way, screw you!"

A savvy vendor could make a fortune selling motion sickness pills outside the mandatory monthly staff meetings. Maybe that could be the ticket that finally leads me towards retirement.

Throw in expanding regulations from a government that thinks it knows medicine better than those of us who have practiced it for decades, coupled with steadily decreasing revenue and the ever present risk of lawsuits, and sometimes it just doesn't add up. It's fortunate that I can't remember how many times I have convinced myself to call it quits if one more three hundred pound patient comes into my office and tells me, "I just don't eat that much, Doc. There must be something wrong with my hormones."

I guess their bodies don't follow the same thermodynamic laws that govern the rest of us. Then there's the ceaseless parade of drug seekers and hypochondriacs, and I'm more and more often thinking it's time for a new career; maybe ice-road trucking?

Today, however, was one of those days where it all made sense. For the last week or so, I'd been battling the *Harvester* for the life of a sixteen-year-old girl. She'd left school Monday morning, telling her teacher, "it's just a headache. I'm sure I'll be back tomorrow."

By the time her mom came home, the normally vivacious teen was barely breathing and was covered with a rash that could only mean one thing: bacterial meningitis. A simple organism, *Neisseria meningitides;* it measures less than a thousandth of a millimeter. A million of them could fit happily on the period at the end of a sentence, and have plenty of room for more. Under the microscope, *Neisseria* looks like two marshmallows engaged in an intense mating frenzy. It scours our high schools and universities, where victims are just approaching the primes of their lives. Under the best circumstances, the fatality rate approaches 25 percent. Those who survive can face devastating permanent effects—deafness, kidney failure, fingers and toes amputated to bare stubs. Even the lucky ones can be faced with months of rehab. It is one of the most heartbreaking illnesses I see.

It looked bad for Jennifer. Nonstop seizures shook her body, eventually leading to coma. Her blood pressure, already dangerously low, dropped to a state of severe shock. Twice, I called her parents to come in and say their good-byes, thinking there was nothing left to be done, but somehow she'd kept going.

A steady stream of friends camped in her room, braving the threat of a highly contagious illness. They brought handmade get well cards and talked to her endlessly, discussing classes and future plans. Her walls were adorned with inspirational posters and playful pictures of her mongrel puppy, Fusion. It turns out she was president of the Science Club, as well as captain of the volleyball team and odds-on favorite for prom queen.

She came off the life support machine today, muscles wasted away like a concentration camp survivor. Her athletic body was easily down twenty or thirty pounds, and she was covered in bruises, needle tracks, and marks where tape had been ripped off, but she was alive.

"Jenny?" I asked hopefully. "Can you hear me?"

She opened her eyes, examining her surroundings. "Where am I?"

"You're in the hospital," I replied. "You found a way to miss a week of school. All your friends are so jealous. How are you feeling?"

She glanced around the room, taking in all the decorations covering the uninspiring brown walls, and saw that her parents weren't there. "I feel like shit. What happened?"

"You had meningitis, a brain infection. Things were pretty grim for a while, but you look great now."

"Yeah," she managed. "Great." She tried to smile, but her dried lips made it too painful. The best she could do was a weak shrug of her shoulders, but again, she was alive.

With illness of this magnitude, mental function can be seriously damaged. Once a patient is up from the constant sedation necessary while on life support, I typically ask a few common-knowledge questions to assess for confusion and disorientation, the bane of survivors of critical illness.

"Jenny, what year is it?"

"2010." She thought a moment. "October, I think. It seems like there was a football game on the TV while I was in and out, but I could have been dreaming. I've been doing a lot of that."

I was examining her heart and lungs while we talked. No signs of pneumonia or problems from being on the ventilator, other than a slightly scratchy voice.

"Who's the president?"

She rolled her eyes. "That guy with the made-up birth certificate. Mom voted for him. Dad still hasn't forgiven her!"

She'd be fine. Cases like this make the long nights and daily frustrations worthwhile and keep all the personal morbidities of the field at bay. They are the royal flush that keeps the gamblers coming back to the tables, the pot of gold that keeps us all chasing rainbows.

The rest of the day finished uneventfully and I was still floating in ecstasy as I turned off the bypass and pointed my car home.

My wife, Aurora, had already gone to bed by the time I got there. Yeah, I know, Aurora. She says her parents were scientists, but I think they worshipped the earth in other ways. I barely met them; they were gone in a car crash shortly after I met the best thing they ever did. A teenager coming home from the Friday night football game crossed the center line and there were two more statistics in the war on drunk drivers. Aurora and I were on our second date when it happened. Fate again, I guess. We spent the night in the hospital instead of at the drive-in horror fest we had planned, and have been together since.

Aurora will usually wait up for me, but my beeper had been going off so much lately that it had been at least a week since her last night of good sleep. Not a pretty picture; she can get irritable when she doesn't get as much as she needs. Me, too, but that's a different issue. I glanced into the bedroom. She was making up for lack of sleep now, performing a medley of her patented dainty 'girly snores.' She always denies these—"I do *not* snore!"—as if it would be some major character flaw if she did.

I, however, take after my father in that department.

Mom suffered hearing loss as she got older, always blaming it on dad. "It's like sleeping next to a construction site," she complained, "or a chainsaw symphony." We all laughed at the thought, but recent research has shown that she was right.

My own snoring is so bad that I have been thrown out of some pretty respectable motels, for breaking their noise ordinances. My buddies in elk camp had to take defensive measures; I was banished to an extra tent on the far side of the clearing. "If you're going to be calling grizzlies down from Canada, we aren't going to be in the tent to bail you out." I think they are just a bunch of girly-men, but what's a guy to do?

With Aurora already in bed, dinner would be alone. It was disappointing, but not enough to bring me down from the cloud of euphoria from seeing Jenny come back in such good shape. After dinner, there would be a few minutes with the new novel I'd been hoping to start, and then I'd probably fall fast asleep in my recliner. There would be no waking to the panicked shrill of my pager tonight. Call duties belonged to Dr. Gallows. He actually pronounces his name more phonetically correctly as DeGelos, but I suspect he's about the only one in the hospital doing so.

As tired as Aurora has been, tonight's fare would probably be some kind of staple—spaghetti with sauce from a jar, or that macaroni-and-cheese tuna casserole I lived on in medical school. That stuff can even be fried into patties in the morning to make a passable breakfast, and with enough hot peppers, the leftovers can be eaten for days.

When I'm off duty, the two of us work together in the kitchen. Aurora will show off her incredible talents, coming up with great stuff that could make anyone's dreams come true. Other times we just cook.

Opening the refrigerator, I was surprised to see a rare

treat—one of my favorite meals. A cheese-laden pastry shell waited, stuffed with a scallop and crab and shrimp filling. After warming in the microwave, it would be bathed in a thick vodka cream sauce. It's like a gourmet seafood version of beef Wellington.

Dessert was something new. I always liked it when Aurora experimented with me. She had made an airy cream-puff with what looked like a cream-cheese filling, lightly dusted with confectioner's sugar and with a fresh fruit compote ready to be drizzled on the side—it looked like heaven on earth. She must have worked all day to surprise me with such involved recipes. No wonder she was snoring. No sleep all week and slaving in the kitchen all afternoon, preparing a special treat for her war weary husband. Someday I'll have to tell her what a great find she is.

As the microwave poured out its delightful aromas, and I waited for the come-and-get-me chime, the doorbell rang. Nobody likes a phone call or front door visitor at that time of night. What are the odds of its being anything but bad news, unless it's really bad news?

There had been a lot of crimes committed in the area lately, and everyone was on the lookout. Looking back, I realize a hopped-up criminal gang would have been a far better option than what waited on my porch. I grabbed my Glock 19, my favorite pistol, and tucked it inside the belt in the small of my back. Should circumstances dictate, there would be no hesitation in putting it to use. I spend a lot of my recreational time target shooting and have done some IPSC competitions, a practical shooting sport that emphasizes a number of skills, some of which apply to self-defense situations.

Unfortunately, the bum on my doorstep was no career criminal, at least not in the common use of the term. He asked those dreaded words. "Are you Dr. Hastings?"

"Yes …"

He put forth an envelope, which I reflexively grabbed, only to hear him announce, "you've been served!"

I swear, he looked like he enjoyed doing it, and even though he was only the messenger, I had a wild thought of making it so he would never ruin another person's perfect evening. I might have even started reaching toward my back, but perhaps it was just a small scratch.

CHAPTER FOUR

This was my first time facing one of these. There is no easy way to describe the horror of a malpractice suit. They say that if you chose a life in medicine, you will be sued. I had naively believed that if I did things right, treated patients with respect and stayed current on the latest research, that I would be spared—the one doctor who escaped the lawsuit dragnet. Of course, I also had a belief that the Bears might someday repeat their 1985 season and bring back the Super Bowl Shuffle. A competent neurologist might conclude that there was something amiss upstairs.

Many of my colleagues had suffered through suits and I had seen what it did to them. All got depressed. Some felt their careers were ruined, and most radically changed the way they practiced—no longer treating their patients like friends, and doing every imaginable unnecessary test to avoid ever being sued again. It was defensive medicine, and it clogged up the system and made it vastly more expensive for everyone.

"Yes, Ms. Jones, I know we did that a few months ago, but you can never be too careful. You never know what a new CAT scan might show, and with all the cancer-causing foods in our diets, you can never have too many colonoscopies."

Some drank. Marriages failed. Some even quit practice altogether, losing all enthusiasm for the field they had formerly loved. Why go to all this extreme—years of intense training, delayed gratification, mountainous debt and hideously long hours—only to have some evolutionarily challenged, low-limbed lawyer stand before a jury and tell them that you are the worst thing humanity has ever put forward, and that it's their duty to punish you with a record setting judgment. Nobody got through one of these unscathed.

Making things worse, sometimes the local daily would publish the story, always in great one-sided detail, and always as reported by the plaintiff. Gwen Jones, a popular local pediatrician, had a tragic case a few years ago where a six-year-old child died. Meningitis there, too, if I remember. She did everything right, but it wasn't enough, and the poor girl didn't make it. Gwen grieved with the family and was even invited to the wake, but then a local sleazebag lawyer convinced them that the case must have been mishandled, and their daughter could have lived under the care of a capable physician.

The story in the paper made Gwen look utterly incompetent, an example of someone who should have never been allowed in the medical profession. Friends and patients dropped her faster than a politician leaving a sinking car and she wasted away into a pitiful apparition of the beautiful and caring person she had been.

I saw her coming out of Walmart one Saturday, empty-handed and crying. She looked terrible. Her normal trend setting clothes had been replaced by what Aurora referred to as 'fat pants,' something between pajamas and sweat pants, and designed for sitting in front of the TV or doing dishes, certainly not for wearing in public. Gwen's hair hadn't seen a beauty parlor in far too long, and she had the devastated appearance of someone who had been ruined and was ready to give up.

"Gwen," I said, alarmed. "What's going on?"

She went on without stopping, but then changed her mind and turned back.

"I'm sorry, Jack. It's that damned lawsuit and that article in the paper a few weeks ago. Everyone thinks the worst. I saw Aviv Einik in there. She's been one of my favorite patients for years. I went to her bat mitzvah. She started to talk to me, but her mom rushed over, grabbed her arm and dragged her away, looking at me as if I was some kind of a germ."

"I'm sorry, Gwen. I don't. . ."

"Why can't they just realize I did everything I could?" she cried.

I wanted to do something—wrap my arms around her slumped shoulders, hold her and tell her that everything was going to be okay, but the hopeless, anguished look on her face made me freeze. What she had wasn't contagious, but on some primordial survival level, my body wouldn't allow me to go forward. Looking back, I wish I would have done more.

Gwen seemed to understand. "She was just too sick, Jack. No one could have saved her."

She spun around and left without waiting for my reply. I don't know what I would have said anyway, but seeing her retreating back broke my heart. It was the last I'd see her.

Gwen's practice dried up. She couldn't even afford to pay

the malpractice tail coverage required to close her doors. It usually costs three years of premiums, billed as a lump sum, and is required by law. No exceptions. For a pediatrician in our area, that would be in the neighborhood of two hundred thousand bucks, probably more for her, with the ongoing suit.

She went off the roof of her office building, holding last year's family Christmas portrait in hand. The roof was a floor or two too low, denying her from reaching her objective, and now she is a permanent resident in a nursing home in Portland, breathing through a size 6 tracheotomy. Her daily nutrition is provided through a plastic tube snaking through her belly, her wastes leaving through a similar device.

She and her husband Bill had been guests at our house a few times. They seemed to have a storybook marriage. He wanted to sue the plaintiff's attorney but couldn't find another willing counsel to take the case. Professional courtesy or something, I guess. He works two jobs now, so he can afford gas to go see Gwen on weekends, and when I saw him a while back, he looked like he was pushing empty. If it weren't for the kids, I'm sure he would have found a taller building, himself.

The story isn't a complete loss. The girl's mother used the proceeds of the suit to build a two story, six thousand square foot monument to her daughter, far more stimulating to the regional economy than two economic reinvestment acts. The home was complete with a well-stocked wine cellar and a hot tub that could have been the envy of Hugh Hefner. Building the house required two lots. They were located diagonally behind my place, and if I didn't pull my curtains, I could see that she had found plenty of ways to help drown her sorrows. From the smiling faces of the men I'd see passing through the fake marble Greek columns framing her front door, I could see she was also doing her part to stimulate the local morale.

All this went through my mind in a matter of moments, compounded by the shame involved. No matter how innocent I was, meticulously following best-practice guidelines and stressing over details, there would be those who assumed that I was guilty of practicing inferior medicine. I thought once more about tracking down the subpoena man. It was just an idea, but it did provide a very brief moment of cheer.

The cold high desert air swirling past my feet brought me back to reality. In shock, my world had temporarily ceased and I had forgotten to close the door. I backed into the house, envelope in hand, still wondering how this could have happened. My first priority had always been the best interests of my patients, and as I mentioned, I had always assumed that I'd be the one physician who made it through. Life and other dreams, I guess.

CHAPTER FIVE

There was nothing outwardly special about the envelope. It was just like the other thousands that have come through my mailbox over the years, but its contents were about to transform my life. More than I would have dreamed, it turned out, and that's how I ended up here today, a curiosity for the nation. (And perhaps, somewhat of a hero, too?)

The return address showed Warren Moon, Attorney-at-Law. He was an adversary as dangerous as anything I battled at work; the varsity player of malpractice litigation in southern Oregon. Moon was a scumbag. There was no polite way to say it; he was as bad as they come. His presence could make spoiled milk smell like a fresh spring day, a summertime outhouse seem like a refreshing picnic spot. If there was a bad, he was a worse.

There was no catchy "Moon, Piederson and Steppleton." Even his own type couldn't stand him; they all thought he brought shame on the profession.

Moon did nothing but malpractice, and would file any claim any time. He was like the old fisherman—the truth was never in him. His ethical laissez-faire, coupled with citywide billboards and taxi signs won him an annual spot in the highest of the tax brackets. Going up against him in court was said to be the low point in a doctor's life, and cases were often settled needlessly, just to avoid the experience. The wonderful life I was enjoying a few minutes ago had just taken a huge step in the wrong direction.

I turned the envelope back and forth, afraid to open it. My mind raced to think of who might be doing this. Had I done something wrong? I'd be devastated if I'd really harmed someone. Sure, we all make mistakes, but I had always been so careful. I couldn't come up with anything. Of course, the malpractice statute of limitations was something like three years, so it could be from way back. And sometimes when a doctor gets sued, it isn't even him in the crosshairs. When a case is filed, everyone whose name shows up in the chart gets a dose of the fun, not just the one who supposedly did the horrific deed. Maybe it was from something Gallows had done and I was just a name along. I'd ask to be dismissed and go back to being the suit-proof doctor of my dreams, celebrating victories like todays for years to come.

Regardless, the envelope had to be opened. There was no way I was going to bed until I saw where this was coming from, and where it might be heading.

The last time my hands had shaken like this had been more than twenty years ago, and for a much better reason.

"Aurora," I had asked. "Will you make me the happiest man on the planet? Will you be my wife?" It's a wonder I didn't get a class 3 paper cut trying to get the damn thing open.

I pulled forth a sheaf of stapled papers, nearly a quarter inch thick accusation. I forgot to breathe as I unfolded it, tight heaviness constricting my chest as I straightened the creases and prepared to read Moon's allegations. Would this be a simple attempt at extortion, or could it be a legitimate claim of malfeasance?

Whereupon August 30, 2009, Mr. Leon Henry entrusted the defendant, Dr. Jack Hastings, licensed physician at Intermountain Medical Center, to perform lifesaving treatments, and with said defendant's carelessness and negligence leading to the tragic premature death of Mr. Henry, the court recognizes Mrs. Pamela Henry as the personal and official representative of the decedent in filing for compensation—

Eleven pages of being told in nearly undecipherable legalese what a worthless piece of excrement I was. The hospital was named for having granted me the privilege of treating patients and would doubtlessly soon be knocking on my door. The requested sum of 1.5 million punitive dollars, plus actual damages, of course, would apparently help to assuage Mrs. Henry's grief and allow her to achieve peace in this world.

Mr. Henry had been a nice guy. I remembered him clearly. We had gotten along well while he was hospitalized, even playing a few rounds of cribbage over the noon hour, at a penny a point. Good thing he got healed when he did, or I would have had to raise my rates to cover the losses. He laughed at my jokes, which the nurses generally refuse to do. (I'm sure it's because the serious nature of what they do has taken a toll on their sense of humor. I can't think of any other reason.)

He had suffered an acute PE, pulmonary embolism—several of them, actually. PEs are ill-formed blood clots that travel through the heart and lodge in the lung where they cause all manner of mischief. I remember reading in a specialty journal that they were one of the leading causes for malpractice claims. They can be extraordinarily hard to diagnose and are often not found until autopsy.

I gave expert opinion on a case a few years ago, convincing the malpractice carrier to settle. The doctor had fatally mishandled a massive embolism. The insurance company was grateful for my input, as I saved them the cost of the trial which they would have surely lost, and a significant judgment.

Treating pulmonary emboli can be just as difficult as diagnosing them. The blood clots themselves are dangerous, of course, but the blood thinner used to treat them can be almost as bad. It's actually rat poison, but in an attempt to get patients to comply with therapy, we generally refer to it by its medical name, warfarin. Prescribing too small of a dose can allow new clots to form, but the other extreme, overdosing, can lead to life-threatening bleeding. The required dose changes frequently, so constant monitoring is required, and even when perfectly prescribed, bleeding can still happen. We're interfering with one of the body's most important life-sustaining functions, the ability to stop bleeding—the results of doing that can be spectacular; the medication is truly a joy to manage.

Memories of the case were flooding back to me. Mr. Henry had died at home, shortly after leaving the hospital. He was happy with the care he'd received, but his estranged wife, Pauline, living in Portland with her new "roommate," was grief-stricken. When her next monthly support check didn't arrive on time, she tried to contact him. An emotional entry on page two of the lawsuit noted that she had been just about to contact her sorely missed husband, to reinvigorate their marriage, but now would never get the chance—forever denied the opportunity to mend what had once been the best marriage ever seen on earth.

My night of drifting off in my easy chair took a jet-stream cruise out the window, and all the day's happy thoughts went along for the ride. I reviewed the case in my mind, going over details again and again, searching to see if I had made any mistakes, but it was no use. I had tortured myself for days after he passed, searching the records for any clue as to something I might have missed or done wrong, but had found nothing. Mr. Henry had been the unfortunate victim of bad luck.

I turned on the television, but the mindless parade of late-night shows gave no solace; even the infomercials, my normal last-resort soporific, failed to produce sleep. I thumbed open my new adventure novel, guaranteed to be the best summer beach read of the year, but couldn't concentrate enough to get involved. I found myself reading and rereading each paragraph, not remembering what had just happened, and finally gave up.

I finally gave up trying to distract myself and went to take my chances in bed. I had quit watching the clock, but it was somewhere around the point where military recruits are getting ready to do more than most people do in a single day.

That didn't work out too well either. My tossing and turning led Aurora to offer a choice; I could either get out of bed or lose something very important—a sequel to the Bobbitt story seemed to be in the making. I wanted no part of that and decided to try out the new couch in my den. It hadn't been broken in yet. This might be the perfect time.

CHAPTER SIX

Somehow, the next day arrived, though it wasn't off to a very good start. Between the lack of sleep and the emotional trauma of the lawsuit, it was like coming back from a bad concussion or suffering the after effect headaches of a youthful all-weekend party. Of course, earning those had been a lot more fun. I must have had a few moments of shuteye, though, snuck in somewhere between when Aurora kicked me out of bed and the rising of the sun—enough to twist my neck into a sour funk, but not anywhere near enough to provide any sense of rest.

My first tranquil pot of freshly brewed coffee is normally the breath of life for my mornings. I jokingly call the programmable space-age brewing outfit Aurora bought me for Christmas my life-support machine. It had frequently rescued me after long nights, providing enough caffeine to get me out the door.

On more restful days, the first few cups ushered in the awakening in a splendid fashion, the highlight of the morning. In medical school, coffee was a different story. I used it strictly in a medicinal fashion, something I grudgingly choked down to stave off the inevitable sleep-deprived collapse, something to allow a few last minutes of studying before giving up on the day. It wasn't savored, it was I dosed. Now, coffee is the major component of my bloodstream, and I am seldom far from a cup. Juan Valdez is definitely on to something.

That day, my morning cups tasted as bland as the afternoon lounge dregs that so often got me through to the finish line, the high-end beans completely wasted. My mouth was too dry to even try a bagel, as if I had an appetite, and I struggled to find any excuse to avoid going to work. The only person I wanted to see was Aurora.

That's when I remembered my dinner. It had languished all night in the microwave. My heart was broken, throwing it out, and I resolved to tell Aurora that it had been spectacular, the best ever. It would turn out to be the first real lie I ever told her—there would be plenty more.

CHAPTER SEVEN

◆

I hated to do it. Aurora needs her beauty sleep more than most, but I felt I had to wake her and let her know what was happening. Repeated, gradually more insistent shakes brought her eyelids to half-mast. "Huh? Jack? What are you doing?—it's early."

"Good morning, honey," I said. "I'm sorry to get you up, but we've got a problem."

That woke her up. The long-standing rule was, don't disturb Aurora in the morning unless the house is ablaze or Ed McMahon is at the door. And I'm not entirely sure even the latter would pass. I learned this early in our marriage, and the kids had it down before their second birthdays. Even the pets that had crossed through our lives learned. It was just a fact of nature, something not to be questioned or messed with.

"What's going on?" she repeated, sitting up in alarm. "Did something happen with the kids?"

"No, nothing like that," I assured her, gently nudging her over so I could sit down. "I got served with a subpoena last night. I'm being sued. Some lady I've never even met is trying to collect a ransom off her dead husband's back. I almost woke you last night, but you were snoring so peacefully that I didn't have the heart. Dinner was great, though," I added.

Aurora took it better than I had. She even let the snoring comment go by as she gave me a lengthy hug. My platonic response, so out of my usual character, gave further evidence of the deep impact this suit was having.

"You look horrible, Jack, but this happens to everyone. You went a lot of years without a suit, longer than most. You're a great doctor and a great husband. You'll get through this."

"Thanks, but I don't know. Truthfully, I want to kill that son of a bitch Moon. I've never felt this way about anyone before, and I don't like it, but if he was here, I'd wrap my hands around his neck and wouldn't stop until I had choked every bit of life out of him."

"He's a real piece," Aurora said, "if even half the stuff I have heard about him is true. Isn't he the one who sued Gwen?"

"Yeah, and the bastard didn't even apologize after she jumped. He's a soulless sociopath. I suppose that's perfect for what he does."

"Well, you're going to be the one who beats him. Now, go to work and try to pretend none of this is happening. You'll do fine, once you get going."

I reluctantly drove myself to work, wishing I had the same confidence my wife had. The swirling gray skies and dripping rain matched my mood perfectly. Pulling into Intermountain's parking lot, I realized that I didn't even remember the trip. I had driven in some kind of dissociative state where I functioned, but without awareness of my surroundings. I shuddered, thinking of what could have happened. Innocent kids, cats frolicking in the street, all had been at risk, not realizing the malignant potential of the approaching car. Try explaining that to a grieving parent or to a kid who just saw his favorite pet smashed in to road kill.

The ICU nurses knew instantly that something was wrong.

"Good morning, Jack."

Typically, I would respond with a new one-liner or a flirtatious suggestion that they would studiously ignore. Today, their greetings fell on deaf ears.

Della, our superstar head nurse, looked up with concern on her face. "Lawdy, somebody musta put decaf in the docta's cup this mawnin'!" Getting no response, she went on, "Can someone *please* get Dr. Hastings? This 'body snatcher' alien imposter just ain't gonna do!"

I smiled. "I'm sorry, Della. Things aren't going so well all of a sudden. I'll get over it."

"See to it that you do, then, son!" She dropped her affectation. "What's going on, Jack? I've never seen you look like this. Is Aurora okay? Is there anything I can do?"

"No, Della," I said, reaching for my first chart, "but thanks for asking. I always know I can count on you."

I stumbled through my ICU rounds—no one died, and I escaped to the office. Rachel, my nurse and Maggie, my receptionist/organizer/stand-in mother, could tell something was wrong. They refused to budge until they had leveraged the story. It took them about five minutes, but I finally caved.

Maggie was indignant. "This just isn't right!" she said.

"Listen," added Rachel. She had been with me for years, and it was rare to see her so serious. Her irreverent sense of humor matched mine, and many patients had commented that having her there made coming to the doctor a pleasant experience. Some even said they came here just to see her.

"There isn't a better doctor in this town," she said. "No one cares more for their patients or works any harder for them. They all know that, and so do we. It's why we love working for you. You're going to win this, Jack, and everything will get back to normal."

"Thanks for the vote of confidence," I said. "It means a lot, but they picked Warren Moon for their attorney; it doesn't get any worse than that."

Grabbing me by the arm, Rachel said, "Let's worry about that later. We need to take care of a few patients. That waiting room is full, and they aren't going to see themselves."

I tried to get through the schedule, but it was impossible. I couldn't conjure up the normal upbeat, happy tempo my patients were used to. The joking and casual banter were replaced by a strict business-like approach. The patients I had loved for so long had been transformed into enemies, all seeking creative ways to destroy me. Even the simplest problems became major evaluations—the headache got a CT scan, the dyspeptic stomach was sent to the ER for a surgery consult. Everyone got labs or other testing. Rational thought and problem solving were fully replaced by technology and passing the buck—'sharing the risk' in the common vernacular.

Finally, when I asked Rachel to call 911 for a patient with a mild asthma attack, she and Maggie had had enough. They sent the rest of the patient's home and gave me clear instructions. "Come back tomorrow when you're ready to be a doctor again." Both had worked with me long enough to be safe saying something like that, and they were probably right. This would be a day better spent at home, tying flies or working in the yard, instead of inflicting my misery on those around me.

CHAPTER EIGHT

Over the next several months, very little happened with the suit. My lawyer, assigned through my malpractice carrier, had been through this too many times. He called periodically with an update, such as going over expert witness lists or potential deposition dates, but in reality, it was usually just an excuse to check up on me. He had represented Gwen and, like the rest of us, completely missed her warning signals. He didn't want a repeat performance.

After the initial shock had worn off, the suit became a nuisance in the background—a toothache that would occasionally flare, or a hemorrhoid—always there, quiet but ready to erupt. No newspaper articles came forth, and there were no hushed looks at the grocery store or people crossing the street to avoid talking to me. Nothing could slow the pace of my practice, though sometimes I wished it would. At times,

I would even forget the suit was out there, regaining some of the love I had previously held for my profession, but then I'd see Moon's arrogant face on a billboard or a television commercial and it would be right back as the dominant force in my life.

The annual request to renew my medical license came at the end of November. It was a strong-arm tactic; pay the state five hundred dollars a year so it could deem me acceptable to continue practicing the fine art of medicine. It's robbery, but there's no getting around it. This time, though, things were a little different. There was a spot on the questionnaire that I'd gone over so often that it didn't normally even register, something passed by year after year with no thought.

Question 7: Are you or have you ever been named in a lawsuit? If so, give all details—name of patient, date of occurrence, allegations and settlement amount. Provide copies of all applicable court records. They didn't even say please! All this was available to them with a few touches on a keyboard, through the National Practitioner Data Bank, but instead, they wanted the practitioner to regurgitate it to them in some kind of sadistic ritual.

I could picture them at the Board's headquarters in Salem as they reviewed the applications:

"Guys, check this one out. A podiatrist got sued. I win this year!"

"Yeah, well, I got a guy here who was sued twice, by the same patient! What kind of idiot would take care of his own mother-in-law?"

From now on, every time I filled out a license renewal or requested hospital privileges, signed up to be a provider for an insurance program or did anything that required credentialing, I'd have to go through all of this again. It would be out there for everyone to see and wonder if I had screwed up. The medical profession's scarlet letter would be stamped forever between my eyes.

This is where I started to think that killing Warren Moon might be a good idea. I had considered it a few times, but always in the most extreme abstract. When I'd see him driving around in his Maserati, or at the club working on his handicap, it seemed like such an awesome idea. Sweet revenge, and I'd be making the world a better place at the same time, but it had been just a wild fantasy—the dream of doctors across the country, I'm sure, but just that, a dream.

There were no truly serious thoughts in that direction, but the idea refused to completely die. I felt ashamed, but at the same time exited. Moon spent his days destroying other people's lives; no different from any other criminal, except that instead of going to jail he was getting phenomenally wealthy in the process. I knew that I could fix that, and maybe keep another Gwen from happening. The medical world would be grateful, and if I got away with it, I could even turn it into a new business—killthelawyer, or jurygonesolutions—.com. How about *Malpractice Disposition, Inc.,* eliminating problem lawyers since 2010. No job too small or too large. Call 1 (800) EAT-DIRT.

It had been a fun way to spend those long insomniac hours that had become my norm, a fanciful dream, but now, after filling out the license renewal forms I was actually thinking more seriously about it.

It's amazing how easily a man can convince himself of the rationality of an irrational action. Moon was a true pathology of the human race, a waste of skin. He was raining all over my life and would continue doing it to others as well, unless something was done. If there was some way he could be convinced to stop using the oxygen that someone else could put to better use, why shouldn't I do it?

Many scenarios went through my mind over the next several months. I dreamed that one day Moon would get sick and end up in my ICU, his miserable life placed in my hands. I know lots of nursing students who need practice with their enemas, and the residents have to learn somewhere too. Statistics say medical mistakes kill enough people to populate a small town every year—what's one more? Probably the only one who'd miss the old son of a bitch would be the tax man, and he didn't collect too much sympathy in this part of the country. His numerous ex-wives certainly wouldn't shed many tears.

The only problem would be finding a way to off him without it looking suspicious. ICUs are designed to save lives, not to bring them to an early end. Even if it were more practical, the odds of him finding a place in my ICU were too small to justify spending much time dreaming of how to capitalize on. If I was really serious about the idea, and I was starting to feel that I was, the next step would have to be more self-directed. An obituary space labeled Moon was sounding better every day. It was time to start thinking of how to make it happen.

I considered something showy, like the bomb-under-the-car plan, where everyone would know Moon's death was intentional. That would be incredibly satisfying, but hard to get away with. The cops would go through the long list of people who wanted him dead and eventually come to my doorstep.

I'm not a very good liar; maybe the old how much I'll love you in the morning line, but not to the practiced arm of the law. They'd catch me before we got past the introductions. The popular wisdom is that jail time has evolved from punishment to a near vacation status, but it's still not how I want to spend my last few decades. I have fishing trips to take, and someday I might actually see an elk on one of my fall hunts. The shower sex scenes don't work so well for me, either.

No, as much as I would love for Moon's death to be a shining example to the other malpractice purveyors, a subtle, natural-looking exit would probably be the best choice.

Chapter Nine

I talked myself out of killing Moon at least a dozen times, but the idea refused to die. In April, the two opposing sides in the suit had a meeting. Stan Martin, my attorney, briefed me that this was just a formality. We'd ask for a dismissal, and Moon's side would offer a ridiculous settlement amount that neither side expected to be accepted, and then we'd try to set a schedule and exchange lists of expert witnesses and go through all the other boring pre-trial necessities.

Stan warned me not to speak except when asked a direct question, and to answer in the simplest possible terms. Everything was to be recorded by a stenographer and would be admissible in trial—I was not to give them any unnecessary material. He tried to be reassuring, but I knew that at 0-3, Stan was no match for Moon. I could decline his services and hire my own counsel, but a quick check showed the cost to be prohibitive. The cheapest recommended lawyer charged three hundred and fifty dollars per hour, and required a twenty thousand dollar retainer. It looked like I would be going in to this trial seriously under gunned.

Moon was a bombastic prick throughout the meeting, trying every trick to set me off, but I played my role well, at least until he cornered me in the restroom.

"I know everything about you, Hastings," he said. "I know where you bank, where you eat, and where your wife shops while you're at work. I know the route your son takes to school and where his girlfriend lives. There is *nothing* I won't do to win this case. I suggest you think about coming to terms today."

I was about to reply in kind when I saw the edge of a tape recorder under his suit. Clever bastard; he'd have had me except for that. I leaned forward as I walked past, speaking directly into his recorder. "See you in court, my friend."

I told Stan about the encounter and how close I'd come to falling for his trap.

"Damn," he said. "He's escalating. This is a new low, and for Moon, that's quite an accomplishment. He must have a new divorce on the way or maybe some debts at the track. He usually saves the theatrics for the courtroom. I suggest you watch your back. I don't know if you are aware, but he does have a criminal background. It's why he had to leave his first job. He had been an up-and-coming defense attorney and was starting to get some A-list clients when he got busted for assault and battery.

The cops were thrilled when he had to drop down to civil law. His best criminal defense had been to ruthlessly attack the involved officers. He ruined several careers. The cops hated him so much that there were rumors of a contract going out on his life. This guy really is bad news; don't take him lightly."

CHAPTER TEN

I was in the office after the meeting. I had been unable to relax since the bathroom encounter with Moon and after hearing Stan's words of caution, I warned Aurora and our youngest son, Zach. Both had agreed to avoid any kind of contact with him.

I was about to head for my first exam room when a good friend, Griff Reeder, showed up. Zombies from a B-grade Hollywood movie looked more full of life than he did. Griff dropped in to the chair facing my desk, the one I use when I have to give patients especially bad news—cancer, AIDS, the cafeteria is serving menudo, that kind of thing.

"Jack, they're suing me!" he cried. "The bastards served me *right* in the office. Timed it so I'd be right in front of my patients and my staff! They made me look like a fucking criminal! I didn't do anything wrong. Why are they doing this?"

"That's pretty low, Griff," I agreed, settling into my own chair. The patients could wait.

"Its worse, Jack. They hired that bastard Moon—no one ever beats him. We work our asses off day and night, and he comes along and gets the benefit." Griff dropped his head into his hands. "He doesn't care who he hurts or how much he damage he does, all he wants is his next payday. I don't know what to do. I can't go back and face my patients, there's no way I'm up to that." He paused, a sudden realization.

"Oh, God!" he said. "How am I going to tell Linda?"

I remembered what it was like the day I was served, and wondered how much worse it would have been to have been served in such a humiliating manner.

"Take the day off, Griff," I said. "I'll cover your patients. Take Linda out for dinner and then go home and try to relax. Get some sleep."

"How can I relax?" he asked, holding out his trembling hands. "Look at me! I want to kill that bastard. I could take him out in the desert right now, and put a bullet through his arrogant head!"

I scrawled him a prescription for a half dozen Xanax, something I would have killed to have had in my medicine cabinet when I was served. It would be enough to get him a little peace but not enough to hurt himself, if he got any crazy ideas. "I've had similar thoughts, my friend." I smiled. In my mind, it was the final straw. There would be no more doubts, no more back-and-forth moral wrestling. Warren Moon was going down, and the world was going to become a better place.

CHAPTER ELEVEN

In my early daydreaming, I had already decided on the first step, that a natural-appearing, "non-homicide" death would be the way to go. Figuring a way to make it happen, though, took more effort than I would have imagined. A fake suicide would never work. The man had no conscience, so no one would ever believe that he felt guilty enough about anything to end his miserable life. A sneak attack with 10 milligrams of vecuronium would work, and be a particularly gruesome way for him to exit this world. Vecuronium is a modern-day synthetic in the curare family, producing a rapid and complete paralysis of all voluntary muscles. It serves a vital role in the ICU, but is not so beneficial elsewhere. Moon would go down like a ton of bricks, unable to beg for help or even to breathe. And while it eliminates muscle function, it has no effect on the mind or the heart—death would come slowly and in a most unpleasant fashion.

I wasn't sure I had the heart for that degree of malevolence, though. Even when I have to kill a cockroach, I try to do it swiftly so it doesn't suffer. I'm just that kind of a guy. And with all the effort to educate the public on CPR, some well-meaning Good Samaritan could pump his chest and keep him alive until the paramedics arrived, under the mistaken impression that they were doing something good. Moon would recover, and tell the police about the needle stick in his ass, and next thing, they'd be knocking on my door, looking for someone with a grudge and access to ICU medications.

A massive overdose of potassium would work. His worthless heart would beat its last, and his demise would look completely natural. It would be a peaceful exit, too, far better than he deserved, but one less troubling for my conscience than the paralytic. It would be the potassium, then, though getting him to comply with the treatment plan might be a problem. It had to be injected intravenously to have the desired effect.

"Hey, Warren, how ya doing? Could you do me a favor? Pop up a good vein there on your forearm. Yeah, that one looks great, then shoot this in for me? That's it. Right up to the hub. Thanks, man, you're the greatest!"—probably not going to happen.

The solution came when I was doing the ritual office clean-up, something I do every year or two. (Or three) And yes, I can clean, I just don't make a habit of it—bad for the male image. I found a brown paper sack, folded and carefully 'filed away' in the back corner of a cabinet in Rachel's room. Georgia Rains had brought it by after her husband died. He had been a favorite patient, always sharing a story or dirty joke. Georgia smiled disapprovingly, but it was obvious they had that old-fashioned kind of love we all hope for.

"Dr. Hastings," she had said the day she brought the medications by. "I just had to thank you one more time for all you did for Herschel. You made it so nice as that cancer got all through him, and I swear, it seemed like you were taking care of me at the same time. I've told everyone how wonderful you are. Thank you so much. I wish the world was filled with people like you."

I smiled, thinking back to my last house call at their ranch. Herschel was clearly dying but wouldn't consider not sitting with Georgia and me at their rustic dining room table. We reminisced about their life in the country. They both insisted that I stay for coffee and who knows how many rounds of her unbelievably delicious coffee cake. I heard about cougars and droughts and harsh winters where they had been cut off from town for weeks at a time. They recounted a bit of history I had forgotten, about a manhunt that ended on their place in the early 1960s.

A mass murderer had escaped from a transport train, killing three guards with his bare hands. He led the authorities on a bloody chase through several states, but picked the wrong place to hide when he got to Oregon. Georgia was hunting rabbits when she came across his footprints in the snow. She followed them to an old mining cave at the back of the property. The escapee was just finishing an act of nature when Georgia arrived. She trained her rabbit gun on his private parts, and marched him shivering and naked back to the house, where she and Herschel held him until the police arrived.

Herschel got a lot of good-natured grief for letting his wife defend the ranch. They declined the reward, telling the police that it was just the way people did things around here, but accepted a certificate of valor. It was presented at a ceremony in Washington, DC, signed by J. Edgar Hoover. It held a place of honor above their fireplace.

Hours had gone by before they let me leave. I had eaten so much of Georgia's coffee cake that it was all I could do to waddle to my car. Fastening the seatbelt across my greatly expanded waist was too painful, so I let it retract back into the holder. My ride home was a mental endurance exercise, listening to the ever more strident warnings of the car's automatic conscience. I couldn't eat the dinner Aurora had prepared, coincidentally, and unfortunately another gourmet effort she had spent hours on. She understood completely, though it was tough to understand her clenched words through the locked bathroom door.

"Georgia," I had replied, taking the bag. "I haven't touched a piece of coffee cake since that evening at your place. There's just no point in going on, once you've had perfection."

She blushed with pride, and then pointed to the bag full of Herchel's medicines. "Please give these to someone less fortunate. They are so expensive that I can't bring myself to throw them out."

I looked into her smiling face and couldn't bear to tell her that it was technically illegal for me to pass them on. "Thanks, Georgia," I replied. "I'll see they get some good use."

CHAPTER TWELVE

That Saturday was typical for my free weekends. If I had been on call, it would have been sunny and mild, with nothing more than the gentlest suggestion of a stirring breeze. In the spring, butterflies would be gently drifting from one flower to another. In the fall, kids would be playing make-up football games, and lovers would be basking in final days of sunshine. Give me a few days off, however, and it will inevitably drop twenty degrees below the fictional *average* temperature the weather propagandists keep putting out there for us, and the sun might or might not make a cameo appearance.

The temptation to stay in bed had been almost hypnotic. Aurora was feeling it too. I had a moment of hope when she turned over to me and said she had found the perfect way to spend the day. I was about to tell her I'd send our last remaining at-home son on an all-day errand, when she squashed my very much non-platonic dreams.

"I thought we could get out the home movies. It will be a perfect day. We can pop some Orville Redenbacher and invite the neighbors. They could bring their movies, start up a new tradition."

I suppressed my first response—"what did the Clements ever do to make you hate them so?" just before it escaped my lips, possibly preventing an embarrassing trip to the ER. The ability to think quickly and calmly in emergency situations is what separates the great doctors from the ordinary ones. It can't be taught in class, you either have it or you don't. I had always excelled, and it had saved the day over and over. That Saturday was one of those.

"Honey, that's an awesome idea. I've never heard better, but I've been planning to clean my office this weekend. Did I forget to mention that?" I was dressed and out the door before her disbelieving look could force a confession—my second lie.

The easy cleaning was almost done, but I still had some time to kill before it would be safe to return home. By now, Aurora would have figured things out, and a cooling-off period was in order. That's when I came across Herschel's bag of medications. Sitting on the floor, I upended it, and the bottles spread out like a Halloween night's overkill bounty. Looking through the swarm, I found a nearly full prescription of alprazolam, the generic name for Xanax—Momma's little helper. It was a tranquilizer so powerful that it made Valium look like yesterday's news.

A handful of those down Moon's throat, and the potassium problem would be solved. Then I could get a needle the size of a tent stake into any vein I wanted, and give him his final vaccination. Those magic pills produce such a state of tranquility that Moon would probably even help. One step closer, but another step raised, rather ironically.

For years, I have battled patients' constant begging for Xanax. They have tried every excuse imaginable to get me to write a prescription or to get an existing prescription filled ahead of schedule. Pills had been stolen; they'd been "miscounted" at the pharmacy; they were flushed down the toilet—not sure how that one happens, but it's a favorite. It never seems to happen with blood-pressure pills or cholesterol drugs, though. I've had people ask for refills because they were called away for an emergency family funeral (again) and even had one claim that the cat had peed on his pills.

"You can't expect me to take those, can you?"

Now I had a situation where I desperately *wanted* someone to take them, and I had no good ideas of how to make it happen. If I could break into his house, I could spike his iced tea, and then hide out until they took effect. It would be tough to do without leaving evidence, but it was the best I could come up with.

I staked out his place in Clarksdale Woods, a quiet, high-end neighborhood, one of the most expensive in town. Tasteful lawn ornaments decorated acre-sized lots, with carefully manicured stems of bluegrass surrounding sculpted shrubbery displays and marble fountains. There was a complete absence of pink flamingos and dismantled side-yard auto projects, and no one clung to last year's Christmas light displays, like they do in my neighborhood. "Why take them down?" my neighbor had asked, his theory very similar to my attitude toward hanging up laundry when I was single. "I'll just have to put them up again at the end of the year."

Criminal activity is fresh ground for me. I didn't grow up in a family of habitual lawbreakers. There would be no wise mentors showing me the way. I was going to have to learn this on my own, though at least I had a small head start. Aurora and I are enthusiastic readers. I can get so wrapped up in a good novel that sometimes I feel as if I'm there as the main character, dodging danger and finding my way through impossible mazes.

Crime novels are a staple for Aurora, to the point that I sometimes wonder if she is studying to learn how to commit the perfect murder. I slept lightly for a week when she finished Kathy Lette's *How to Kill Your Husband*. Aurora swore it was a simple, lighthearted comedy, and she did laugh until she cried a few times, but there were other times when I caught her giving me an unusual, thoughtful look. And usually, when she finishes a book she really likes, she suggests I have a go at it. I asked her to put it on my shelf when she was done but she replied, perhaps a little too quickly, "its more of a woman's book, honey. You wouldn't get it."

She also loves *CSI* and its thousand spinoffs (at least if there isn't a more intellectually stimulating reality show airing), so I had those to go on, too. Unfortunately, the criminal, no matter how clever, always seems to get caught. Not the endpoint I was after, but they did have a lot of information on how the cops figure things out.

Over the years, I had learned from these, but for the most part, it was going to come down to homework and common sense. Moon had to die and it had to look natural. If I screwed it up and the police suspected homicide, medical professionals would have top spot on the list of suspects—our town is woefully short on criminal gangs randomly doing charitable homicide work. Doctors such as myself, who were his recent targets, would head the list.

One necessary skill would be lock-picking. I had to have

some way to get into Moon's house. I scoured the local book-stores until I found a few good references.

"We don't sell many copies of lock picking books," the clerk said. "Starting kind of late in life to begin a criminal career, aren't you?" Fortunately, she was smiling as she asked. Not intrusive, just conversational in the light-hearted manner that sets a good employee above those who are just putting time on the clock.

I smiled back. "You caught me! Where did I go wrong?"

"It was that cagey look," she smirked. "I've seen it a million times."

I think she liked me.

"Actually," I said, "I've gotten tired of spending my week-ends fighting the dandelion wars. For years I've thought about writing a book. I've finally decided to go for it. These are to get some details to make it more realistic."

I counted out the cash and smiled broadly at her. "And if the book fails, house-breaking can become my fall back career! That is, if the lumbago doesn't keep me down."

It was an easy lie. Writing has actually been a dream of mine for years. The few times I got started, something always got in the way, or my plot would fizzle out. I once got a good start on one, in which I was a globe-trotting, wealthy, playboy sex-aholic, but Aurora told me I didn't have the background research to pull it off. I assume she was talking about the travel.

A spy story failed from the start, and I fell asleep writing my autobiography, doubtlessly saving my audience from the same fate. I wasn't seeing international acclaim sneaking up on me. My best effort was a post-apocalyptic novel with starving zombies chasing resourceful heroes, but even that died after a dozen chapters. I kept reading it and rewriting everything I'd done, searching for perfection until I got sick of it. I think it's still on a shelf somewhere. Maybe I'll go back to it later, but for now, I'm going to have to stick with medicine.

"Can I have a copy when it's finished?" the clerk asked. "I love to read, and it would be great to know an actual author."

Yep. She definitely liked me, but then, who could blame her?

"First copy off the press is yours!"

No place in town sold lock picks. Perhaps I should have a chat with the chamber of commerce. They always want us to buy locally instead of relying on the Internet or traveling over the mountains to Medford, yet you can't find the most basic items! I used a computer at the library, hoping no one tracked the user's ID, and had a set delivered to a post office box I had registered under an assumed name. While waiting for its arrival, I studied the instruction books until I felt confident I had the fundamentals. I couldn't wait to spring my first lock.

The confidence booster that I really needed was the opportunity to practice on Moon's lock, but I assumed he'd object if I asked. All the homes in his division had been constructed by one contractor. I actually took care of him in my office once, when it looked like he might have lung cancer. He was thrilled when I gave him a clean result, and he offered to build a home for me at a tremendous discount, but it was still a little out of my comfort zone. Anyway, with just the one builder, it seemed logical to assume that the houses would have similar locks.

I devised a plan, drove to Moon's neighborhood, and selected a house two doors down from his. A lovely elderly lady met me at the front door. I felt terrible about deceiving her, but I needed to see what I would be up against when I made my move against Moon.

"I'm sorry, ma'am," I said, gasping for breath. "I hate to

bother you, but I was walking my daughter's dog—little white Jack Russell?" I briefly spread my hands out, about shoulder-width apart, and dangled the leash I had just purchased. I returned my hands to my knees, still breathless—"I can't believe I let her off the leash. She just loves that, you know, and I always pick up after her, but a stray came along and chased her off. She's such a coward. Anyway, I feel terrible. I chased her until I couldn't keep going, but lost her some-where around here. Have you seen her?" Without waiting for her reply, I spun around. "Clarabelle! Here, Belly! Where are you? Come to Daddy!"

Her distress was so evident that it made my guilt over the deception even worse.

"You poor dear," she said. "I haven't seen her, but I'll look about. Let me get you some water. You look like you are about to fall over."

As she disappeared toward her kitchen, I stole a quick look at her lock. Kwikset, excellent. I thanked her for the water and then set off down the block, looking for Miss Clarabelle.

I bought several Kwikset models, from different stores, and set about learning to pick them. At first, my efforts were noisy and slow, but with practice, I got to where I felt completely at home with them, even practicing in the dark.

With entry into his house solved, I still had to find a way to get him to take enough Xanax to make him more recep-tive to his terminal electrolyte infusion. I was coming up with frustratingly few ideas, and none that seemed reliable enough to stake my future liberty on.

I was starting to think it might be time to explore some new options, but one thing was certain. Moon's reign of terror had come to an end. There would be no more Gwen's leaping from roofs, no more Griff's being intentionally humiliated in front of an office full of patients and staff. No matter how it happened, the ambulance-chasing fraternity would soon be down by one.

CHAPTER THIRTEEN

Do you believe in luck? Coming home from a late call back to the ICU, I passed by Gilligan's Bar and Grill. Its location, just a few blocks down Sixth Street, literally in the shadow of the hospital, was fortunate. It provided a steady stream of customers for the emergency room, lining up for their genital swabs and antibiotic injections. I wish I had stock in the company that makes Rocephin, with so many short term romantics coming in with their painful drips, but I generally kept my investing away from pharmaceuticals to avoid any appearance of a conflict of interest. Not that I had enough to invest anywhere seriously enough to make a difference, it was just the appearance. So many doctors have their own labs and X-ray facilities. I wonder how often they are tempted to do a few more tests than are really called for, to help the bottom line. It was a road I didn't want to go down.

A silver-gray Maserati Gran Cabrio was parked in front of Gilligan's, conspicuously placed where all inside could see. There couldn't be too many people in southern Oregon driving cars with insurance premiums higher than most of our mortgages. It looked like Warren Moon was on the prowl. My court date hadn't been set yet, and if he died tonight, it might never be. It would feel so good filling out my future license applications to go back to checking no in the lawsuit portion.

Entering Gilligan's, I saw it was indeed Warren, and he was in full swing, taking a shot at the most attractive girl at the bar. He was dressed in an expensive shirt—I wouldn't know an Armani from a Versace, but I could tell it was way beyond the norm for our part of the world, where camouflage was the rule and where cowboy boots outnumbered work shoes by a sizable margin.

Moon's shoes looked like they belonged to someone who took style seriously, and the gold chain around his neck must have finished the look he was going for, as he seemed to be feeling pretty good about what it all did for him. I'm not sure what it is about some middle-aged men that makes them think that they could sweep a twenty year old calendar girl from her feet, but Moon clearly thought he could be the one. I have been married and out of circulation for a while, so I suppose it's possible the dating rules have changed. Moon had a good-sized pot belly developing; perhaps that had become the new sex symbol. Maybe, but I was a little skeptical.

Moon was a touch inebriated, and I've heard that can have a bit of an effect on a man's perceptions of a woman's interest. The object of his desires was listening to his tales about whatever he thought was so wonderful about himself when her boyfriend came back from the head. Things were about to get a whole lot more interesting.

Posturing with his steroid-enhanced physique, the boyfriend barrel-chested up to Moon in a classic male dominance display. I was reminded me of something I'd seen on an episode of Marlin Perkins' *Wild Kingdom*.

"Who the hell are you, asshole, and what do you think you're doing?" the boyfriend snarled.

I looked around for the videographer.

"Are you trying to start something with my girl?"

Moon was backed up against the bar, struggling to keep his balance. His dream girl was glowing in the limelight of her beau's jealousy.

"Whoa, kimosabe," Moon said, sidling down the rail. "Do you have any idea who you're dealing with?"

Not impressed with the bravado, Mr. Biceps edged Moon further, literally bending him over the bar. I'd be in traction for a month, positioned like that, but Warren had a fair amount of liquid muscle relaxer flowing through his veins and seemed to be handling it fairly well. Still, there could be no doubt who would be left standing if things went physical.

"Okay, okay," Moon said. "I was just asking her if she had the time. It's all good here!"

There was a moment when everyone was turned in that direction, and before I even had a time to think it through, Warren's amber-filled glass of 'exuberance on the rocks' was now itself in a highly intoxicated state, loaded with several milligrams of alprazolam. I might have overdone it a little, not having a lot of time to meter out a more appropriate dose, but he was a big man. Who says he couldn't handle ten times the normal dose?

If Moon made it home alive, he was mine. If not, the problem would be solved just the same. Either way, his next appearance in the newspaper would bring joy to physicians across the region.

I had plenty of time to see this through to its finish. It had been late when I left the hospital, so I hadn't called to tell Aurora that I was heading home. I didn't want to run the risk of waking her. If she was still up, which was doubtful, she'd assume that I was hard at work, desperately trying to save someone's life—her husband, the hero! The contradiction brought on one of those famous shit-eating grins. I'm not quite sure where the expression came from, a face full of crap wouldn't make me grin, but regardless, there hadn't been very many of them lately and it felt really good.

The perpetrator of my misery had backed down before the much younger and highly motivated foe. He polished off his drink, and went back to his first prospect of the evening, where it looked like he had better odds. There were fewer years between them, and she was a little wobbly on her stool, as if the night hadn't been too kind to her. Warren signaled the bartender, probably to order an insurance round—"the wedge," as an old roommate used to call it. He had just gotten the bartender's attention when the ultimate date-rape drug hit.

I'll have to give Moon credit; he started for his keys, thinking in some slack-jawed way that he'd drive himself home, and then decided against it. The MADD ads might have made an impression. Either that, or when the keys slipped through his fingers and he sprawled next to them on the floor, a ray of common sense might have entered his brain. Three times, he tried to stand, staggering sideways into chairs, customers, even the bar before abandoning hope. Driving himself home wasn't going to happen.

Realizing the situation, the younger and much more

sober victor showed a bit of class, helping Moon to his feet. Ed and his fall back date listed into each other, yet somehow worked their way out to a cab, earning enthusiastic applause from the bar crowd. I wonder how he managed to get his address to the driver, as he could barely get the back door open and slump in before surrendering completely to my magic potion. There was a very real chance the potassium wouldn't be needed.

Reality hit as I watched the cab pull out, the realization of what I was about to become. Twenty years earlier, graduating from medical school I had taken an oath. Now I was ready to turn my back on it, to become a murderer. I was setting out with a clear head with the intent of ending a life. There was no coming back from that, but there would never be another chance like this. It was tonight, or forget the idea entirely. If I didn't follow through, would I curse myself every time a colleague was dragged through the hell that had become my life, or when Moon had my jury in his rapture, making them believe that I had callously allowed Mrs. Henry's husband to die? Would I look back at this night and wonder what had possessed me to let him go? I was circulating these thoughts, but realized that I was following his cab as I did so. My body was on autopilot—it appeared that the decision had been made.

It wouldn't do for the cabbie to see headlights follow him to Moon's house. The cops were bound to question him, at least superficially, so I turned off and chose a different route, parking in the shadows a short distance away from Moon's house. I hoped they would arrive soon, before I had a chance to think this through again. I should have been agonizing over my decision, but a strange peace had come over me, a sense of calm, of destiny, and I wanted nothing to interfere with it.

The dick-skin lawyer had to go down, and tonight was going to be the night.

Another question rose as the cab pulled up. What would I do with Warren's date? I had no interest in making this a 'Two for Tuesday' homicide special, and even if I could cross that moral hurdle, there would be no way to make two deaths look natural. Fortunately, by the time they arrived, Moon's friend must have realized the night wasn't going to go as she had planned. She never even got out of the cab. Home alone for her tonight, and it was a good thing—for both of us.

Moon woke up enough to make it inside on his own. His liver must have had some background in this sort of thing. The taxi driver, to his credit, made sure his charge made it through the front door before taking off to deliver his second fare. I would give Moon a few minutes, but it shouldn't take him long to get to bed, if he even got that far.

I grabbed my picks and syringe of potassium, glanced around the neighborhood, and then made my first serious mistake of the evening. Opening my truck's door, I was bathed in light. I hadn't thought to disable the dome light. Search-lights probing for King Kong could have been no less reveal-ing, and anyone on the street would have no problem giving a description of the man with the medical bag outside the dead lawyer's house.

Good fortune reigned again, though. At such a late hour, and on a school night, the streets were empty. Moon's porch light was off, also perfect for the occasion. Picking locks is done by feel. The only advantage to having a light on would be to lessen the risk of marring the lock's surface, a detail sure to arouse suspicion. The only thing that could stop me now would be if Moon had engaged a deadbolt, an obstacle I hadn't completely thought my way around. It turned out none of it mattered. The inebriated Lothario had left the door unlocked, an invitation to all who might wish to enter.

My one-night life of crime couldn't have gotten off to a better start, or so it seemed at the time. Warren's date had gone home, the taxi driver had witnessed Moon, so intoxicated that he literally fell out of the car, and I hadn't even had to pick the lock. And, from the sonorous sounds coming down the marble staircase, a well-anesthetized lawyer was waiting for a very unique house call. Warren Moon had filed his last malpractice case, and southern Oregon would once more be safe for practitioners of the healing arts.

I followed the snoring to his room and had my first disappointment of the night. He was still fully clothed. Don't get any ideas; as I mentioned earlier, alprazolam is an effective date-rape drug, but my interests were not in that direction. I'd just hoped that he'd have gotten down to his skivvies before passing out. It would have made the rest of the job that much easier.

I almost injected through his shirt into the brachial vein—a direct line to the heart, but realized just in time that the needle would leave a bloodstain on his fancy shirt. Even in Mayberry, that would be the end of my deception. The homicide learning curve, I was learning, is a steep one. The slightest little mistake could end up leading to the clang of a barred door and the end of my life of freedom.

The most logical approach would be the femoral vein, a large vessel in the groin. It was easy to find, and with Moon's layers of soft fat, a needle stick there would be easy to miss in a casual forensic inspection, especially if Moon hadn't signed on to the man-scaping trend. I gently pulled his pants down and found my target, well secluded in what he must have thought was a proud, masculine embrace of hair. A quick poke with the hypodermic, a flash of aspirated blood to confirm the placement of my needle, and with a quick depression of the plunger, the electrolytes were on their way. There would be no pulling back now.

A tiny spot of blood appeared when I pulled the needle out. It was easily handled with a toilet-paper compress. Moon's eyes opened for a moment, startling me, but he had clearly reached the end of his shelf life. I was relieved to see there were no obvious signs of distress; his exit would be far more pleasant than what he had done to so many of my colleagues. If I had asked them, I'm sure there would have been plenty of suggestions for a more dramatic end, but I had no interest in torture. I felt bad that the last thing he saw before moving on was my face and not the romantic conquest he had lined up, but beyond that, he didn't suffer.

CHAPTER FOURTEEN

That should have been the end of it, but sometimes what should be isn't the same as what is, and this was about to enter that unfortunate category. I double checked his bedroom to make sure I hadn't left sign of my intrusion. I left a Ziploc bag with a few more alprazolam, rubbing his fingerprints all over it before putting it in his pocket. I flushed the toilet paper with its pinprick of blood and replaced his pants about where they had been. With no visible sign of the needle stick, I felt good about the death-came-naturally look. The bartender and cab driver would give a good cover story and it would look like a straightforward case of his time simply being up, another victim of over indulgence. The coroner might even sign off without an autopsy, as I had staged things so convincingly. I even had a suspicion that the cops might not look too hard for evidence, once they found out who it was. They were probably still sore over the tactics he used, back when he was doing criminal law. I seriously doubted there would be much grieving down at HQ.

I slipped out the door and headed for my car, right into the arms of Moon's neighbor, George Bicknell, MD. George was a casual colleague. We were friendly on a hallway basis, but not much more than that. I did know that he was having a terrible time at home these days, with the ever-present doctor's wife issues. Word was that he was taking it pretty hard.

George had obviously been spending some quality time with his single malt scotch library. Now, at one o'clock in the morning, it was time to return the spirits to nature—a watery circle of life. He chose to bless his least favorite neighbor's yard. His micturition/irrigation action was intended to be a benign insult, but unfortunately, the slight might be my ruin. All those hours of careful planning and flawless execution, and I was about to be brought down by a full bladder.

"Jac-c-ck," he slurred, "what're you doin' at Ed's place? He throwin' a party?" He looked up, unsteady on his feet. "And why're all his lights off?" A moment of realization showed on his face. "Oops. Hey, I'm sorry, man. I had no idea—you with that bitchin' hot wife of yours and kids and all. It's none of my business, really, I just never would have guessed."

I couldn't think of a convincing story to explain my early morning departure from the formally breathing lawyer's house. Proud as I was of my accomplishment, it didn't seem wise to play it up. ("Hey, George, you'll never guess who I just offed.")

I wasn't too thrilled at what George was suggesting, either, but if it would solve the problem, I could live with it. Unfortunately, nothing was going to change the fact that in a few hours, the coroner would be carting away his dead neighbor, and the questions were bound to follow. My best hope was that George was deep enough into his cup that he wouldn't remember our encounter.

Watching him struggle to keep his balance and not fall in to the Warren's prize roses, a solution did come to mind. It was dismissed just as fast. I couldn't bring myself to kill again, especially a colleague. It looked like I might be spending my forever-more in an alternate living facility, dressed in grey and eating industrialized food.

"Morning, George," I said, "just passing through the neighborhood. The stars are so much clearer up here. My neighborhood has all those damn Christmas lights, they block everything out. I should probably head home and get some rest, though. Why don't you go have a few fingers of Macallan and do the same?"

If I had any of the Xanax left, I would have offered him one. It has incredible amnestic powers, and when combined with the inebriants already flowing through his system, it might have been my ticket to freedom.

I could predict how the rest of the day would go. When Moon didn't show up for work the police would be summoned. They would check his house and the time of death would be established. Routine inquiries would be made, of course. George would be included, and he would remember that he had seen me skulking from Moon's home around the same time that Moon had died.

"And now that I think of it, officer, isn't Jack being sued by him. You don't suppose he had anything to do with this?"

Next would come the knock at my door, then a trip downtown. I fully expected this would be my last day as a free man. I would need a good lawyer; ironic, considering what

I would be charged with. A mental defense might help—temporary insanity caused by the stress of the suit? Probably not. A sympathetic jury might help, but there was no way the prosecution would allow doctors or nurses to sit on it. Perhaps we could stock it with single young ladies. I could charm them with my wit and humor, but then, of course, I'd just have to deal with Aurora—prison might be the better choice.

Of course, there was still the small hope that George would take my advice on the single-malt nightcap. Scotch has its own amnestic capabilities, if consumed in adequate doses. What ended up happening, though, makes for a slightly different story.

CHAPTER FIFTEEN

Other than being tired from my late night, which sadly was a common experience, the next day passed uneventfully. My homicidal wanderings brought no untoward consequences, though every time I turned around I fully expected to be staring at a set of double wrist bracelets. It was actually an easy day and I made it home early. Aurora met me at the door, wearing a huge smile. She asked me if I had heard the terrible good news. Warren Moon was dead! She was having a glass of white Zinfandel.

"I know it's wrong to be celebrating," she said, "and I hope God will forgive me, but I just can't help myself." She was slightly inebriated, and was practically dancing. "After seeing what his lawsuit was doing to you and remembering what happened with Gwen and her failed leap, I think it's a blessing to have him gone."

Refilling her glass, Aurora turned into my arms, a smirking, self-reproachful look lighting her face. "Does it bother you that I'm so happy?"

Stupid question! What could bother me when my gorgeous wife is held tightly against my chest? It's better than being dealt a pair of aces against the dealer's six. "Are you kidding? Having Moon gone is like having one of those annoying buzzing flies escape out the window. It's the best news in months!"

Aurora hesitated a moment, locking her captivating eyes on mine. "Can I tell you something horrible?"

Still half-expecting this would be our last night together, there was nothing I was going to say to lessen my chance to spend some quality time with my wife. "Shoot."

"I saw him walking downtown a few weeks ago," she said in a soft, conspiratorial tone. "He was right out in the street, crossing on a red. I caught my foot just as it was heading for the gas. I was going to run him over, just like you did with my poor Scooter."

Scooter had been her multi-heritage mutt. She named him Myles when she adopted him from the pound, but his annoying habit of dragging his butt along the carpet as a hygiene measure led to my giving him a more appropriate name. Shortly after I found one of his skid marks on my pillow, Scooter committed suicide under my car. I've been hearing about it ever since. It will probably be emblazoned across my tombstone.

The temptation to tell Aurora what had really happened was almost beyond my abilities to resist. I still wonder if it would have been better if I had, but I expected it would be out soon for everyone to see, and so I spared her for the evening. And, of course, there was that other issue I wanted to consider for my last night of freedom—finding out that her husband was a murderer might squelch that.

The evening wore on, and after Aurora's third glass of blush, other thoughts replaced her guilt. My last night before going away to jail looked like it was going to be all that I had hoped.

As we lay entwined, basking in an incredible afterglow, I asked Aurora if she could be okay without me. With no response, I looked over and saw that she was fast asleep, an angelic smile I'd remember forever etched across her beautiful face.

CHAPTER SIXTEEN

The next day, hospital rounds went smoothly. Two easy days in a row, it was almost unheard of. A few people were talking about Moon's death, but if you hadn't ever been in his sights, he was just an annoying face on a billboard. I was having a cup of coffee before heading to the office when George Bicknell stopped by.

He leaned a hand on the chair opposite mine. "Hey, Jack," he said. "How about you and I do lunch?"

I got the distinct impression that turning him down would be a bad idea. "Sure, George, any place special in mind?"

"Placer's? At noon?"

Sven had made it big in Alaska. He had found an unusually productive claim, producing enough gold to set him up for life. He loved it there, but eventually decided he needed to come to the lower forty-eight, where the men didn't outnumber the women by a four to one margin. The move must have worked, because he was seldom seen without a full on smile—not the look of a man hopelessly enmeshed in a celibate lifestyle. He couldn't quite get the Klondike out of his system, though, and had set up Placer's, his diner, to remind him of home. Everything had a rustic feel. Hand-spliced hardwood chairs rested on an unpolished plank floor, tables to match. The walls were adorned with mining memorabilia and old black-and-white street photos from turn-of-the-century Fairbanks—a time when the bars and brothels seemed to outnumber the residents.

A nugget the size of a walnut graced his ring. It had fascinated my son into thinking of an Alaskan life himself. Either that, or it was the constant smile. Teenagers notice these things.

Placer's was also a place you could go for a quiet conversation, and it didn't take much imagination to figure out the topic for the day. Since George hadn't gone to the police, there was only one other likelihood: blackmail. It had been a relief that I was no longer going to be screwed by Moon, but now I feared it was about to happen anyway, from a colleague. I wondered how much he was going to try to take me for.

I was the first to arrive, selecting an out-of-the-way booth. Lost in thought, I almost missed the waitress. She was asking what she could get me. She finally got through and went off with an order for a tall iced tea with extra lemon. Lunch wasn't really on my mind, but I'd go along with George if he ordered.

George was running late. His office had probably gotten behind. Either that, or he was trying to sweat me, soften me up for the meeting.

As I waited, another thought intruded—a thought worse than blackmail. George might be working with the police. He could be setting me up, hoping to record a confession. Had any customers come in since I had arrived, choosing a spot where they could keep an eye on me instead of Sven's waitresses, all of whom had been selected for their obvious physical attributes?

If that were the case, where would the cops do the takedown, once George had helped them get their evidence? Probably on the street; I was not a habitually violent man, but they might not know that and would do their best to avoid putting the other lunch-goers in danger.

Surveying a room without looking like that's what you're doing is a difficult task. Patterns and interactions have to be examined—a subtle acknowledgment between two seemingly separate people, someone who casually positions himself looking away, but within hearing range, or between you and an escape route. Each individual in the room must be examined for inconsistencies such as a look held too long, a quick glance away, or a magazine reader who never seems to turn a page. There are so many things to look for, but it all has to be done without giving away any of the same clues, yourself.

One young thing thought I was paying her too much attention—not such a bad idea, but not what I had in mind. She gave me a look I had gotten quite familiar with when I was single, the old "not on your life, chump" gaze. Actually, I still get that on a fairly regular basis. My paunch must not be up to modern standards.

My gaze went several times to a man a few tables over. He came in shortly after I did and didn't fit in with the typical profile for Placer's. His table had a clear view of mine, and though he was not physically imposing, I had him pegged as the one who would do the arrest. Each time I glanced his way, I could see that he had been keeping an eye on me. "Dr. Hastings," he'd say. "You are under arrest for the death of Warren Moon. You have the right to remain—" All of a sudden, separating from a little blackmail money was sounding better than Sunday morning sex.

Every time I glanced toward the door, it was clear that "Mr. Obvious," as I had named him, was still keeping an eye on me. The more I tried to not pay attention to him, the more obvious my scrutiny became and the more obvious his attention to me. My tax dollars at work for a cop who couldn't even tail a first-time criminal without being spotted; I was definitely going to file a complaint with City Hall.

I was startled when he got up and worked his way over. He didn't walk like a cop, ready to bust a suspect's chops. I couldn't see how he fit with either of the scenarios I had imagined.

"Hi," he said, holding out his hand. "I'm Seth. I've got the style shop across the street—Seth's Buff and Cut? I do nails too, but hair is my specialty. I wondered if you needed a new place to be coiffed. I'm *sure* I can raise you to a new standard, one you've never imagined."

He smiled at his double entendre. "Cutting hair is not what I'm going to do forever, though. I'm going to be a fashion designer, in California. I just sent my portfolio in. This is just to get me by until that comes through."

Seth must have misinterpreted my relieved smile, as he started to sit down. Ordinarily, I'd have had a much different response, but I was suddenly in a much more charitable mood.

I quickly raised the universal slow-down-a-minute hand. "I'm meeting someone in a few minutes," I said. "Sorry if I gave you the wrong impression."

Seth handed me his card, "in case you change your mind," and then went back to his table with a disappointed look.

Back to the matter at hand. I guess I've always had a love for clichés. Some people think they're trite, old hat, not worth the paper they're printed on, but sometimes a good cliché will really speak what's on your mind. I make a point of never passing up the opportunity to trot one out. Anyway, I needed some way to figure out if I was going to be set up for exaction, or if George was planning to help the police, ready to secretly record everything I said to be played for the amusement of the jury at my death penalty hearing.

"Can you believe he was so stupid as to let them record all that?"

"I know, and he's a doctor! What a maroon."

"I'm glad I never went to him."

I had no idea how I was going to figure this out. Grabbing George in a bear hug and frisking him wouldn't work so well. That would attract more attention than desired; plus, I didn't want to make Seth jealous. If I asked him if he was recording us, he'd just say no, and if there really was a tape, anyone listening would know that I was up to something, simply by the fact that I had asked; worrying about hidden tape recorders wouldn't be a normal conversation starter. I'd just have to see how it went.

In the meantime, the sweating thing was definitely working. I should have taken a beta-blocker. They block the effects of adrenaline; even the most frightened public speaker can appear calm on stage with enough Inderal in his system. One of those magic alprazolams would have been great, too. There were still a few left at the office, but I was going to need my sharpest wits today, and those two things don't go together well.

George came in about fifteen minutes late, all two hundred and fifty pounds of him. He apologized, and explained that he had gotten behind on patients. He was all smiles, but I noted when I shook his hand that he was a little shaky, too. It would be decaf all around.

I had it figured that this meeting would be like a chess match. I'd see George's opening move, wonder what it meant, counter, and eventually it would be clear which direction we were heading. His opening gambit might be along the lines of "nice night for looking at stars, yesterday," or "I've always loved the early morning for walking—so much less traffic." Perhaps a more direct opening.

"It's so unsettling, Jack, having my next-door neighbor die suddenly like that. Those cops sure were asking a lot of questions. I really didn't quite know what to say to them, seeing you coming out of his house, and all." That would get the ball rolling in the right direction.

George was never one for too much subtlety, though. His upfront demeanor and unwavering criticism of the hospital administration had earned him a permanent membership on Intermountain Regional Medical Center's unofficial, but well-recognized black list. Not that he was the only one who felt that way; it was widely held that the search for intelligent life could easily bypass the upper echelons of our hospital's leadership, but most of the doctors were more circumspect in their criticism.

George had accomplished the honor of being the only doctor permanently excused from hospital committee meetings after he asked the CEO if his mother and father were brother and sister, and accused the board, after a particularly heated policy disagreement, of recruiting the vice-president from the annual "Best Dressed of Walmart" calendar.

It was easy to see why he felt that way. The VP, Henry Oliver, almost got arrested for disturbing the peace the previous year. He had grown increasingly irate at the delay in getting his Big Mac one day. The drive-through line behind him was growing equally impatient. Henry finally got out of his Beamer and was about to launch a full-scale frontal assault on the poor minimum wage staff, when the store's manager pointed out that he had ordered through the trash can, and would he, "please pull forward to the microphone?"

Oliver was the type to try gambling with round dice, or to bet on a rerun of the previous week's football game, always wondering why he lost. He functioned well, however, in his current capacity as the mindless hitman for Hal Logan, the CEO.

Dr. Bicknell could always be counted on to call things the way he saw them and that didn't go over too well with the commissars running the hospital.

"Hey, Jack," he greeted me. "Nice job on Moon this morning."

Classic George, straight to the punch. It was not quite the gambit I had expected, though, and I was caught a little off guard.

"Uh-h-h, yeah, George, . . . thanks." No denials. No "I don't know what you're talking about," or "I haven't seen that damn asshole for weeks" ploy. None of the point/counterpoint strategy I'd been working on. I might as well have just come right out and said, "Yep, snuffed the bastard. He pissed me off, and I nailed his ass!" This was going to be one short criminal career.

"A permanent muffler for that bastard has been long overdue, Jack. I'm just a little surprised that you're the one with the cojones to do it. Definitely well played, though; the cops think it was all natural; they have no idea"

He signaled the waitress, pausing the discussion while he ordered a glass of sun tea and an appetizer platter, then continuing in a hushed tone. "My wife called yesterday and mentioned that she had gone over to see what the police were doing at Warren's place. They told her Moon was dead and asked her a bunch of questions. The police want to talk to me, but Joyce told them that I was too busy with work. They agreed to wait until this afternoon."

He caught another waitress's eye and winked. They seemed to know each other. "I'm just not sure of what I should tell them, Jack. I know they'd be happy to talk to you. Ask about why you were coming out of his place so early that morning and how he can't go to work filing suits against doctors anymore, since he is no longer among the living." He smiled benignly but his look was like that of a cobra. "They might even be curious that he had a case about to go forward with you."

So there it was: blackmail. He was going to bleed me like an eighteenth-century physician. I breathed a sigh of relief, actually relieved. "So George," I said. "What do you think it would take to tell the cops that you had a great night's sleep Saturday, and that as a neighbor and skilled physician, you'd been trying for years to tell Moon to quit drinking and to get a little exercise?"

I gave a worried grin. "With things the way they are with my practice, I don't have a lot saved up. All I see in the ICU these days are Medicare patients and unemployed meth heads, and with the downturn in the economy and all, my financial picture has gotten a little sketchy. Still, I think we can work something out to our mutual benefit."

He laughed. "How well do you know me, Jack?"

Where was he going with this? I just wanted an answer—what would it cost to keep my feet out of San Quentin, and he was getting all philosophical. "Well, George, you're well respected. Honorable." A little flattery couldn't hurt. "And didn't you say you wanted to sail the world or something like that? I might be able to help you move forward on that boat."

Laughing and dismissively waving his hand, George said, "hold the phone, Jack. I don't need your money. My patients are the cream of the crop, they have great insurance—finances are not a problem. I even took care of Moon, confidentiality being less of an issue now. No," he went on, now assuming a more conspiratorial tone. I have another problem, and I think you're the perfect one to help."

I hoped he wasn't looking to move into fashion design. I have my limits.

"Do you golf?" he asked.

"I swing a club now and again, but I don't live for it or anything. Spend most of my time hitting out of someone else's fairway or wandering around in the rough."

"Well, Joyce has taken it up in a big way, and her pro seems to like spending time in the rough, too. It's not the first time this has happened, but this time she has been bleeding me. I let her run our finances. I'm always working and don't have a head for that stuff, anyway, but recently I've noticed that things weren't right. Our account was way down from where it should have been. Then one day I had to stop by home early and was surprised to find a separate bank statement, addressed in her name. I steamed it open and found that she has diverted a sizeable sum of our money. It looks like she's setting herself up for a life lived happily ever after with the pro."

He looked around the restaurant, then leaned forward

over the table and whispered. "I want you to kill that little bitch and the shagger too, if you can pull it off. Send them both on a one way ticket to hell."

I was shocked. I'd never heard George swear before! It looked like the brief criminal aspect of my life was about to come back for an encore performance. Such a short time ago, my goal was to keep people out of the undertaker's hands; now, it looked like I was aiming for first place on their Christmas card list.

George wanted an answer, and it was actually a fairly easy decision. I'd never liked Joyce—she had a tendency to look down on anyone not up to her perceived status. I had never understood why George had married her, nor why he stayed with her. Her constant belittlement of others, and her steadfast griping about the 'complete lack of culture in this God-forsaken hell hole' she was forced to live in was a steady embarrassment in a community where the doctors drove pick-up trucks and economy cars instead of ones she would consider more suitable.

George was offering a get-out-of-jail-free card. It was within my reach, if I could do this one thing for him. Plus, I knew that if I did this, he'd never be able to threaten me again over Warren's murder—he'd go down just as hard as me, if he turned me in. A brief handshake, a nod of the head, and George and I were friends for life.

CHAPTER SEVENTEEN

George and I got together later at his house, where we could get more into detail. He hadn't been kidding when he said his practice was successful. His basement was every man's dream come true; marble-topped wet bar, full-sized pool table, and an official-looking dart board. Signed posters from the glory years of the Dallas Cowboys' cheerleaders adorned the walls, wishing him well. They were seductively lit from the antique Tiffany-style beer hall lamp suspended over his pool table— one even sported an open-mouth lipstick kiss and an invitation to 'come back any time, Sweetie!'

Thursday night football was about to begin. The Bears were trying out their twentieth quarterback of the decade. It was late in the season, but they hadn't been put out yet, and long-suffering fans were thinking towards the playoffs. Someone had a lithium deficiency, I'm afraid, letting their bipolar dreams triumph over years of repeated history, but it has been a better season than most.

"George," I said, settling in before his widescreen with one of his home-brewed beers. "This is going to be a lot tougher than Moon. Two unexpected deaths in neighboring houses a few days apart are going to be a tough sell. We might want to wait a while."

"Unfortunately, we can't do that, Jack. Time is a factor. I think Joyce is about to file for divorce. Splitting my assets doesn't fit my retirement plans, especially with what she has put me through these past few years. I need a solution, and I need it soon. I also want back the money she stole, and that might be tough if she lives long enough to get the papers filed."

"Not to mention," I said, "if a divorce is in progress when we kill her, you'll be suspect number one, and I'll be riding your coattails to the electric chair. Let's get a plan in place tonight, and get this done."

George agreed. "Can you think of a way to get them both and still have it look like an accident?"

"I've been thinking of that," I said, "but I'm coming up short. Getting both of them like that would be tough, especially on such short notice." I am not mechanical enough to sabotage a car to simulate a credible accident, and multi-forked lightning strikes are out of my jurisdiction. I couldn't think of much else. I don't have a long record of plotting murder, and didn't have a lot to work with. Also, the brain does slow with the passing of the years, as Aurora has pointed out so many times.

"I think it's best if we just take care of Joyce," I said. "That will take care of the main problem."

"I really wanted to get that country club bastard, too," George said. "Are you sure there's no way?"

"We can talk about the pro later, when things have cooled down, but you'll still get your revenge. He thought he had it all figured out—the trophy girlfriend, and getting half of your money. He'll suffer a while, and then we can take our time and get him later, when everyone has forgotten about Joyce."

That cheered him up. I've always been good at convincing others to see things my way.

"How do you think you'll do it?" George asked. "We could just have her disappear. No body, no crime."

"That's been done a thousand times, George. The cops always know it's the husband. You'd be all over the news, and even if they couldn't prove it was you, her family would sue you in civil court and your life would be turned to hell."

"How about a robbery? You sneak in and strangle her or stab her or find some other suitably painful way to kill her."

He leaned back in his chair as the plan unfolded in his mind. "You could give me a superficial injury and then get out the back door. When the police arrive, I'll tell them I woke up to a noise and found someone standing over Joyce's body. I fought back, but he was too much for me. I'll come off looking like a hero."

"That has been done to death, too. No one is going fall for that script." It was becoming clear that there was a shortage of untried ways for getting rid of a problem spouse. Maybe that could be the book I've always wanted to write.

I got up for another of his beers. They were pretty good, though his customized label seemed a little self-aggrandizing—it still was just a basement brew. "A home invasion might work, though. Steal some jewelry, a few guns, and Joyce dies in the process. Of course, they'll always go back to that first rule of homicide investigation, look at the spouse. Wonder why that is? Anyway, we could distract some of the suspicion by getting some lowlife to pawn her jewels down the road in Idaho, or Nevada."

"What about a fake suicide?" George suggested. This was starting to sound a lot like the debate I had with myself while deciding on Moon's fate. "I could tell people how worried I've been about her," he said, "that she just hasn't been herself lately, and that I've been afraid to leave her at home."

"Tough to pull off, George. I hate to say it, but she seems pretty damn happy these days. Plus, with all the money she's been pooling, the future she's planning doesn't include your becoming a widower. I think that would be a short cut to the Green Mile."

It took a while, but a plan finally came together. And, the Bears won.

CHAPTER EIGHTTEEN

George had a CME—continuing medical education conference scheduled in San Diego for next week. It had been set for months, and no one would think twice about his being gone. While he was out of town, his personal problem would vanish and we'd both be free, unless he decided to follow through with the golf pro, and that would be well down the road. My conscience should have bothered me more, and the fact that it *didn't* bother me was a little upsetting, but somehow everything seemed justifiable.

I had performed a huge service for the medical community, society in general, really, by getting rid of the worst malpractice lawyer in the state. I shouldn't have to fear being punished for that. It was too bad that someone else would have to go too, but whoever said life had to be fair?

I arranged to have time by myself when George left for San Diego. Aurora had jumped at the opportunity to see her sister in Boston. I assured her there would be no problems. Zach wouldn't starve, and the laundry wouldn't stage a bloody revolution in her absence. "Besides," I told her, "I'll have time to catch up on a few things that need doing."

Darkness came early at this time of year, especially with the pall of clouds that had plagued us lately. Snow was predicted but so far hadn't materialized. I parked a few blocks away from the Bicknell's home, and this time remembered to pull the bulb from the dome light. The brain may have slowed, but I can still learn from past mistakes.

I showed up on Joyce's doorstep, bottle of bubbly in hand.

"Hello, Joyce," I slurred. I had doused myself liberally with cheap scotch to convince her that I'd already started an evening of merriment. "Did George make it off for his conference?"

She was surprised to see me. We were barely acquaintances, and like I said, we didn't get along terribly well. Surprised, and perhaps a little disappointed too, seeing the downturn of her smile. She had probably come to the door hoping to find her golfing buddy, looking for some R&R while her husband was out of town.

Joyce recovered quickly, giving me a halfhearted greeting, but not inviting me in. Her demeanor made it clear; she wanted no part of me, but when I mentioned that I thought we should talk about her golf course extracurricular activities, she became much more receptive. We went to her kitchen and she got a couple of glasses for the champagne. Sitting down, I made sure she saw that my eyes were all over her, which wasn't all that hard to do. She was beautiful, having all the right bumps in all the right places, not that Aurora gave up anything there, either.

I had followed Joyce and Caldwell, her pro, from the country club to his place one day and had taken a few candid shots—she was impressed with my photographic skills.

"If George sees these," I said, holding the photos up, "your easy street life is going to come crashing down, and I guarantee you, a golf pro isn't going to be able to keep you in the style you're accustomed to. Say good-bye to your Lexus and your weekly spa sessions. Be ready to sell some of your jewelry, too, unless you have an awfully good divorce lawyer. You'll need the money to eat."

She drained her champagne and leaned forward, "You wouldn't—"

"This *could* be our little secret," I hinted. "I've always admired you, Joyce. I did everything I could think of to keep you from seeing that. I didn't want to upset you, but I've always felt that George wasn't man enough for someone as beautiful as you."

"Aurora is in Boston for a few days, visiting her sister. I thought maybe we could get to know each other a little better." I let my eyes wander down her cleavage again. Joyce reached across the table and took my hand, twining her fingers between mine. She was a fast student—it didn't take long for her to figure that a night with me would be a small price to ensure her future.

A bottle of France's finest later, consumed more by her than me, she was ready to go upstairs to pay her toll. "I've always hoped you'd come over sometime," she cooed, "but I was always too afraid to ask. That's why I've always seemed so distant. I was afraid of what I'd do if I got close to you."

Right!

We formed a two-person conga line and went upstairs for the main event. Her appointment, however, was with destiny, not a coerced carnal adventure with a lustful pulmonologist. At the top of the stairs, I turned around and gave her a hard shove. No time to think about it, just get it done. The look of shock on her face was horrible. It transitioned to sheer terror as she scrabbled, trying to regain her balance. It looked like George would be getting the other part of his wish, the part I hadn't agreed to where Joyce suffered for her sins.

Her descent would earn no Olympic accolades. It was characterized by a series of gruesome snapping sounds, along with another noise, something wet that I'd prefer to forget. She made it almost to the bottom landing, coming to rest in a most unnatural pose.

A trained doctor can tell when a person has gone to the other side, but unfortunately, Joyce was only part way there. I couldn't imagine that she had landed so akimbo and not be dead, but there was no doubt. I had a bargain to fulfill, and going halfway on a deal like this wasn't an option. I hoisted her over my shoulder and started once more up the stairs. Doing so, I was reminded that I had never gone through with my recurring New Year's resolution, the one where I joined a gym and got into shape. Next year, for sure.

We made it to the top of the stairs again, but I had to use the handrail for support. Her second trip finished where the first had failed. Her head was turned to a most unnatural angle and several fingers were, too. Seeing her like this was had more effect on me than I would have thought, and I was glad I'd put my dinner off until later.

The preparation for the police would be more involved this time. My fingerprints, on file from when I applied for my medical license, were all over the handrail. I have no idea if these are entered into any kind of law enforcement database or just used for a criminal background check and discarded, but I didn't want to find out the hard way. The police might never even check the handrail, if they bought the scenario that this was just an accident, but if they did dust, and they identified my prints, it would be tough to explain. Wiping the rail clean would be even worse, a clear sign that someone had been there and was covering his tracks. Either way could lead to trouble.

I searched around until I found a glove, put it on, and used it to go lightly up and down the rail. It should smudge the fingerprints, but leave remnants in place. At least, that was my hope. I then set about the rest of the scene.

There are so many ways to fall down with a task like this, that it's almost impossible to achieve the 'perfect murder.' I should remember to tell that to Aurora. I took my champagne glass, washed and dried it, and put it back in the cabinet, then wiped down the bottle, put her prints back on it and dropped it in the trash. Getting those finger prints on the bottle without letting traces of blood get on wasn't easy, but overall, my crime scene décor seemed quite passable. There were no neighbors 'watering' the yard when I left this time, and I was home, unobserved, in time for the evening news.

George made a few calls from San Diego that night, just to say hello at first, and then, when Joyce didn't answer, he started calling a little more often. It created a nice impression of a husband who was gradually getting more alarmed, the messages left on the answering machine well scripted for when the police came on the scene.

We both felt bad about the next part, having to involve his nurse. Rose had been a fixture since George opened his office. She was as sweet as a person could be, and George had come to rely so heavily on her that it was assumed he would have to close shop if she ever decided to retire. Bringing Rose in on this was regrettable, but couldn't be avoided.

She picked up on the third or fourth ring.

"Rose," George said. "I hate to call you at home. I hope you're not busy."

"No, sir," she said. She refused George's constant entreaties to address him less formally, stating that it just wouldn't be proper. "The dishes are done, and it's just rerun night. What's going on? You don't sound so good."

Rose's husband Andros had had a devastating stroke several months back. She was unwilling to put him in a nursing facility, insisting instead that he could be better cared for at home. The rehab program was eating through their finances, but his progress was undeniable.

George admired Rose's devotion and dedication—she worked a full schedule at the office and then went home to repeat the day's physical therapy exercises one more time with her husband. She was frequently exhausted, but never complained, or brought her problems to work. George found a way to slip a few extra bucks her way, always under the table so the other employees wouldn't get jealous: an envelope slipped through a car window or dropped in her purse, reimbursement for office items she hadn't purchased. Neither said a word about the arrangement, and I wouldn't have even known about it, except I caught him doing the drop one day. He was evasive when I asked, not wanting to call attention to his good deed, but he finally relented and the truth was out.

A few times a week, Rose and Andros skipped the evening exercises and watched DVD reruns of the shows they had watched together in healthier times. Tonight was their night of fun, and George and I were about to rain destruction all over it.

"I'm sure sorry to be calling so late, but I've been trying to call Joyce all evening, and she's not answering. It's probably nothing," he told her, "but I'm starting to get a little worried. She might have just gone out for dinner or maybe just drank a little too much; she's been doing that a lot lately. I'm going to talk to her about it when I get back, but didn't want to create a row before I left. She probably just fell asleep on the couch or something, but could you go and check on her, then call me back? I'll sleep so much better if I know she's safe."

"I'm happy to do it, sir. It's not that far to your place. I'll call you right back!"

George smiled but kept a slightly worried tone in his voice as he thanked her and assured her that he would be waiting for her call.

When Officer Tolliver called back with the horrible news, George sobbed convincingly. It was a lot easier without anyone there to actually see the act. With several wracking breaths, he was finally able to tell him that he would return home immediately, "but officer," George asked, "how can life be so unfair?"

The police inquest was perfunctory. Caldwell, the golf club romantic, tried to tell them that Joyce's death didn't look right, but our plan was bulletproof and the execution had been almost flawless.

As far as the police were concerned, Joyce had gotten drunk and had broken her neck falling down the stairs. (Twice, but who's counting?) Her husband had been in California on a long-scheduled business trip. The police checked his accounts, looking to see if he had made any five-figure withdrawals, but the only significant drawdowns had gone to the victim's account—unlike doctors, hitmen don't routinely go for the free charity jobs.

Other than Caldwell's objections, there was nothing to create suspicion. They did ask about her new bank account, but it was easy to explain.

"She always felt so bad," George said, "having to ask for permission to buy things. We decided that she should have some money of her own, in a separate account to give her a little freedom." He noted that she might have gone a little overboard with it lately, but, he cried—"I would happily give ten times that if only it would bring Joyce back."

The money, of course, would be returned, now that Joyce would no longer be needing it. Her death was ruled an accident, case closed. Rose might need a little therapy, but George would help with that. Joyce's life insurance paid off; it wasn't enough to raise any red flags, but was plenty to cover Rose for a few months with the best PTSD counselor in town.

CHAPTER NINETEEN

After Joyce's murder, life started moving back to where it was supposed to be. Aurora came home from a delightful Beantown visit, regaling me with stories of exploits with her sister. Faneuil Hall, the Old North Church and Bunker Hill—all were seen and conquered. They enjoyed nightly lobster dinners and had run amuck, flirting with hopeful guys at all the popular nightclubs—they even paid homage to Cheers' imaginary home. It was like being free and young again.

Aurora hadn't wanted to say anything before, seeing how affected I had been by all that was going on, but now she let on that she hadn't been happy at home for quite some time. The trip to Boston had been just the solution she had needed. And, it helped that she returned to find a version of her old, happier husband waiting. Things were going to be 'spot-on' right again.

"Someday," she suggested, "we should go back together and see the Boston sights."

"I'm delighted you had fun," I teased, "but there's really no reason to go to all that trouble travelling. I see Old Ironsides first thing every day, when I wake up!"

As I was putting the jury-rigged ice pack over my blackening eye, I told Aurora that I, too, had just needed a little time to sort things out, but that it was all good now. "I know I haven't been myself ever since that damn subpoena showed up on our doorstep, but guess what? The malpractice insurance carrier called while you were gone. Mrs. Henry couldn't find another lawyer willing to take over after Moon's death. None of them felt she had a case; they actually said it looked more like an extortion attempt than a legitimate claim. The lawsuit is gone, we're free!"

Aurora and I ate at Chateaubriand that night. She was tired from her trip but the excitement of being out from under the lawsuit and of having her happier husband back more than compensated for the time changes and the hours spent in the air. We had their signature dish, the chateaubriand, medium rare. Tender béarnaise asparagus and the creamiest garlic mashed potatoes imaginable, drizzled with glorious melted Brie and powdered with just enough smoky red paprika to give them character sat on the side. A towering inferno of cherries jubilee finished the meal in a splendid fashion.

The incredible dessert was accompanied by a seventy five year old cognac. There is no other way to say it, the cognac defied description. It was poured from a hand blown bottle, painted with the distiller's coat of arms. The bottle itself was worth well more than I'd normally spend for an entire evening, even at a fine restaurant. I didn't feel a bit bad paying the tab. Aurora and I raced home where we made love like newlyweds until the sun showed its first glorious morning rays.

I showed up at the office the next morning in jubilant spirits, but immediately recognized that something was wrong. Rachel was nowhere to be seen, and Maggie was practically hiding under her desk as she handed me the schedule. A full day waited, and at the end of the list was the worst albatross of my practice, Henrietta Peabody—a hypochondriac of world-class caliber. She was just on the right side of the three hundred pound mark, and there wasn't a disease that she hadn't diagnosed herself with, including several she had invented entirely from scratch.

Ms. Peabody had called this morning, very worried about a change in the color of her bowel movements. As usual, her primary care provider was "too busy" to get her on the schedule, and suggested she call my office. The girls had drawn straws. Rachel lost, and was stuck being the one to break the news.

Ordinarily, having Henrietta on the schedule with one of her imaginary ailments would prompt me to thoughts of ritual suicide. Today, I smiled and said, "thank you, Rachel," then went to my office to sort through a stack of charts before starting in on the real work.

If these on-top-of-the-world happy feelings could be condensed into a pill, à la Huey Lewis, major corporations would drop their small time operations and go into full production. Wars would end, cats would dance in the street with junkyard dogs and the members of Congress would work together to solve all our nation's troubles. The ladies looked at each other, unsure of what to do, having never before seen anything quite so remarkable.

I heard Rachel tell Maggie that she was going all in on lottery tickets over the noon hour. Maggie, a strictly conservative Baptist who thought games of chance were the devil's work, gave Rachel five dollars, with a request that she not to tell anyone about her journey into the world of sin.

CHAPTER TWENTY

From here on, it was supposed to have been back to the good old boring Jack Hastings, MD; healer of the sick and broken-hearted. With the suit out of the way, I gradually got back my enjoyment of life. Before, all the things I used to love had fallen prey to an unending, abject dolor. The Rolling Stones' *Paint It Black* had become my new theme song, circulating through my mind on an unending, continuous loop, coloring all my thoughts. I had forgotten for too long what it was like to enjoy life, having settled into my new existence with little hope and living just to get through to the next day, with the expectation that it would be no better than the last or the one to follow. Now, the old Dr. Hastings was starting to return. Tender shoots of hope rising phoenix-like from the ashes of the fire that had come so close to destroying me.

Not that there had been that much about me that was that special. Before I took a shot at living on the dark side, and aside from my spectacular daily performances in stand-up comedy, I was just another doc. I lived within a few miles of where I had been born, fished the same streams with the same hand-tied dry flies I had used through high school. My previous life paled next to the excitement of some of the other physicians, but it had always been good enough for me.

Each fall I traveled across the state on an enjoyable, but never successful elk hunt. Unsuccessful, that is, in that I never came home with fresh venison, but I always came back a little better for the time spent in the mountains. I had my own private campsite accommodations, well away from where everyone else slept, but I think I mentioned that earlier.

I did a little semi-gourmet cooking, which now and again produced something worth eating, and I worked on being a good dad and husband, when work allowed. I drove an average suburban car until I splurged on a new F-150 a year or two back, and seldom drove more than five or ten miles per hour above the posted safe and legal limit. I occasionally dabbled in the social clubs, but never too seriously and more out of a sense of societal obligation than any true desire. I did dream of being that author at the top of the *New York Times* list, but so far there had been no progress in that direction.

Aurora had given us three great children, all boys. Gill, Harper, and Zach, each as different from the others as could possibly come from two parents. They were gone now or at least close enough; passed through the complete dependency phase, the want-to-do-things-with-dad stage, and the high school "parents? What parents?" part.

Gill was starting an engineering career in Portland, struggling against a political tide a world from his own. His car had been keyed three times before he finally listened to my advice and took his conservative opinions off his bumper. He was disillusioned, but ultimately realistic.

"So much for tolerance and diversity, huh Dad?"

Harper was a beach bum somewhere in Florida. That sounded bad, but he was probably the happiest of the lot. He checked in once in a while, and I have to admit, at times I've been a little jealous. He lived each day to its fullest, with no worries of the ups and downs of the stock market, no concerns about mortgages, just living life. That didn't keep me from preaching to him about the importance of getting a real job someday, but my heart really wasn't in it. He was living the dream that so many of us pictured, before the realities of the world hammered us down to become senseless conform-ist work-a-day Joes.

And Zach? Still ostensibly living at home, but with a new driver's license and a steady girlfriend, Aurora and I might as well have been empty-nesters. Having Zach still at home was a little like having Bigfoot around. Once in a while, there would be a suggestion that he was out there, but visual sightings were rare.

The most consistent evidence of his existence would be what he called music, the auditory excrements that pounded out from under his bedroom door. I have a pretty good command of the English language for a never published would-be author, but was at a loss to adequately describe these sounds. Permanent physical damage could be suffered just from getting too close.

When I was teaching Zach to drive, he tried endlessly to convert me.

"Dad, how could you *not* like Uberdeath?" And "'Chains of Wrath' is the best they ever did, don't you think?" Obviously, he had listened to my instructions to keep his eyes on the road. If he had looked in my direction when I made the mistake of actually listening to the words of Uberdeath's famous melody, he wouldn't have needed to ask. Word of advice: it's a *good* thing that most of these songs are easier to feel than to hear. As unpleasant as the auditory intrusion is, it's far better than if you actually pay enough attention to hear what's being put forward to our willing high-school audiences. I expect this will be our last generation.

I have always been someone who reads a lot, and at this point, my interests were back to my usual—espionage thrillers, horror stories, an occasional *New England Journal* article, and of course, my specialty pulmonary and critical care magazines. No more lock-picking manuals, and I left the crime stories to Aurora. After living them for the last month or so, the excitement had faded.

I also used to love politics, but now, with one election starting the day after the last was posted, the joy had been taken out of it—too much of a good thing, similar to the way my wife thinks about my favorite activity.

"If it's there all the time," she once told me, "it will be less special. I'm only thinking of you."

Nice of her to be so concerned, but I'd love the chance to find out. She seems pretty resolute, though, so I'll keep up with my other hobbies for now.

One thing I tried in my pre-hitman stage was a little different—a brief spell with homemade pyrotechnics. The children and I felt it was fun, and the results were spectacular. It was also a little dangerous, more from Aurora's disapproval than from the concussive effects of our creations.

I wanted to keep this bonding experience between the four of us, but Aurora came home from a shopping expedition one afternoon, earlier than I had expected. She was curious what the four of us were up to, hiding behind the closed door of my study. Before I could stop him, Gill, the soon-to-be engineer, started to explain the physics involved in getting the best blast effect from our devices.

"Hi, Mom. Dad's teaching us how to blow stuff up! We get an *awesome* explosion if we reinforce the cases..."

Big mistake.

"You're teaching the kids to make bombs?" Talk about an exothermic reaction. Our little creations couldn't come close to the splendor coming forth from my normally placid wife. The kids were enthralled, both with the scene erupting in front of them and the actual explosive-making process.

The children's enthusiasm made the situation with Aurora even worse, and it took all my persuasive skills to explain the benefits of exposing the children to science. She did calm down, though I think it was a week or two later, and allowed us to continue, but she demanded that I do all the dangerous parts.

"You're insured, after all," she said, "and I can always get a new husband if you do something stupid, but if you let anything happen to the kids—"

Her admonitions sounded a lot like what she told me when I took the boys on safari in Africa. I had been instructed to not bother coming home if a lion or an elephant or any other of God's creations hurt 'one of her babies.'

Our chemistry experiments came to a halt after 9/11. It didn't seem wise to have the kids going to school, telling everyone about the cool bombs their dad made. Our neighborhood was fine without the black Suburbans and stealth helicopters.

With the end of the bomb making, I was back to the

basics. Work had always been a joy, before the suit. Sure, I groused a little now and then about the perpetual, never satisfied complainers, the drug-seekers and the hypochondriacs. Intermountain's administrators were a constant source of discontent, and the never-ending stream of pointless government regulations led to a frustrated complaint now and again, especially with their new mandate forcing doctors' offices and hospitals to go to electronic records. Having grown up in the days before computers, I'm not that comfortable with them, nor very trusting.

The insurance companies were a steady nuisance, too, but overall, I really couldn't think of any other way I would rather make a living. Okay, maybe as a high-profile porn star or a fly-fishing guide (at a Montana nudist camp?) but realistically, I loved what I did and expected to go on with it until the day I died, leaving the world with a smile on my face that would make St. Peter proud. The lawsuit had stolen so much of that joy, but now it was like a new day had begun.

One slight problem did arise. My sleep was occasionally interrupted by lurching drunken lawyers and cartwheeling housewives. Though I didn't regret what I'd done, there must have been an element of guilt in there somewhere. I'd grown up in a family without religious inclinations and had generally figured that those superstitious sentiments were for those too weak to make it through life on their own; a crutch, and nothing more. I wasn't worried about any kind of comeuppance in the afterlife. Converts had proselytized to me a number of times, even some of the other doctors, whom I thought should know better, but the preaching had never taken hold.

Getting hit with the lawsuit reinforced my skepticism. What kind of benevolent God would allow someone like

Moon to prey on the people like me who were doing something good in the world? Still, even without divine threat, I knew on some level that it was wrong to go around killing people, even malpractice lawyers.

Long after I'd started my supplemental career in homicide, I took another look at the whole heaven and hell issue. A dying, in fact, hopelessly dying young patient had made a miraculous recovery. I tried to find a rational medical explanation, but it wasn't there. He went from a guaranteed reservation in the morgue to sitting up and playing video games with his sister. His family had repeatedly told me that God would save their son, but I had gently corrected them on their miscalculation. I had tried to be patient, considering their situation, but I was starting to get a little annoyed at their failure to give up their ridiculous hopes.

"Science never lies," I finally told them, when they failed to see reason, then stalked off to see other patients.

When he made his miraculous recovery, I expected a smug "we told you so" or similar reproach from his family, but they simply smiled and thanked me for my efforts. "We knew he'd be fine."

Still dumbfounded at his recovery, and not knowing what else to do, I returned their thanks. It looks like I'm going to have to rely heavily on that forgiveness clause, but again, this epiphany didn't come around until well down the road.

CHAPTER TWENTY-ONE

It was a few months later that George showed up in my office. He didn't call ahead, and I wasn't terribly pleased to see him. We occasionally passed in the lunch line but, by unspoken agreement had little to do with each other. We would exchange the stereotypically insincere hallway greetings, the ones everyone hopes won't lead to an actual conversation, and occasionally had an unofficial sidebar consultation, but little else. Since he had been permanently excused from staff meetings, I didn't even see him there, and he seldom saw patients in the ICU. I did go to Joyce's memorial, to show support for him in his time of need, but that had been the extent of our contact.

And now he was in my office. Maggie had escorted him back while I was tending a patient with especially difficult asthma. There was a new treatment option finishing its testing and she was interested in getting in to its final trial. When I came out to do my charting and to try to get her enrolled in the study, George was there, smiling and admiring my office.

My shelves were filled with curios and novelties. They were threatening to edge out the relics from two decades of vacations, and Father's Day grade school projects. A few items were in danger of falling to the floor if someone closed the door too forcefully. The walls were also at full capacity, with thumb-tacked team photos memorializing years of Babe Ruth dreams. An original *Star Wars* poster, lovingly preserved behind low-glare glass, held a position of honor in front of my desk. Princess Leia, the object of my childhood passions, stood next to that interloper Luke, my competitor for her affections. According to some pawnshop reality television show, the poster was worth several hundred dollars, but there was no way I was going to part with my first love.

My office was a snapshot of life, a brief reflection of peace on those busy days where the work hours outpaced the day. It was a scene probably reflected in cubicles across the country. Center stage (next to Leia) was a caricature of Aurora, drawn by a street artist in Nassau. The kids had stayed with their grandparents, and it had been a vacation to remember—days and nights spent frolicking on the beaches with warm sand trickling between our toes, diving for lobsters and soaking up the tropical sun in a state of pure relaxation.

Cell phones were still in their infancy, a time before instantaneous contact was the expectation. Aurora and I had 5 days of selfish together time. We bought a hidden treasure map from a street corner pirate, both knowing we were being taken, and spent magical hours hunting for the long-lost treasure of Phillipe Bequel, a 17th century privateer who had plied the local waters. It was a week spent living life to its fullest.

I looked again at the picture of Aurora and wondered if George had any pictures of Joyce on his office walls.

"George?"

"Hey, Jack. Thought I'd come by and see how you were doing, catch up a little."

Things seemed to be going well in his new life. He'd lost a few pounds, and that early ruddy glow had faded off his face. Rumor had it that he had a new girlfriend, stereotypically young. He was standing tall, smiling, and looking very much like a man who was truly enjoying life; about the way I had been feeling until he showed up in my office.

It wasn't hard to tell that there was more than a social theme for George's visit. He walked around behind me and nudged the door shut with a loafer-clad toe, keeping eye contact as he settled into a chair and smiling like a politician on a voting safari. "Jack," he said, "I've got a business idea I want to put in front of you."

I started to raise my hand to cut him off.

"No land in Florida or funny stock ideas," he laughed. "I'm serious—hear me out."

He leaned forward and dropped his voice to a conspiratorial level. "Do you know Al Thorpe?" Noting the negative shake of my head, he explained. "Al is a friend from my residency days. He's an internist in Redding now, and he's a great doc; everyone loves him. Anyway, he called last night, so completely sloshed that he could barely talk. Someone is suing the hell out of him. Four million bucks. That's a lot of zeros, Jack, and his policy only covers half that.

In California, they give out big awards like Halloween candy, even more if the plaintiff gets a sympathetic jury. It's just like your case. He did nothing wrong, but the patient died and his son, who hadn't seen him in years saw an opportunity to make a big score. Al's insurance company wants him to settle. If he doesn't and loses at trial, they'll make him pay a huge part of the damages—maybe even some of the expenses. And remember, they are pulling the jury pool from the state where they bought that argument about the glove that didn't fit! He doesn't want to do that and have it look like he did something wrong, but he's afraid of the risk if he doesn't. He made a mistake once before and got sued, losing in court, so this is his second go-round. And, his insurance carrier is threatening to drop him or raise his rates to some even more ridiculous level. You know what they already charge down there."

"I've heard horror stories," I admitted.

"He can't afford much more overhead, but doesn't want to close the practice he built and finish his working life slinging chamois at some family carwash. He doesn't know what to do. That son of a bitch is one of the toughest men I know, Jack, the type who'd do the running of the bulls, going upstream on a dare! Man, did we have some fun in med school. He's broken now. I couldn't believe it; he almost broke down crying on the phone. It broke my heart."

"I understand his problem," I said, "but I'm not sure where you're going with this. I don't see any kind of investment opportunity here."

"It's not really an investment," George went on, "as it is a new business. I sort of mentioned that there might be a way to bring things to a different, more satisfactory conclusion. No mention of your name or anything, nothing to put you at risk—I just told him that I knew a guy who terminated his plaintiff's attorney, and that the case went to the land of nevermore. Al said he'd thought about doing something like that but figured he'd get caught. He thought, even then, that it might almost be worth it, taking one for the team. To hear that someone had actually done it really lifted his spirits."

Now it was my turn to sit down. I didn't like the direction this conversation was going.

"He was just calling to commiserate," George said. "Having a possible solution drop into his lap did more than the double-dose of Prozac he has been self-prescribing. He has some money hidden away for that famous special occasion we all dream about and wondered if this could be it. He offered me a finder's fee if I could get the two of you in touch. Your cut would be twenty thousand."

George picked up the scorpion paperweight I found on a trip to Arizona a few years back, and tilted it to watch the sun rays prism across my desk. "That's a lot of nights in the ICU, Jack. You could tell everyone you were going on a quick vacation, do the job and be back in a couple of days, a richer man for the experience and knowing you had done something truly good for a fellow human being and for the medical profession."

I started to tell him I wasn't a hired hitman, but he wasn't done with the sales pitch.

"He'll give you the choice, Jack—the lawyer or the plaintiff. I like the lawyer idea myself. We could take this thing and run with it. There have to be docs all over the country who'd pay to get rid of problem attorneys. Think what it might be worth to a plastic surgeon or to an orthopedist. And we both know there is no way the politicians are ever going to pass tort reform. Their re-election coffers would dry up and they might be forced to get honest jobs. This would be our own version of reform."

He made a picture frame with his hands. "Picture slimy malpractice whores dropping like flies, from one coast to the other! It would take a few, but eventually the rest would notice and start thinking of taking a lengthy vacation, maybe even a career change."

"George," I told him, "my killing days are over. I got away with it twice and don't have too many regrets, but I don't see it as a full-time career."

He didn't show any sign of getting up to leave. Grinning, he said, "as far as the laws concerning murder go, Jack, after the first few, the rest are free."

He was right about that. "Even if I was interested, which I'm not, how could we ever make a business like that grow enough to be worthwhile? I don't think the Yellow Pages has a "Killer for Hire" section, unless maybe Dr. Gallows counts."

His laughter showed his agreement with my assessment. "It's all referrals. Nothing lost for advertising expenses. We provide a service, a lawsuit goes away and the client thinks of a friend in a similar spot. He buys him a few drinks, and our next prospect is on the phone. And," he pointed out, "no income tax. Do you like keeping every receipt for every meal and motel when you go on a business trip? Fuggettaboutit! Get a receipt for gas in Sacramento, or for a hotel in Memphis, and you can use it to light up your favorite Cohiba while Angel or Mystique swirls around the shiny pole to *New Sensation*."

He was starting to make sense.

Then he dropped the clincher. "Did I mention that Al has three hundred acres on the Sacramento? It's been in the family for years and he never lets anyone in. It's practically virgin fishing. I mentioned that my friend who might be in a position to help liked to toss a fly around, and he offered not only to let you fish, but to even show you the best holes."

Well, the Sacramento was a great stream. I'd meant for years to give it a try. That train wreck and contamination in the 1990s spoiled a trip I'd been anticipating for months. The vacation time had already been set before the spill. If I remember, it was spent in a shopping mall in Southern California. I still have the mental scars.

I can't remember what spilled. Sulfuric acid or pesticides or some other equally toxic material, but miles of the river had been sterilized. It was now supposed to be back to full aquatic health and I had thought a few times about trying again, but like so many of my plans, it never seemed to get past the thinking stage.

It could be an interesting trip. I'd tried a few "cast and blast" trips on the Rogue River. Drifting slowly downstream, swinging Green Butt Skunks through the deep aquamarine runs for winter steelhead and shooting at passing greenheads. George was proposing a "cast and murder" weekend, something I'd never seen in an adventure travel guide, but there might be something to it. Probably need a 5-weight rod, perhaps a 6 for the trout. For the lawyer, I'd need something a little more substantial. I suddenly realized I was picturing it in my head, even as I had been telling George that I wasn't interested. Access to private water on the Sac was an impressive selling point.

The financial benefit also deserved some consideration. With a few thousand extra dollars in the bank, Aurora could cut back on some long term cost-control measures, like recycling her dental floss, and I could picture retirement while I still had control of my bodily functions.

"Tell Al he's got a deal—one dead lawyer, coming up!"

Rachel's impatient knock brought our meeting to an end. After George left, she mentioned how good he looked, so soon after his terrible loss. "He's an inspiration to us all."

CHAPTER TWENTY-TWO

The next few days were too busy for George and me to meet, though I did spend some time trying to put the pieces together for a successful California assassination. It was likely to be tougher than the local ones.

"With Moon," I said, when we finally had the chance to get together, "I had all the time in the world to find a plan to make his end look like natural selection. With Joyce, there wasn't much time, but it was still local. This time, with the distance involved, it's going to be harder to plan. I'm thinking that a simple, violent death would be the best way to go. Not too much planning or finesse; just get down there and get it done."

"I agree," George said. "We could use it as a test case. A savage death would send a clear message. CNN or FOX might pick it up, and then the other networks would follow.

Malpractice lawyers all across the States would see the story and wonder if doctors had finally decided to stand up for themselves and end the abuse."

I did some research and found that this lawyer, Allen Blackman, was also without partners as he fought his battle against all that is good in this country. He was a sole practitioner, just like Moon. I also found that he had sued so many doctors in the last few years that there were at least a dozen the police would have to look at as suspects. He also did some other legal work, including a fairly well-known product liability case. He got a $2.3 million settlement for someone who broke his neck driving with a windshield sunshade in place. The "Don't drive with screen in place" warning tag we all laugh about is a direct outreach of that case. Who says lawyers don't make a contribution to society?

I found a newspaper article that said he actually got death threats while he tried that one. I think he also wanted to sue the distiller whose product befuddled his plaintiff's judgment to the point that he would even use a sunscreen on a cloudy day, let alone hit the highway with it still in place, but unfortunately, the poor guy couldn't remember if it was the Jack or the Jim that day, so they couldn't figure who to file against. The injustice of it all!

So, Mr. Blackman, attorney-at-law and persecutor of the medical profession, was going to go down in a spectacular fashion, and I was going to get a go at the feisty wild rainbows of the Sacramento River. Lawyers across the country would start to think twice before suing my colleagues, and there would be a nice tax-free check heading my way. Where was the downside?

CHAPTER TWENTY-THREE

I had the next week free from call. It didn't give much time for planning, but an unsophisticated hit like this couldn't be that hard for a man who had fooled the police twice, in his own backyard. Unfortunately, Aurora had extracted a promise for a new coat of paint on my next set of days off. Her recreation room was a time capsule from the seventies, when the house was built, doubtlessly under the influence of someone who had too much fun in the sixties. It was in desperate need of a facelift.

My suggestion that she keep the room as a museum, a tribute to Timothy Leary, didn't even get the dignity of a response. Aurora had already picked an outlandishly expensive replacement for the worn gold shag, figuring we'd saved enough by not replacing it the first twenty or so times she had asked. I made a half-hearted objection but had to admit, it had been put off as long as it reasonably could.

"Okay, okay," I'd said. "You win. But let's get the painting done before they put it in. Besides, for carpet in that price range, they'll probably have to do a credit check." Stupid comment, I know, but I have a well-established track record in that department.

I had promised and retracted the painting project so many times, that it had become a private joke. Aurora was about to hire the "Yes, ma'am!" man, the gleeful handyman who for a small fee would perform whatever task your incapable or unreliable husband had failed to do. I hated his commercials and never let them go by without a scathing remark. Usually, I punched the radio off, or at least dimmed the volume when they came on. Aurora knew that if she ever wanted to really hurt me, she'd have to do nothing more than call 1 800 YES-DEAR. The idea of calling another man to do your husband's job just doesn't seem right.

The biggest challenge for this trip might be finding a way to once more delay the indoor masterpiece. It was especially bad this time, considering the efforts Aurora went through to extract the latest promise. As we shopped for paint samples, I was contemplating a few escape scenarios, most of which involved expensive jewelry or weekend shopping trips, when providence intervened.

A family showed up in the ER in various stages of respiratory failure, prompting a panicked call to the local pulmonologist. There was no time to even get home and change clothes.

A policeman tried to pull me over as I sped to the ER. He followed me all the way, lights and sirens pushing my adrenaline to life-threatening levels, but there was no way I was pulling over. All three patients were turning blue when I arrived, saliva drooling down their chins and panic registering plainly on their faces. They were fading into paralysis.

I asked the mother, the only one with enough strength left to hold her head up, if they canned their own food. From her stricken look, I could see that they did, and that she understood the question—botulism. We had three advanced cases. The ER doctor and I got them all on life support, though the husband had a brief period of cardiac arrest.

The rest of the week was a chaotic mare's nest of disasters, with one setback after another: the mother and the child got pneumonia from aspirating contents from their mouths, and the father developed a blood clot, followed by HIT—heparin-induced thrombocytopenia. HIT is a dreaded complication where a patient's platelets drop from a reaction to heparin, the medicine we use to fight the clots. Paradoxically, this leads to more blood clots, even more dangerous than the ones that started to process. Its a condition we truly hate to see.

All three family members eventually survived, but it took everything I had, especially since there were already two other highly involved patients in the ICU before they arrived. By the end of the week, when I was set to have those days free, I was run so ragged that Aurora actually *suggested* I take a few days off.

"Go and do something fun and relaxing," she had said. "You can worry about the painting later."

"But honey, you know I'd love to do that; I could use the rest, and there's a million things I'd love to do, but I have been promising that I'd get that room done forever. I think I'd better just get to work."

I thought about throwing in a plaintive sigh, but decided it might be pushing things a little too far.

She saw it for what it was, but bless her heart, she played

along. "We can do the painting anytime, Jack. You have to take care of yourself. All work and no play, you know! I don't want to come home some day and find you chopping up Miss Daisy from next door, while singing 'Polly Wolly Doodle All the Day' as you stuff her into a case of mason jars. Go do something fun. You've earned it."

"Well, if you really think I should. Someone did offer a chance to spend a few days fishing down in California, on the Sacramento. I was going to turn him down, but. . ."

"Go," she said. "You're incorrigible."

CHAPTER TWENTY-FOUR

Mount Shasta grew in my windshield the next morning, its snow-covered slopes shining through the early icy mists. I had left home early in hopes of seeing the sun rise behind it, supposedly one of the more spectacular regional sights. The effect was as dazzling as advertised, the icy crags and shadowy valleys changing before my eyes in the rapidly growing light. People actually climb that mountain for fun, all fourteen thousand and some feet of it. That looks too much like work for me. I'd much rather ply its glacial melts, swinging the perfect dry fly into their hidden pools and matching wits with the native rainbows and brook trout that live there. They have highly tuned survival instincts, and are much more challenging than the hatchery stockings people in most parts of the country are forced to pursue. That exercise/adventure stuff was for a younger generation.

Shasta, and its little sister Shastina, went by as I passed through Weed and Dunsmuir where I joined up with the hordes traveling down I-5. The northbound lanes were worse, congested with skiers looking for a last few runs before the spring shutdown. It would come a week ahead of schedule this year, according to an alarmed article in the *Daily Register*. The San Francisco intellectuals were decrying it as another example of the ever-increasing effects of global warming as they demanded a government cure. The newspaper recommended that anyone who liked to ski should get it out of his system, as there would be little chance in the coming years.

Andrea "Abby" Norton, the peoples' eternally re-elected representative, would fly again from Washington on a private jet, preen before the masses, and win points looking like she cared, all while treating herself to every obscene luxury item available on the tax-payers' dollar. It was a great scam. I've actually thought about running for office myself, but would have to find a way past my disability—I have a compelling need to tell the truth.

In the guise of saving the earth, taxes would be raised to subsidize more electric cars and wind turbines, she'd get re-elected for the fifth or sixth time, (or was it the seventh?) and all would be well. It truly is a great country.

When I retraced the trip, driving back past the mountains on a northerly course, California would have one less lawyer. That could be my contribution to the climate issue. It would be a small reduction in greenhouse gasses, to be sure, and not my main motivation, but we all have to do our part. Think globally and act locally, right?

The enormity of what I was contemplating sobered me; murder for money. But as the road wove back and forth across the Sacramento, and I was treated to brief glimpses of its fish laden pools and riffles, the effect didn't last. By the time I exited in Redding, I was fully back in lawyer killing mode.

CHAPTER TWENTY-FIVE

In retrospect, picking the plaza outside the courthouse to be Blackman's termination point probably wasn't the smartest thing I've ever done, but the symbolic appeal couldn't be dismissed. I could see the headline: "Lawyer's final judgment rendered on courthouse stairs." I should have been a journalist.

It was the final day in a trial where there had been a bad outcome during an obstetrical case. Why would a meth-smoking sixteen-year-old high school dropout have anything but a healthy baby, unless the obstetrician had utterly and carelessly failed to uphold the basic standards of medical care? I was curious to see how Blackman would spin it, but didn't dare go inside for the trial. There was too much chance that someone might see my face.

A reporter stepped out for a smoke. The deeply etched wrinkles surrounding her mouth suggested that she'd been at it for a long time. I hadn't smoked for years, having given it up at Aurora's insistence, but felt that a little smoker's camaraderie would be a good way to find out what was going on inside. Smokers are so ostracized these days, that the chance to share with another from the brotherhood provided an instant bond, a measure of solidarity.

She was happy to talk about the trial, and made it sound like Blackman was going for the throat on this one. After hearing the defaming accusations put forth—'greedy and uncaring,' 'an incompetent charlatan, only looking out for his bottom line, upset at having to delivery yet another welfare baby,' the physician had actually come from behind his table and launched an attack, failing at the last moment when the stunned bailiff recovered and pulled him back.

"Blackman ate it up," she said, "acting as if his sensibilities had been wounded by the attack." Then, with theatrical flair and her best statesman affectation, she pantomimed Blackman's final arguments:

Ladies and Gentlemen of the jury, the greatest gift you can give this state is to grant a judgment so large that this uncaring physician will never be able to harm another unborn child. Or, and here she turned dramatically to face me, as if I was the jury, *those trying to defend them.*

Blackman must have gone to the same law school as Moon. A few years ago, one of his physician defendants had been taken out of trial by ambulance, suffering a devastating stroke after listening to testimony similar to what he had put forth today. Rumor had it that he kept a framed copy of the newspaper article describing the event, placed high on his office wall for all to see. It had apparently been one of Blackman's proudest moments.

Did I say I'd struggled with the moral aspect of killing him? After hearing from the reporter I was feeling more like an exterminator than a criminal. Too bad I couldn't frame a copy of tomorrow's front page for my office. It would bring a smile every time I looked up, but might raise uncomfortable questions.

Northern California's righteous judgment-maker finally came out of court for lunch. He was surrounded by syco-phants, and in control of his surroundings, or so he thought. I infiltrated his ranks. Instead of the corned beef on rye he had been expecting, Blackman got a stomach full of double-edged high-carbon stainless-steel surprise. I stood so close to his body as I struck with the knife that no one else could see the blow. When he fell, clutching his mid-section, the crowd's initial reaction was to gather around their fallen hero, calling desperately for CPR. It didn't take long, however, for the situ-ation to clarify. That's when the real excitement began.

Centered in front of the courthouse, it should have crossed my mind that there would be a certain degree of police presence. Maybe I was thinking too much about the beautiful rainbows I'd soon be chasing, or maybe it was sleep depriva-tion or the senescent effects of my advancing years. Anyway, Johnny Law came out the ornate courthouse door just as Blackman hit the ground for his final public performance. I moved away as inconspicuously as possible, while the cop ran to provide assistance. The initial panicked response and the shouting for CPR gave some cover, but only briefly, and I knew I was going to have to get out as quickly as possible.

As people pulled back, staring in horror at the spread-ing stain of lawyer and realizing this wasn't a simple heart attack, the officer saw me heading away. A younger cop might not have put it together so quickly, but this one realized that there was something wrong. Why would a bystander be fleeing the scene of a simple medical condition, and why would he be looking worriedly over his shoulder, prepared to run as he did?

He locked eyes on me as he fumbled for his radio. That was all I needed. I haven't run for anything since high school, and not particularly well there, but I put everything I had into a dash to my escape car. I had an old import I'd stolen earlier that morning, one of those generics that looks just like everyone else's. The owner had trusted a magnetic key holder to protect his spare, conveniently and predictably hidden in the wheel well. I left the car parked where it would be easy to get to, a few blocks from the courthouse. My plan had been to drive it to my truck, switch, and be on my way. Problem was, the 'hood had descended.

Why would a group of teenage gangsters be hanging out around my piece-of-shit car—okay, around someone else's piece-of-shit car? A few blocks away, every lawyer in town had his Lexus sedan or Mercedes or low-slung two-door BMW chick magnet car lined up like a Vegas luxury sales lot. Yet here they were, surrounding mine, and standing between me and freedom. There was no way I could fight my way through, and the cop would be coming around the corner any second. I was done.

The gang had a tire iron. They were about to break out the rear window when I remembered the brown paper package. It had been partially wedged under the driver's seat, but wouldn't fit all the way. It had been getting in the way of my feet, so I tossed it into the back. There had been a vague but familiar odor coming from it, but my mind had been focused elsewhere, and it hadn't fully registered. Now, I realized I'd been carting a stash of Humbolt County Gold, California's finest. I hollered at them and hit the unlock button just as they began their back swing, and told them to help themselves, barely saving the window.

My generosity with the weed, or perhaps some street cred from the blood-tinged jacket I was wearing, was enough for them to get out of my way. In moments, my trusty import was fired up and downtown Redding was disappearing in my rearview mirror.

Looking back, I could see my newfound friends were running interference. Go team!

I couldn't get back to my truck fast enough. Patrol cars were coming from all over. It was like I had kicked a beehive, an experience I am unfortunately too familiar with. A couple of the cops took a second look at me, and one even flashed his brakes before changing his mind and heading on to the courthouse. They must not have had much of a description, but I couldn't count on it staying that way. I needed to ditch the car as soon as possible, and to find a different way to get to my truck.

The parking lot for a plasma donation station served as a good place to hide the car. It was already loaded with others just like mine. As they say, the best place to hide a Christmas tree is in a forest. Leaving it there left me several blocks from where my truck was parked, but I felt too vulnerable staying with it.

I left the spare key in the ashtray, wiped away my fingerprints, and made for my truck. My blood-soaked overcoat was deposited in a dumpster, after I double checked to make certain I had left no identifying items in its pockets.

The lure of the river had been temporarily replaced by a simple desire to survive. I walked a few blocks to the west, to get away from the drug-mule car, and then stepped into a bar to consider my options. Celebrity sightings would be few and far between, but it was right in line with area standards. The customers appeared to be there with a single-minded purpose, to leave the cares of the world behind. They eyed me with suspicion, obviously an outsider.

Would it be better to hole up here for a few hours, or to press on? If the police found the escape car, they would focus their search, and eventually they would have a more accurate description. That would be disastrous, and from the way I was regarded by the midday regulars, I couldn't count on them to give me any kind of break. I'd take my chances on the street.

Making an effort to appear normal, I left the bar and slowly closed the distance to my truck. As I got close, I saw a policeman approaching it, reaching for his radio to call it in. He was alert, but not particularly on edge.

"Afternoon, officer," I said, friendly, respectful—slightly deferential. "Problem with my parking?"

"No, sir. We're investigating a disturbance near the courthouse. Have you seen anything suspicious?" He was eyeing my Oregon tags. I was glad to see the Policeman's Benevolent Association fund-raiser decal. They had made a cold call solicitation a few weeks ago. I was on the way out the door to the ICU and almost didn't answer. The twenty-five dollar donation might be the best money I've ever spent.

"Well," I began, "I'm not from around here, so it might be a little tough for me to notice, but nothing seems obviously out of the ordinary. Well, wait a minute. There was that one guy I passed a few blocks back. He kept looking back over his shoulder, and he didn't even respond when I tried to say hello, not even a simple nod. I thought he was just crazy, you know, but maybe not. What happened?"

He started around my car, looking in the windows. "We had a homicide," he finally admitted. "They've called in practically every cop in the city; must have been someone important."

"Oh, man. Do I think that might have been him I saw? That gives me the creeps."

He had gotten around to the driver's side window. I did a quick mental inventory and couldn't think of anything incriminating. "Would you like to take a quick look inside? I don't mind, if it will help."

"Nah, I don't think so. You don't look like the type. Besides, you're on a fishing trip. Hate to get in the way of that, just wish I could go. My dad and I used to hit Whiskeytown every weekend. I sure do miss him. Anyway, you don't really look like the guy we're after. He was fairly athletic." He was taking a look at my waistline as he said it. "He outran one of our officers."

"I'll keep an eye out," I said, "especially if I see that guy again. And I think I'll stop talking to strangers for a while. Do you have any other description that might help, in case it wasn't him?"

"Not much. A couple of teenage gangster wannabes gave us a little something. Said he was a tough-looking dude, someone they wouldn't want to mess with, maybe ex-Special Forces or something, but not much description beyond that. We're interviewing other witnesses—there's at least a dozen. A TV reporter was there and never even thought to turn on his damn camera. Can you believe that? Everyone gave a different story. Tall, short, heavy, thin. One swore that he had a scar across his cheek, and several even disagreed about his skin color. How do they expect us to do much with that?"

I wondered what the conversation would be like when they talked to my smoking buddy; she must have some idea of what had happened.

"I'll call 911 if I see something, Officer … uh … Rodriguez. I hope you catch the guy. This world sure has gone crazy."

He didn't think to ask what a fisherman was doing parked on a seedy downtown street, and I didn't stick around long enough to give him a second chance. The rest of my trip out of town was uneventful, but Officer Rodriquez was right about the reinforcements. Killing someone on the cop's home turf didn't go over so well, something to file away for future reference.

Getting the rest of the way out of town hadn't been hard, but I was glad to be spending a few days on the river. Trying to head home before the heat died down would be asking for trouble. I-5 would be crawling with law enforcement, and I didn't dare take a back road. Anything that went wrong, a flat tire or even a stop to drain the morning coffee could get a cop's attention. They'd ask why I was taking the long way home instead of I-5, and I'd be in it deep. By then, they would probably have a better description, and every law enforcement officer in northern California would be out to bust the hitman with the balls of steel.

I hadn't really put it in those words before, but that's what I had become. Moon had been goal-directed, and killing Joyce had been for self-preservation, but this one was strictly for the bank. Dr. Jack Hastings, hit man. Murderer for hire.

The directions to Al's ranch were easy. A few turns on the padlock, a hemorrhoid-rattling trip down a two track studded with basalt boulders ideally spaced to cause maximum spinal damage, and I was staring at fishing paradise.

CHAPTER TWENTY-SIX

My short stay on the river was a tantalizing glance at what life could be. Thorpe had a small A-frame cabin. I named it my Valium Villa. It looked like a giant upside down V. When people look at a pill now, and see a V they think of Viagra, but when I was in training, that meant Valium, the original Momma's little helper.

The cabin's similarity of effect couldn't have been any more pronounced, even if it had been stocked with a year's supply of those magic pills. Gazing at it, I could feel the layers of stress peeling off my back. For a moment, I did nothing but stand there and take it all in.

An extra surprise awaited me just downstream. A natural hot spring bubbled up right next to the river. I could rest my weary bones in hot water, freshly percolated from the depths of the earth, and have my hands in the cold Sacramento River at the same time. The spring was isolated from the highway, so my lack of a swimsuit was of no concern.

I was exhausted from my time in the ICU, and also from the stress and drama of the murder and my escape from Redding. The fishing could wait a few minutes.

Those few minutes magically changed into the rest of the afternoon. The lullaby of the river and the soothing warmth of the mineral-rich waters pulled me into an amazingly refreshing sleep. I awoke hours later to the sounds of trout feasting on the evening mayfly hatch, with trout slurping them one after another, literally at my eye level. It was a sight few have ever had the chance to see. Normally, when faced with a rise like that, I would be scrambling like a teenager on his first real date, trying to get my rod put together before it got too dark to fish, but tonight, it was enough to just sit back and watch it happen.

I stayed in the water, enjoying the experience until Orion started his nightly journey, hunting across the sky. That was when I realized that I had made a small, painful mistake. My Boy Scout leader would have been disappointed. I hadn't thought to bring a flashlight, breaking the "Be Prepared" rule, one of the first tenets of Scouting.

My poor, water-wrinkled city dweller feet didn't do well on the broken rocks lining the path back to Al's cabin. In the daylight it had been easy—I had been able to pick and choose where I stepped, but in the dark, every step was an adventure. Still, it was a minor issue. I wasn't going to lose any sleep over it. In fact, in the splendor of this magnificent canyon I wasn't going to lose sleep over *anything*.

Not ready to give up on one of the finest evenings I had seen in a long time, I started a fire. Crackling flames were soon dancing in Al's natural stone fireplace. My feet were propped on a bearskin ottoman and an escapist novel was perched on my lap. It had been a perfect evening, and as I settled in front of the fire, I realized that it was getting even better.

In the morning, I would awaken on a soft down mattress. Freshly ground coffee beans would be placed in the French press, ready to give up their essence for my day's first delightful cup. It would be savored on the front porch as the first rays sunshine brought in the new day—a day to be spent entirely at my leisure. There would be no pagers or emergencies, no waiting in line for marginal cafeteria food, all the while counting the minutes, knowing that I needed to be getting back to my patients. It would be a day with sole access to a spectacular mountain fishery. If God does exist, this part of the world must have been made in one of his finer moments.

Morning came, and it was just as I had imagined. The Sacramento's long, gently twisting stretches of riffles and pocket water created a natural symphony—a morning lullaby that set a tranquil tone for the rest of the day. The river was lined on both sides by deeply undercut banks, ideal places where the big trout would hide. They'd be safe from airborne predators while they waited in ambush for their next meal.

After flowing past the cabin, the river dropped down in to a deep, turbulent pool which then transitioned to a shallow, beautiful calm next to the hot spring. That calm would come alive with rising trout when the sun finished its daily journey, it's finally rays lighting the sky as it settled over the dramatic rocky crags to the west. I could so easily picture my hand-tied elk-hair caddis flies dipping out of sight in the center of a trout's ripple that I startled myself, raising my arm to set the imaginary hook.

I couldn't help smiling again—the next few days were going to be me and Mother Nature. Looking up, I saw that osprey had rule of the sky; they are my favorite bird. I could almost feel myself up there with them, sun on my back, cool air slipping below my taut wings as I watched the world go by—nothing but freedom, and the anticipation of my next meal, a heavy silver trout struggling in my talons as I struggled to fly back to my nest.

Awakening from my daydream, I slipped my favorite fly rod, a delicate 2-weight, out of its protective case. It had been given to me by a favorite patient.

He had been on his deathbed, emaciated from the relentless advance of a cancer diagnosed only a few months earlier. Our dreams of another season spent dancing dry flies in front of Gearhart Mountain's wild trout were replaced by the stark reality of his impending death. He had gifted the rod to me, smiling as he pictured the adventures we had over the years. It would be perfect for the dry-fly action of the early evening, a fitting memorial for a wonderful friend.

As he was dying, I smuggled some of his favorite scotch into the ICU. It was a clear violation of hospital policy, and it had to be spooned into his mouth, but the smile as he emerged briefly from his stupor was priceless; another one of those moments that make my career worthwhile—my lawful career, that is. I wonder what Harry would have thought of my more recent activities.

A more substantial rod would be needed for the bigger prey, the ones hiding in those undercut banks. I had a 5-weight for those, one that I had built as a senior project in high school. It didn't compare to the high tech rods being put out now, but it had always served me well.

After both rods were strung, I realized I had forgotten to call Aurora last night. A hot tub under the stars will do that. Reception was sparse, an intermittent two bars, but I managed to get through.

"Hi, honey. I made it safely. It's absolutely beautiful! The only thing missing that could make it more perfect would be having you here!"

"Nice try, suck-up, but I think you'll be just fine on your own."

She tried to give a brief update on her day, but we kept losing the call. We eventually gave up, after every attempt at redialing gave the same result. I did get through that I might stay an extra day, since it was so relaxing. Could she call the office and tell them? I left the part off about letting the police dragnet settle down before hitting the road home.

"When those patients hit the office Tuesday, I'll be ready to rock and roll."

The call dropped again, but she did get through that she would tell Maggie.

After having checked in with the boss it was time to fish. I knew exactly where I was going to start, if I could find the right fly. A few years ago, I had spent an evening tying the most time-consuming pattern I'd ever attempted—a spun deer-hair field mouse. It was made of layer after layer of tightly spun hair, wrapped around the hook and then trimmed to shape and finished with a cute set of chamois ears and a wrapped-thread nose. The ears were my touch, completely unnecessary, but I couldn't resist. They added that special touch that would be sure to bring a smile. Working all night, I could only finish three, but they were truly works of art.

My original plan had been to use these fishing for large-mouth bass in a Kansas farm pond, but that trip, like so many others, never came to be. They sat around for years, neglected and unused. If I could find them, it would be time for their inaugural voyage. The rainbows and brook trout I normally pursue love a good meal of insects, but the brown trout, especially the big ones that live under the banks, love a meal they can sink their teeth in to. The mouse pattern should be perfect.

My fishing equipment lived in the same state of disorganization as most everything else in my life. Finding the right screwdriver or wrench for a given task can be a half hour search. Typically, it comes to the same embarrassing point. "Aurora, have you seen my stethoscope (hammer, shoes, brain)? I can't find it anywhere." It goes from bad to ugly when I try to gather the records for doing our taxes.

Searching through the chaos of my fishing gear, I finally found the fly box I'd been looking for. There they were, my three field mouse flies, as beautiful as the day I tied them. No trout would be able to resist. I tied on the most seductive one and headed to the river, looking for just the right spot; a nice undercut bank where the currents were not too tricky. If you cast across fast water, the current grabs the loose line and pulls it down stream, dragging the fly across the surface like a reckless water skier with no resemblance to the helpless drifting meal a trout would be looking for. A single cast with bad drag can send a trout off in alarm—there is no second chance.

I found the spot just upstream from the Valium Villa. Glancing again at my mouse and recalling the loving hours spent creating it, I almost hated to put it in harm's way. But, it was brought into this world for a specific purpose and it's time had come. I cast it just onto the far bank, slightly upstream from my target. A few subtle twitches worked it through the weeds, and it plopped into the slack water, a perfect landing.

What happened next was spectacular. A huge, thick-sided brown trout materialized from the depths and launched itself at my defenseless mouse, rising halfway out of the water in a savage, twisting attack. At the sting of the hook, it took off downstream, screaming line off my reel, the drag singing like pissed off hornets.

The fish couldn't be controlled and I had to take off downstream after it. I almost broke my ankle in the process, but when it got to the deep pool and out of the fast current, it dove to the bottom and things became a lot more manageable.

The brown trout is one of the most beautiful creatures on the planet, but frustratingly elusive. I seldom caught one, so was seldom able to admire them up close. Now, not only was I in a position to do so, but it was the biggest trout I had ever fought. After it had rested a few minutes at the bottom of the pool, it resumed the fight, breaking the surface over and over like an enraged tarpon, and then crashing back down with depth-charge fury. It took deep runs back to the bottom of the pool, where it would sulk for a few minutes before tearing off again.

It couldn't get past the rocks at the end of the pool, so I was safe from another downstream journey, but it did try to go back upstream. It even made it part way, but the current helped my struggle this time, and I was finally able to subdue it.

I brought the trout close to shore, where I was able to take a few pictures. One showed the trout's colors in brilliant fashion, and showed the deer hair mouse in great profile. The sun was in a perfect position, and even Gill, always critical of my camera skills, would have been impressed. I would have the shot enlarged, and it would have a position of honor on my office wall.

Something would have to go to make room. Princess Leia would be the most obvious choice—she was making Aurora jealous, despite my protests that she was number two in my life. Putting the picture of the trout up in the princess's place might smooth some fences. The other option would be to remove the vacation caricature of Aurora. She had never liked it, but odds were that if I took it down and kept Leia I'd be spending a lot more time on the couch in my den. It would be the princess.

The fly would be retired. There was no way it would ever match the thrill I had achieved on its first cast. It would be the first entry into the Jack Hastings Fly-Tying Hall of Fame.

The hook came out easily, and a textbook-perfect catch-and-release was accomplished. I'm not opposed to eating a trout now and then, but this magnificent fish would live to terrorize field mice another day. Slightly winded from the excitement, I lay down in the soft grass and watched the world go by. The sun was warm, and it wasn't long before I was doing an impressive Rip Van Winkle imitation.

My somnolence was interrupted by a firm nudging in the small of my back. What was Aurora doing in my fish camp? I turned to see if it was a dream, and if not, to see what else might come from the situation, only to stare straight into the eyes of an equally surprised black bear. Who'd have ever thought that the world's largest bear would be living in northern California? This thing probably snacked on grizzlies when it got bored with normal bear fare, and used telephone poles as toothpicks—an ursine Babe, the Blue Ox and it was standing right over me.

With its poor eyesight, the bear must have that thought that I was a log it might turn over to find a few grubs. The log, however, came to life at its nudge. I screamed, and the bear bit down before turning to beat feet out of the area. I was left with four very sore holes in my butt and a great story to tell at the next cocktail party. I'm just glad I wasn't sleeping face down!

When the shock wore off, and I had a chance to survey

the damage, I found that the wounds weren't too bad. Bears don't carry rabies, and there was nothing that would require more than a tetanus shot, which I had been needing, but putting off for years anyway. With a generous portion of Advil, I was able to finish the fishing day, though it did take a moment for my hands to stop shaking enough to change flies to match the evening hatch. Trout were rising avidly, and it made for the perfect ending to a sort of perfect day.

CHAPTER TWENTY-SEVEN

Saturday morning got off to a leisurely start. I was surprisingly sore from my 'bear attack,' and my shoulder was a little stiff from fighting the huge trout. It must have taken close to half an hour to land it, and I'm not in exactly in prize-fighting shape these days, despite what my ganja-smoking friends told the police. I thought about the hot springs but decided instead to have a simple breakfast and then stretch my legs. I didn't get enough exercise, and the fish would still be there when I got back, so I set off to explore the canyon.

The day passed in idyllic fashion; I even got a mild sunburn, sure to set me apart from the whitewashed masses at home. The rock walls of the canyon offered a challenge too tempting to pass up. They proved to be a little more intimidating than they had appeared from below, but I was able to find a route, and by mid-morning, I had an osprey's view of the river from the top. As an added bonus, I found a unique artifact.

A small indentation in the face of the rock served as home for a marmot, or perhaps a packrat. One stick in the nest didn't fit with the others—it was too straight. Further excavation revealed it to be the broken shaft of an arrow. The tip was fully intact and was partially embedded in the vertebra of a large animal. It prompted visions of life a few hundred years ago, when Native Americans ruled.

The area would have made a perfect home. Clean water and a climate suitable for crops, if they chose to grow them. I'm not sure which tribes lived here; some did farm, while others were pure hunters, living a nomadic life. For them, there was plenty of game, including bears the size of a teepee. They would have done well here.

The trip down was more treacherous, and the possibility of a second fatality for the trip loomed, especially when a shale of loose rock slipped free under my feet, sending me sliding to the edge of a drop. With a final desperate reach, I was able to wedge my arm into a small crack, bringing my fall in an abrupt, painful halt.

Unfortunately, the relic tumbled over the edge.

I had planned to give it to Zach. Before he discovered girls, he was all over rocks and lizards and history. We spent our free days searching miles of beaches, scouring the desert and chasing rattlesnakes. Ghost towns were researched and explored, and seldom did we come home without a rusted mining artifact, unique rock or other memento. Aurora wasn't terribly pleased with our treasures, but I think she secretly liked the time we spent together. Plus, it got me out of her hair.

I was saddened to miss the opportunity to reconnect with him. We had little to do with each other these days, and we had never found anything so unique; that, and the fact that this was a tremendous archeological find, and in museum quality. Still, I figured he'd rather have his dad back than an old bone, no matter how cool it was.

Looking over the edge to see if there was a way down, I was pleasantly surprised. The artifact had caught on a snag—a forlorn growth trying to make it in solid rock. What an example of triumph over difficult circumstances.

With a chance at reclaiming Zach's treasure, I leaned over to the point that blood was starting to pound in my ears, but it remained just out of reach. If I tried to stretch any further, I would have it, though the reunion would be brief and the final result both predictable and unpleasant. Joyce took two trips down the stairs; I was confident that it would only take the one to secure my passage to the happy hunting grounds.

I am insured, though Aurora never misses the opportunity to tell me it should be for more. Someday, when I'm feeling brave, I need to ask if that is because she has such a high opinion of me, or if it's part of her special early retirement plan. Meanwhile, if I wanted the artifact, I was going to have to find another way.

A narrow ledge, no more than five or six inches wide, ran below the survivalist bush. It looked secure. If I could lower myself down, I could position myself within reach of the arrowhead. It would be a risk, but the ledge looked solid, and there was a manageable path from there to the bottom if I could manage one difficult maneuver.

I got a firm hold and swung my feet out over the drop. There was a slight convexity to the wall, which I hadn't appreciated from my initial vantage point, and it put me in a more difficult position than I had anticipated. Unfortunately, at this point I was fully committed. A few decades ago it would have been no problem to pull myself back to safety, but then, a lot of things were different back then.

My arms were starting to give out, trembling from the sustained effort as my toes searched for the ledge. They were reaching the end of their ability to hold me, when I finally found it and transferred my weight as quickly as I could. The ledge was littered with loose rocks, cracks and deep fissures, but it held my weight.

The hidden convexity of the wall put my center of gravity further back than I felt comfortable with, especially with my backpack and my ever-so-slight beer belly. My heels were positioned well over the drop, and I had to support myself on my toes, but again, there was no choice—I could never make it back to the top.

Lessons from my rock climbing days started coming back. Slower is faster. Always keep at least two anchors. Never take a step without making sure there is another secure opportunity to follow, and one of the most important, always maintain focus. Thoughts of seeing Zach's face as I handed the vertebrae to him were pushed out, and I entered the zone. No fear, just a joy at being one with the mountain.

I reached the bush and again marveled at its ability to grow in such harsh conditions. I secured the treasure and then went back to my primary objective, getting off the rock alive. Before starting my descent, I had spotted a chimney, a rock formation almost as good as a staircase for an experienced climber. It looked like it went all the way down, though the foreshadowing from my original perspective had led me to believe it was closer to the bush than it really was. It would require an actual slide of at least ten feet to reach it, a move unacceptable without safety gear.

With no choice, I started back along the ledge. It was even more unnerving from this direction, and the route down would be far more technical than the chimney. Fatigue led me to lose some of the focus that allowed rock climbers to reach their older years. I was thinking that Zach had damn well better appreciate what I was doing, when the ledge gave out from under my left foot. I teetered for a moment, drop but managed at the last second to get a thin handhold, enough to stabilize myself.

The gap from where the ledge had crumbled was too big to cross; I was forced to reverse direction once more. The slide down to the chimney was now my only chance. It was terrifying to let go of all support and start to slide, but I made it to the chimney, where I was able to arrest myself. It was exhilarating, but I wouldn't recommend it. Amusement parks across the country have rides, all well designed to produce a much safer adrenaline rush, and manage to do it without the loss of several layers of skin.

Chimneys have always been my favorite and have been the only significant efforts at free climbing I had ever allowed myself. I made it to the bottom without further mishap and headed back to the cabin. There would be no more excitement today; I was going back to fishing mode.

Two small rainbows found their way to my creel. They were cleaned and dressed in a hazelnut crust. I gathered wild sage and steeped it in a lemon butter sauce. It was drizzled over the top of the trout, providing the final gourmet touch.

Al had stocked the cabin in anticipation of my arrival. I found a treasure trove of dried morel mushrooms, which I sautéed, and fresh fruit which I turned into a salad. A delightful 1986 cabernet completed the meal. I enjoyed it in the spreading warmth of the fireplace. The contrast with the evening's cool, pine-scented air produced an evening of such tranquility as to almost defy description.

Mindful of the previous day's encounter with Godzilla the Bear, I closed the sliding door before curling in bed with my novel. It was probably still running to get away from the man with the bad grammar, but I wasn't taking chances. Sleep interrupted me in mid-paragraph, and the next thing I was aware of was the new day's full sunlight streaming through the bedroom window.

I'd slept past the morning rise, but the fishing was still spectacular. Fish fell to nymphs and small streamers, almost everything I tried, even a steelhead pattern I floated through a riffle on a whim. It was a magical day. As it came to its end, it was time to go back to the 2-weight and dry flies. The evening rise surpassed the previous night's, with mayflies and dancing caddis, ovipositing for future generation. I realized that without intending to, I had quit fishing and was simply watching the nature show in awe. I'd never dreamed I'd have a day of such good fishing that I'd be content to sit back like that, but it was a night I'll always remember.

CHAPTER TWENTY-EIGHT

Monday morning reality hit as another night of blissful sleep surrendered to my internal alarm clock. One last leisurely breakfast and a few last casts in to the upstream pocket waters, and it would be time to head north and get back to my real life. It would be speed limit plus five, all the way home. Besides being the way home for serial lawyer killers, I-5 is a major drug trafficking highway, and is heavily patrolled.

I am constantly amazed at the number of six- and even seven-figure drug busts where the suspect was pulled over for speeding, or some other avoidable violation. We had one a few months back where the genius was driving without a license tag. That one only cost them a few hundred thousand, but really? With the ingenuity of the smugglers, able to build sophisticated tunnels and even homemade submarines, you'd think they could find smarter mules—ones who could get the product the last few steps to the buyers. Instead, they hired flunkies who drove with their headlights off or sped through high narcotic traffic areas, attracting the attention of the law.

I wanted no extra attention. Maybe when I got home some extra attention would be nice, but that's a different story. My fishing gear would provide a reasonable excuse and my digital sure-shot had a few snaps of my conquests in case I did get pulled over. I could show them off and brag about my catch-and-release philosophy— ("I don't want to hurt anything, Officer.") That would, however, require my being able to bring the pictures forth from the depths of the camera's memory, a nearly impossible task for someone from my generation. Without prompting from my son, and with a cop looking over my shoulder, eager to be the one to wrap up the humiliating murder, that might be a problem. Maybe I'd leave the camera out of it—speed limit plus five would be the rule.

The drive went well. Talk radio can be fun for a few hundred miles, and I even thought briefly of calling in to air my opinion on a few subjects, but I lost the nerve. I can eviscerate a lawyer in broad daylight in front of a building full of police, but anonymously talking to a radio host fifteen hundred miles across the country? Maybe another day.

As the miles melted away, and the patrols thinned out, I regained some of the relaxation I'd felt in the last few days and started dreaming of seeing Aurora again. Homecoming was always nice. I loved my adventures, at least my old legal ones, but getting back to the comforts of home and the loving embrace of my wife has always the best part of any trip.

Aurora was happy to see me. She welcomed me home with a loving embrace. That embrace was followed by a stern command. "Now, go get in the shower." She shook her head no when she saw me raise my eyebrow in question. "You're showering alone, fish man!"

Oh, well, still nice to be back. And Zach loved his arrow-head.

The shower out of the way, Aurora asked me if I had heard anything about a high profile murder while I was gone. Lying to my wife isn't something I have much experience with. I'd told her a few times that a dress or a pair of pants didn't make her look fat, or that one more line of French fries wouldn't show, go ahead, but the real stuff—true, meaningful lies; not so much. Technically, since the cabin had no TV or radio, I was okay telling her that I hadn't heard, though I didn't feel good with the deception.

"It was a big-shot malpractice attorney," she said, not seeming to be too upset at his misfortune. "I'll bet there are a lot of Redding doctors going for the back-shelf stuff now!" I almost hugged her again. For the second time, I came so close to telling her what had really happened. It would make it so much easier if I decided to make putting lawyers under the dandelions into a real career. I didn't relish the thought of carrying on a life of deception, having to lie to her every time I went out of town. Plus, she was smart enough that I probably wouldn't get away with it for long, anyway.

With the way she was talking about these deceased lawyers, she might not be too upset to hear that their deaths had come at my hands. She might even want to come along on a few assignments, at least if they took us somewhere nice, like Orlando or maybe New England while the leaves were chang-ing. One of these days, I was going to have to take a chance and tell her.

It wouldn't be today, though—"*Hi, honey, I'm home. It was an incredible trip! I've never caught so many fish. Oh—I gutted a lawyer, too. What's for dinner?*" Probably not the best way to start that discussion, and my other plans for the evening would probably end up on hold; not an acceptable situation.

CHAPTER TWENTY-NINE

I went over to George's the next day. The transformation from the lace and flowers his wife demanded to a comfortable, first-rate bachelor pad had been thorough and amazing. I wonder if Aurora would ever let me have a corner to call my own, though I doubted I could ever approach the level of male sophistication George had achieved. With no consideration at all for the concerns of a wife, he had created a true masterpiece. From that point on, I always insisted we have our meetings there; it gave an artificial sense of having some control in the world.

George was thrilled with my California performance. "You were brilliant!" he said, muting the remote. "There is no way anyone could mistake that for a random act of violence, of Blackman being in the wrong place at the wrong time. ABC, CNN, FOX News, they're all talking about it, wondering if someone has declared open season on lawyers. You're a star!"

"Will there be commercial endorsements? When do I get my footprint on Hollywood Boulevard?"

"No," chuckled George, "you'll have to wait for that, but Al called. He is thrilled with the way things turned out. Every doctor in Redding wants to thank their new hero! The cops have already been by to see him, but like you said, there are so many others who would want to see the man dead that they didn't even push him. He just told them he hadn't even known it had happened until one of his partners stepped in and invited him to a good-bye party a bunch of the other doctors were sponsoring at the Gee Spot."

"Tell him thanks. And tell him his trout fishing is the best I've ever had, minus the bear attack, of course."

"He wanted to know how we want to get paid."

"Ah, the second element of our criminal life," I said. "Kill the lawyer, make a dramatic getaway, and then get filthy rich."

The bank wouldn't do. They are required by the government to report deposits of the magnitude I'd be making. There could be no paper trail connecting me to the crime—not a good way to achieve longevity as a hit man.

I had decided to use an offshore account, but had to do some homework first. Thanks to Al Gore's incredible information-sharing invention, it was an easy task, and I was soon well versed in the offshore banking field. It was actually quite interesting.

There is so much money coursing through these banks that they have become the major share of some regional economies. At least fifty islands and even several land-based countries make these services available, making it a challenge to decide where to go. All offer anonymous security, and some leave it up to the client to report interest income to their countries tax agency, rather than reporting it themselves, as our institutions are required to do.

An additional advantage is that our financial institutions are regulated almost as heavily as the medical field. The offshore banking industry was free of that, allowing them to offer much greater rates of interest. I wasn't looking at this as an investment so much as a safe place to hide my felonious gatherings, but a little interest is still nice.

The concept of off shore banking began when European entrepreneurs grew sufficiently sick of paying the exorbitant, in fact, confiscatory taxes demanded by their governments. They started putting their money into banks in the Channel Islands, off the coast of Normandy, and saw immediate benefits. Security, tax advantages, and complete confidentiality became the hallmark of the industry, and it rapidly became a worldwide enterprise.

Most clients were lawful citizens, just trying for a little edge, but it didn't take long for the criminal element to see the potential. It was the tax man who finally got Al Capone, not the FBI. Lessons like that need to be learned only once. These guys are a lot smarter than the drug runners—they don't get tripped up by the same mistakes over and over. They found off shore banking to be a perfect opportunity for laundering money and, of course, a place to secure their large sums of ill-gotten currency—exactly what I needed.

I settled on the Bailiwick of Guernsey, deciding to put my trust in the Bank of Clarkenshyre. Guernsey is a small agricultural island, described as having an "independent and free-spirited" population. Along with a couple others of the Channel Islands, it has the distinction of being the only British territory occupied by the Germans in World War II. Many of the islanders were interned in POW camps and endured horrific deprivation as slave laborers, forced to work for the Nazi war effort.

Others were exported, most never coming home.

Military fortifications remain scattered over the island. They have become popular tourist attractions. The area's history was fascinating, but the real attraction for me was that besides the romantic notion that the Channel Islands banks were the genesis of the offshore banking industry, they are reputed to be among the world's most secure.

Setting up my account was easy, even with my rudimentary computer skills (a constant source of amusement for my children). Proof of ID was accomplished by e-faxing a copy of my passport and a utility bill, to show my current address. A nine-digit security code was established, along with a list of co-owners, Aurora, and all they needed was my first deposit. They wanted that at the beginning, but I explained that the first funds would be coming from an outside source and would be deposited immediately after the account was active. It was a little nontraditional, but they were happy to work with me. Customer satisfaction seems to rank high on their list of attributes. The process took no more than fifteen minutes— less time than it takes my wife to pick the right pair of shoes for a day at the mall.

George sent my account number to Dr. Thorpe, along with Clarkenshyre's routing number, and I had e-mail confirmation of the deposit later that afternoon. Welcome to the elite offshore club, home to millionaires and billionaires, the jet-set elite, mafia kingpins, . . .and me!

I got up after our meeting, ready to head out the door when George grabbed my arm. "One more thing, Jack. This is going to really tickle your hang-downs. Al mentioned a friend, an orthopedic surgeon, who is in a tough spot. Al mentioned that the lawyer suing him had been killed. His friend congratulated him, and went on to say how much he wished something like that would happen to the lawyer suing him. What do you think, are you ready for another go?"

An orthopod, I thought. *That could be some serious cash.*

That was followed by another of those moments of concern at how easily I'd transitioned from a few reasonably righteous killings to becoming a murderer for hire. These moments of doubt were really getting old. If these lawyers had chosen an honest, respectable way to make a living, they wouldn't *be* in any danger. So far, no one had asked me to kill a teacher, or to off a mailman or a garbage collector. Hospital administrators might be a consideration, and I wouldn't be opposed to branching out to include divorce lawyers—they are sort of in the same family as the malpractice scum I've been working with, but overall, it was easy to convince myself that I was making a positive change as I slowly reduced the dramatic over population of lawyers in our country.

And then there was a new factor to consider. The government has exercised its infinite wisdom—all hospitals and doctors' offices are now required to abandon the traditional paper charting that has worked for generations, and to move to an electronic operating system. Hospitals where the change has been put in place have been generating horror stories. Tasks that took a doctor ten or fifteen minutes now take an hour. Mistakes in patient care have become more common, and physician dissatisfaction has risen nearly to the point of revolution. The cost has also been staggering—well over a hundred million dollars per hospital, dollars that could have been spent expanding patient care or paying their staff properly.

It's the same in doctors' offices. A few medical software vendors had come by, each claiming their product is the only complete, user-friendly version on the market. Their idea of user-friendly is somewhat different from mine, and it was obvious there would have to be a lengthy office shutdown to get any of the systems into play. Poor Rachel, already well into her sixties, was on the verge of having an ulcer at the thought of making the transition.

None of the available office systems would interface with the system the hospital was putting in, the only feature that would have been a benefit to me. Putting even the cheapest and least capable program in place would require serious long-term financing, or a staff reduction—not possible for most of us. We've already cut our offices to the core to compensate for reduced Medicare fees. Most of the sole practitioners I had talked to wanted to simply close their offices and retire, or to sign on with one of the medical "box stores," rather than go to the expense of buying a system, and having to learn a whole new way of taking care of patients.

It's sad to see. No one coming out of medical school, already with a half million dollars of debt, would be willing to buy a practice that isn't already set up for government compliance. They would be forced to join large groups or hospitals. The era of the free-spirited, hang-out-your-shingle independent physician was coming to an end. I had less than a year to decide which direction I would go.

I could easily see myself retiring, if I had the resources to allow it. The prospect of practicing under those nerd-driven systems was making a future in medicine much less attractive. Unfortunately, I wasn't even close to being at that point. A career of murder and mayhem was looking much more attractive.

"Sure, George, I can do it, if it can wait a bit. I need to work on a few things. There were so many ways I had almost gotten caught in Redding—I'm so ridiculously out of shape; that fat cop almost ran me down. And if those gang-bangers hadn't backed away from my car, I'd be a permanent guest of the California Department of Corrections. There's no way I could have fought my way through them. Let me spend some time at the gym and work on a few things and then we'll talk about Al's friend."

George slumped back in his couch, disappointed, but apparently seeing the wisdom of my approach. He didn't want to go down either. "All right, Jack. Take your time. I'll tell Al, and if his friend is still interested down the road, we'll set something up."

The news flashed back to our case, just as I was going once more for the stairs.

"Jack, we're on again," George beamed, undoing the mute. I sat down to revel once more in our accomplishment. A local reporter was being interviewed. He had found that Blackman had built up some impressive gambling debts, and speculated that that might have been the motivation for his murder, not his malpractice work. The story became a lot less interesting, and my media frenzy was at risk of dying off.

I turned to George, shaking my head. "I can't believe it! How many of these sons of bitches am I going to have to kill to make our point?"

CHAPTER THIRTY

The reinvention of Jack Hastings took off at a manic pace. An hour was lopped off the beginning of my office schedule. I told the girls that it was time to start following the advice I had been giving my patients for so long. There was an independent gym near the hospital, Vitality Health Club and Nutrition Center. Lots of the nurses went there. Vitality's television ads featured impossibly Junoesque young ladies sweating ever so slightly as they toned their well-tanned bodies on the latest modern miracle machines. The Swedish bikini team could take lessons. Watching the commercials made me wonder why I had put off this exercise thing for so long. I paid my monthly fee and presented for titillating—I mean, fitness.

There was an unannounced mid-winter sign-up bonus going on, a discount on a personal trainer. Hans (or Franz?), the twenty-something, pumped up pimple faced kid manning the chipped Formica desk, caught up in the eternal arrogance of youth, looked at me and suggested that the trainer *might* be a good way for me to get started. I think he even sneered as he suggested it.

In addition to the gym, where I was now certain I'd be a regular attendee, I had decided to begin martial arts training. I wanted to be the best cold-blooded killer ever produced by a US medical school. And, when I had a few months of kung fu under my belt the condescending front desk Mr. Fitness might be a good place for some real-life practice.

Heading in for my first session, it was obvious that truth in advertising had taken a left turn at the state line. There were four guys for every gal, not that I was looking, and none of the ladies had the faintest resemblance to anyone featured in the ads. In fact, many of them looked like they could have a fair chance trying out for a spot on the Bear's front line. Maybe it was something in the studio lighting, but I was skeptical. Oh, well, it was probably for the best.

The workout machines were an intimidating amalgam that would have made the Marquis de Sade envious. A few were recognizable; the bench press, the leg raise machine and my old favorite, the chin-up bar that the high school gym teacher had used to torment us in front of the girls. One machine, though, had me thoroughly confused. A young lady came along and told me, with a condescending smile, that I was sitting on it backwards. She probably wondered why they even let the old folks in. I thanked her, but assured her that I knew what I was doing and was just trying something different, the way they do it in Europe. When she turned to get back to her routine, I snuck off to another machine, hoping no one else had noticed.

CHAPTER THIRTY-ONE

With my new Adonis-like physical conditioning process underway, the lawsuit gone and a new revenue stream shaping up, life was looking so much better. My old smile was back, the one that made everyone assume I was up to something. No more all day complaining about the various injustices of the world—rotten weather, Satan-spawned hospital administrators and computer programs, etc. The nurses were actually relieved when I started again with my stupid jokes.

I'd been running, working out at the gym, and even the unthinkable—cutting back on the double-layer bacon wrapping and cream cheese pastries. My martial arts training gave me a new rhythmic fluidity; my energy was up, and my shoulders were too. Something was definitely going on with this recently depressed healer.

Aurora was one of the first to start wondering about the changes. One evening, as we were settling down to relax, she shifted on the couch to face me. She was fidgeting with that brunette hair that I so love to run through my fingers, obviously nervous.

"Jack," she said hesitantly. "It was so hard watching you go through that horrible time before Moon died. And when the suit was dropped, I was so happy for you. You quit gaining weight and even seemed like you wanted to live again. But now, something else is different. I can tell. Is there something we need to talk about?"

I tried looking her in the eye as I replied but couldn't quite do it. I ended up running the remote up and down through the channels while answering—I think they would call that the mother of all tells.

"No, dear," I lied. "Everything is great. I just have so much relief at getting out from under that horrible cloud. You can't imagine what it was like. Now I know what my depressed patients have always tried to tell me, but I'm all better now. There's nothing for you to worry about."

She didn't buy it for a second. "Nice try, Jack. Is there someone else? Are you going to be leaving some night in a shiny convertible with your new love, looking for true happiness while it's still within reach? I had lunch with Janie the other day. She told me you remind her of her husband just before he went off with his secretary and their life savings."

"Honey, there's nothing for you to—"

"Remember," she said. "You have kids in this, too."

"There's no one else," I insisted. "Of course not."

This time, I could be honest with her. "You're the only one for me." I held her hand, squeezing it gently. "You're just seeing the new me. I've got so much energy. I feel like I'm ten years younger, ready to take on the world!" I paused, as my attention went back to the remote. "That's all it is."

Her silvery-gray eyes, eyes whose haunting, slightly asymmetric beauty had always captivated me, bore in like hot pokers. Strike two. You can't live with someone for twenty-five years and not recognize when you're being shit-shined with second-hand platitudes.

"You're welcome to talk to me when you get your story straight," she said, turning and settling deeply in to her corner of the couch. It was strike three; conversation over, evening over.

Conversations at dinner became stilted. I could see why she was concerned, and it hurt to be putting her through this. Eventually, she'd have to hear about my new life, I just wasn't sure how to do it. In the meantime, she became more and more convinced that I had some extracurricular activity going on. I'd catch her trying to listen in on my calls, and once, when I left for a late-night ICU trip, she followed me all the way to the doctors' parking lot before turning around, not knowing I'd seen her the whole way.

Eventually, she started to become more direct with her inquiries. "Who is she?" she'd ask, and "Is it someone I know? Is she prettier? Why won't you tell me?"

With my repeated denials and assurances, she eventually quit asking. I don't know if she finally believed me or if she was afraid that someday I'd break down and tell her the truth, something she'd rather not know. Either way, my new career was putting an unacceptable strain on things at home.

Suspicions came up at work as well. Drugs were suspected, or a late transition to a bipolar state. An old residency acquaintance, who ended up in psychiatry, just happened to bump into me in the windowless hallway to the

ICU one morning. It was interesting, as the psych department was at the far end of the hospital campus, in an unattached building. We hadn't even exchanged Christmas cards since the Clinton years, but now he was here, casually asking leading questions like a long-lost friend.

"Jack," he said, pointing to a waiting bench with an open hand. "Long time no see! How's the wife and kids? Anything going on?"

"Well, Phil, there is. My wife has taken up with the pool guy. That sucks. She says she's going to run away with him as soon as he finishes high school. My oldest son is coming up for parole, if he can score that good behavior bonus. Zach thinks he's almost got the meth licked this time, and I'm not sure, but I think we'll be able to keep our house from the bookies for another month or two. But I've still got my health to be thankful for, except those damn anal fissures that keep me itching all day. Enough about me, though." I grabbed his hand in a lumberjack grip. "How are things with you?"

"Well, I ..."

This was a conversation I wanted to keep short. We'd never been more than casual acquaintances, and I didn't want to get into a lengthy interrogation.

"You look good, Phil. Psychiatry must be paying better these days." I patted him on the stomach, "you've even been putting on a little weight!"

"I've been meaning to start at the gym, but. . ."

"One of the nurses mentioned something about you helping to get a new graduate hired. Ingrid, was it? Damned nice of you to help the newcomers along like that, getting them started on the right path."

"Aw, shoot, Jack," he said, his voice quavering. "I had no idea it was getting so late. Gotta go. My first patient is a kleptomaniac; I probably shouldn't keep him waiting in my office."

"Nice seeing ya, Phil. You be sure to say hi to Gayle for me, and the kids, too," but I was talking to his retreating back.

The nurses were also starting to take notice of the changes, but perhaps with more basic interests at heart than my mental well-being. Carol, the delightfully buxom third-floor head nurse, had become much more attentive on morning rounds.

"Jack," she said one day, taking my arm and turning me away from the room I'd been heading to. "I've got some great ideas to help us move forward in the unit. We could go out to lunch one day—there's a great Thai place near where I live. I could run some things by you; see what comes up?"

The other nurses' sideways glances spoke volumes. I politely indicated that I'd love to hear her ideas, and that perhaps we could meet some day in the hospital cafeteria. Her disappointed look confirmed that work-place improvement hadn't been what was on her mind.

There were casual, lingering bumps in the hallway and countless cups of coffee offered. It was all very flattering, and perhaps a little distracting. Once, when I ran late at the gym and didn't have time for a shower, one of the floor nurses paged me back after I had completed my morning rounds. There was something she needed to show me in the med room. The biologists would say it was just a pheromone thing, but I recognized it for what it was—an understandable and irresistible draw towards the hottest hunk of doctor west of the Mississippi. Or at least, that's the way I'll interpret it.

The all-knowing administration had me submit a urine sample, which of course was clean, and invited me for a brief

sit down. It looked like one of those TV show interventions—
a small room full of colleagues, carefully seated in comfortable
chairs, circled around mine. The vice president was there, too.
He was always on the lookout for anything to use against me,
ever since I called for his forced resignation at a county medical society meeting. The man was an embarrassment, even
among our inept leadership, and the common wisdom was
that he was kept around only to make the others look better.
Either that, or he had something on the CEO.

I was able to dissemble enough to put them at ease. They
didn't have my wife's innate lie-detector skills to fall back on.
I explained that I had been through some understandable
depression after the suit, but that I had climbed out of it, using
exercise and deep personal New-age contemplation.

They wondered about the deep bruises and various limps
and shuffles, but those were easily explained. There were no
aggressive loan sharks or marital beatings; I had taken up the
martial arts and the bruises were simply the marks of my initial
introductions to the sport. I did leave out the part about my
chosen kung fu discipline, choy lee fut. It was a particularly
aggressive form, developed in the 1800s, utilizing devastating
kicks and powerful punches, delivering unbelievable amounts
of force—far more than anyone would think possible. This
was not Hollywood choreography kung fu, nor a competitive
Olympic sport, and it certainly wasn't the self-defense strategy
common to many martial art styles; it was combat. Take your
enemy down hard and fast, win at all cost combat.

Finding a place where I could study had not been easy,
but a grateful patient had put me in touch with his friend,
Cho Lin Me. He was a wiry and (I'd find) merciless man who
had "retired" from the Taiwanese National Police Agency. He
had abruptly come to the conclusion that a smallish town in

northwest America would be a good career move, after some unspecified adversity at home.

Early in my instruction, I made the mistake of trying to engage him in polite conversation. "What happened in New Taipei City," I asked, "to make you want to move halfway around the world?"

He wasn't inclined to share about that. His response, in fact, was less than conversational, though well remembered for the rest of the week. There would be no end of the semester apples for this teacher.

His sparring room was the essence of simplicity; fastidiously clean, and almost completely unadorned. I got the impression that his departure for the States hadn't allowed a lot of packing time. A single Buddhist mandala anchored one wall, and the only other decoration was a garish velvet painting of "the King"—Elvis preserved in a style I had never understood. A single bare mat, in places worn almost through to the concrete, completed the picture. My training was intense—I tasted that mat on a regular basis.

Upstairs, simplicity continued to rule, though the always present scent of garlic and ginger gave a sense of this being a home. By our town's standards, Cho Me lived in a pretty rough neighborhood. I feel sorry, though, for anyone foolish enough to try bothering him. A group of hopped up skinhead teenagers had once tried relieving him of his groceries, as he walked back from the Oriental store on Mulberry. It was a one-time mistake.

My martial training, physical and mental, was a transforming experience, almost addictive. I can see why so many parents push their kids to get involved. Perhaps not the choy lee fut style I had chosen, but one of the more conventional forms. The agility and clarity of mind were helpful throughout my day and could only be a blessing to a kid trying to grow up in this crazy world.

As I was working on my body, my literary interests expanded. It's amazing what is out there in the name of relevant self-improvement books. Shelves of books on how to improve your self-esteem, achieve the workplace success you deserve, balance your inner chakra while reaching for the cheese. Volumes had been written on how to wage a personal war against almost any adversary. Financial dirty tricks and character assassination led the long list of ways to ruin another's life; with a little imagination, the world is full of things much worse than a knife to the gut, if you really wanted to damage someone.

I enjoyed *How to Hide in the Urban Jungle*, but *The Home Anarchist* and *The Poor Man's James Bond* were true treasures, destined for literary greatness. I could read and reread them forever, learning something new with every journey. My mind melded so completely into the genre that I was soon coming up with my own bestial ideas. There is no end to the horror that can be inflicted on the life of someone unfortunate enough to have angered an opponent enough to get them to set aside the common laws of decency.

I read all that seemed relevant as winter passed through to the gloomy reaches of what they call spring in southern Oregon. Even without the other motivations, the dreadfully gray skies and the unending snow and rain provided the angst to put me back into the proper mind set for murder. I called my new partner and let him know I was ready to go.

"Set 'em up, and I'll make 'em fall. And by the way, George, is there anyone living someplace warm and sunny who might need killing?"

The list of prospects was short, two. My recent lack of

homicidal activity had kept us from expanding our referral base. There was one new opportunity, also courtesy of our friend in Redding. A psychiatrist who volunteered in an after-hours charity clinic had a patient who killed himself shortly after starting samples of a new antidepressant. The patient's children saw the 1-800-BAD DRUG commercial and were suing for an outrageous amount; enough to set them up for a life of luxury. It was far beyond the limits of the paltry malpractice policy Al's friend could afford, and he could lose everything. He had warned the patient about the small risk of suicide but got busy and forgot to write his warnings down. As we were repeatedly warned in medical school, if you don't write it down, it didn't happen. His care was good, but he knew he was vulnerable and was afraid to go to trial—a simple charting omission, and it could ruin his career.

This was perfect. Exactly the kind of case I had been looking for. Save a well-meaning practitioner from a ridiculous lawsuit that had been put forth by a sub-amoebic yellow livered, toilet-licking excuse of an opportunistic litigator and his scum-sucking, get-rich-quick scumbag plaintiffs. I was tempted to go for the grand slam and get them all, a Darwin award by proxy.

"I'm in." I smiled. "It's perfect!"

"There's a timeline on this one," George mentioned. "The client needs it done soon, and simple revenge won't be enough. He needs the suit completely squashed. It's getting close to the deposition phase and he can't let it to go any further. Is that going to be a problem?"

"Shouldn't be," I said. "Help me think of an excuse to get me out of town without making Aurora more suspicious than she already is, and its game on. Where will I be going?"

"Madison."

He said it in such a nonchalant, matter-of-fact manner that it took a moment to sink in. I searched my limited mental atlas to see if there might be a Madison, Arizona, or Madison, Florida, but I was coming up empty.

"Wisconsin, huh? Damn! Uh … what's the other case?"

"It's the same one Thorpe referred before," George responded. "The orthopedic surgeon, the one who left his patient with a leg a quarter of an inch shorter than the other. It's the case you put off while you pursued your self-improvement program. The case has already passed the point where an intervention on the lawyer would bring it to an end, but the revenge factor is still there."

Orthopedics is one of the most lucrative branches of medicine. Ask anyone who's had the pleasure of needing their services. Half an hour in an orthopedic doctor's office costs about the same as an afternoon in the ICU. They bill more for a hairline fracture than most critical care specialists get for draining a gallon of life-giving blood from a patient's crushed chest or restarting a child's heart after a nonstop two a.m. asthma attack. It doesn't seem right, but that's just the way it is.

"I'm not completely opposed to the idea," I mused, looking up at a spider spinning a web in the corner of George's ceiling. "Revenge isn't quite what we were thinking when we started this, but it would be a great chance to overcome some of that income inequality we're always bitching about."

The hooker here was that the case actually had some merit, making it a bit of a judgment call. With the others, unfortunately including the one in the frozen wasteland of Wisconsin, there was just cause that a moralizing hit man could fall back on; a tenuous grip on that slippery slope. This one would be another step down the moral incline. A small step, perhaps, but I was still having a little problem going there. I'd have to think about it.

"Where does this guy live?" I asked, hoping for a convenient excuse.

"You're going to love it," George said. "He's the president of one of the most prestigious practices in the South, right in the heart of the Big Easy."

Damn! This was going to be a hard one to turn down. "Give me a day or two to think about it, and I'll get back to you."

CHAPTER THIRTY-TWO

I was home, considering my options, when Aurora came into the living room and sat next to me. Southern Oregon had been having a few days of beautiful weather, uncharacteristic for this time of year. The sun was casting gentle warming rays, teasing us as to what might come months down the road. It had been going on long enough to fool the trees to blossom into an early fragrant bloom.

As the weather goes, so goes Aurora. She could be the poster child for seasonal affective disorder. She had just come home from a nice walk, rosy-cheeked and showing that joyful radiance I had fallen in love with so many years ago. She leaned teasingly across my lap to reach the remote, turning on the source of constant family entertainment.

Sadly, the television's default station is our local news channel. The weatherman was just coming on, set to ruin what could have become a very good afternoon.

"Put away your shorts and flip-flops," he moaned. "I hope you enjoyed it while it lasted, but it's time to cover your tomatoes. We're going back tonight to the spring weather we all grew up loving!"

That typical May weather was enough to put suicidal thoughts in the mind of all but the most optimistic. A major Alaskan front was on the way, and it would arrive just in time for the weekend. Our reprieve had been short lived, and so were my dreams for the afternoon. Wind and snow were predicted, along with freezing rain, as if we ever got anything else at this bleak time of year. I couldn't switch channels fast enough to keep Aurora from seeing it. Even the weatherman seemed depressed, and Aurora's playful mood dropped into a deep hibernation. I could see only one option.

Her response was an immediate and enthusiastic "Yes!" when I asked if she'd like a short vacation to New Orleans.

"It will be like a grown-up spring break," she enthused.

The situation got a little more difficult after that. I mentioned that moral decline earlier and the moral compass that had always guided me. The damn thing kept coming back to bite me in the ass. The poor shrink in Madison was the model of what all doctors set out to be, before various realities made us more pragmatic, or whatever we become. He was being sued for everything he had, after giving up his free time to do volunteer work. It just wasn't right, and I couldn't get it out of my head that I could make things better for him. But now I'd really screwed things up by promising Aurora a sunny trip to the Gulf Coast. Why the hell did the psychiatrist have to live someplace even more cold and gloomy than our home? I had to find some way to put that damn altruistic streak back in its rightful spot before it ruined me.

Planning a long-distance assassination in a town you've never visited is not an easy prospect. I saw the result of taking it too lightly when I went to California, and that was an easy trip, just a few hundred road miles from home. I wouldn't be able to spend a few weeks casing the area, forming plans and counter-plans in case things went sideways. Getting the proper murder tools can also be a problem. Now, try to make it a double-header in two towns a thousand miles apart, and take your wife along just to make it a little more interesting. Talk about a Darwin award in the making.

After foolishly offering the New Orleans vacation, Aurora had returned to a grand mood. I couldn't very well tell her I'd changed my mind. I really, truly hate celibacy and don't see any need to court it as an ongoing lifestyle.

Trying to do both assassinations in one trip would be a challenge, but it would be even harder to find an excuse to take two separate vacations so close together, especially one where I didn't take my wife. A continuing medical education trip would work, like when George got rid of Joyce—Aurora would have no interest in that, but Madison in the spring isn't a hot spot for medical tourists. In fact, I think the main thing going on there at this time of year is a sincere effort to raise the U.S. per capita beer consumption. Not a bad idea, necessarily, but that would have to be another trip. No, if I was going to do the honorable thing and accept the second assignment, it would have to be tethered to the New Orleans trip. That meant it was time to have a serious discussion with Aurora.

She obviously was aware that there was something going on anyway, and I felt like a louse, keeping things from her. Also, she was starting to ask those probing questions again, and if I started disappearing for long periods while we were on our vacation, it would get a lot worse. The time had come. There would be no more lies.

It actually felt good, now that I'd made the decision. There might even be some advantage, if she decided to come on board. A second set of hands would come in handy, and she could provide great cover for my travels, telling her friends that the two of us had decided to start enjoying the fruits of my years in the trenches. Having her along might even help with avoiding that celibacy thing. (I hate to keep coming back to that. I'm really not that shallow-minded, but if you met my wife, you'd understand.) The experts at *Cosmo* say a motel room can work magic. It certainly does for me. In fact, it reminds me of a favorite joke that always gets a few laughs:

An Alaska woodpecker gets tired of the cold and takes a trip to Texas. He stops in a local bar where he hears a bunch of arrogant Lone Star wood-heads talking about how they were the toughest beaks around. The Alaskan swaggers over and confronts them—"Woodpeckers from the north are the ten times tougher than you southern wimps."

A serious discussion followed, and they came to the conclusion that there was only one way to settle this. They reconvened at the hardest tree in Texas, a tree so tough that no Texas bird had ever been able to drill it. The Alaska bird perches on the main branch, takes a deep breath and then bores a deep hole, pulls out a grub, and gulps it down. Wiping his grinning beak with the back of his wing, he brags, "any questions?"

The Texas birds are impressed and a little ashamed. "But you ain't seen nuthin'," says the Klondike visitor. "Alaska has a tree so hard that even we can't drill it." They all fly north and the situation is repeated in reverse. A Texas woodpecker buries his beak all the way and pulls out his own tasty grub.

The woodpeckers fly back to the local watering hole to try to figure things out over a couple of beers. How can the Alaska woodpecker drill into the tree that no Texas pecker can bore, and the Texas bird drill in to the one too hard for the Alaskans? They thought and thought, and then it finally hit them: your pecker is always harder when you're away from home!

Telling Aurora about my new career was risky; a degree of finesse would be required. She was going to figure it out eventually, if I kept on as the executioner of the high courts. A lifetime of marriage without a separate vacation, and all of a sudden I'm off somewhere alone, month after month? And don't forget about the new and improved gym-hardened GQ look I was showing off. The questions would intensify all over again, and I'd be back to battling that truthfulness handicap until it all came out; best to do this in a controlled situation.

If Aurora reacted unfavorably, I'd be seeing the world from the confines of an 8 x 11 cell. (I could decorate it a bit—it would be home for a very long time.) A more favorable response and I'd have the cutest traveling partner a 'contractor' could ever ask for, as well as a helpful assistant.

I debated how to bring it up. A straightforward launch into how I'd been killing lawyers for fun and profit seemed unwise. A lighthearted joking manner might work. "Honey," I'd say, "what would you think if I started up a business killing rotten, disgusting malpractice lawyers? We could call it Final Tort Reform, Inc. I'd be the hero of the medical community." If she was shocked, I had an out. ("Come on, you always take

me too seriously. Can't you tell when I'm goofing around?")
I could show her the balance in our Channel Islands account
and transition from there to how much more there could
be, tracking toward a luxury retirement, if she wasn't too
concerned with how it got there.

Then, something she had said earlier came back to my
senescent mind. It seemed like a good springboard to introduce her to the new chapter in my life; hopefully, *our* life. I
would find out which tonight.

Chapter Thirty-three

I was a little nervous that evening when I asked Aurora if we could have a few minutes to talk. She cautiously agreed, nervous herself, expecting the confession she'd been waiting for, an admission of the new love that was going to set her husband free or some other unpleasant marriage ending topic. That's another one of those things like the 2:00 a.m. phone call or the late-night knock at the door. Nobody likes to start an after dinner spousal talk that starts with the 'we've got to talk' opening.

This would be a conversation best held where we wouldn't be interrupted. Zach was in his room but I didn't want to take a chance of his coming out in the midst of our discussion of my homicidal moonlighting. Kids just don't need to be burdened knowing that their father is a hired serial killer, though it might pay off next time I asked him to clean his quarters.

I took Aurora's hand and led her up to my favorite room, the one she seems to think was designed for sleeping. (I have a somewhat different opinion, but I'm sure you can guess who wins that argument.) We sat on the edge of the bed, me staring at the floor, and Aurora wrapped in the protection of our floral comforter, pillows pulled in tight to ward off the coming evil spirits. She had the sad, insecure look of a puppy just pulled from its mother's teat and left alone at the side of the road. I can't remember ever seeing anyone look more vulnerable.

She looked down at her lap and asked, "what did you want to tell me?"

I wrested the blanket from her clenched hand and locked my fingers through hers. "Do you remember how things were when I got served with that lawsuit? How miserable my life was and how I lost all my happy thoughts, my joy? You started to wonder if you even wanted a future with me."

"Of course," she admitted. "You were such a miserable person. Everything was negative. Nothing went by without a complaint. You didn't want to go to work or cook or even get out of bed, some days. You must have gained twenty five pounds, and I'm not the only one who didn't want to be around you. Your attitude made it miserable for everyone."

"I know, and I'm sorry. I wish I could take it back, but life seemed so pointless, and I was so angry." I took a strategic pause, and then went on. "Do you remember how you told me one day that you had seen Moon walking downtown, and that you almost drove over his sorry ass?"

"Oh yes, and I wasn't just thinking about it—I really wanted to do it. He was ruining our lives, just like he had done to so many others. Do you have any idea how many times I regretted not actually hitting the gas instead of the brake? Turns out, though, it wasn't necessary. He got what was coming to him, I'm guilt-free and you're off the hook for the suit—it's perfect!" She smiled at the thought. "I suppose it's wrong to be happy when someone dies, but I can't seem to make myself feel too bad about it." Then she asked, "But what does all this have to do with now? You're happy again," she said, hopefully, "more than I've seen in so long. You're back to the man I fell so in love with."

I was all in at this point. Whether she helped or sent me down the river, I was through not telling her the truth. From now on, if I took a new contract, there would be no more deception. No more lying about where I was going or why. Perhaps I still had a few standards of civilized behavior left in me.

"Well, there's more to the story." I searched her eyes for a moment, paused again—"I killed the bastard."

Silence.

"Nice try," came her cautious response. "Trying to impress me?

"No, it's for real," I said, trying to read her face. "His lawsuit was destroying me, and I decided that his time had come. Someone who could make his living doing that to others needed to just go away. I drugged him and gave him enough potassium to kill Rasputin. It was perfect, and you know what? It felt good. The police decided it was a self-indulgent accident; they never suspected murder. I'm actually rather proud of how it went off, being a first timer and all."

"Why are you telling me this now, since you got away with it?"

"Well, I sort of didn't get completely away with it. You know I've been spending a lot of time with George Bicknell lately? He lived right next to Moon's house. He chose the morning when I did it to take a leak on Moon's yard. He was at it right as I was making my escape. George hates lawyers, Moon in particular, and was kind of making a statement by pissing all over his prized grass. He thought he was getting a good one over on the greedy bastard—I think I one-upped him."

"He couldn't have gone to the police," she said. "You'd be locked up. Is he blackmailing you? Is that what this is all about?"

Here's where it was about to get interesting. "That's how things got started. My price for freedom was to get Joyce out of the picture. She and her golf pro were having a good time behind George's back. Apparently, she needed something to fill her days when they phased out soap operas. She and the country club pro were playing hide the sausage, and they were stealing from him, too. He wanted them both gone."

The shocked look on Aurora's face gave me concern that I'd gone too far. She was suddenly living with a serial killer; not someone who had justifiably disposed of the man who had been destroying our lives, but a homicide frequent flier.

"You killed Joyce?" she asked, pulling back from my grip. "Are there others?"

I reached into my pocket and brought out the offshore account book, showing her the balance.

"Where did that come from?" she asked uncertainly, looking at the twenty-thousand-dollar deposit.

"George has a friend in California, down in Redding. He was in the same position I had been in, getting sued for no reason, but it was even worse. His insurance was trying to force him to settle and save the cost of the trial. He was getting screwed both ways."

Realization began to dawn on her face. "The fishing trip …?"

"Yep. I'm a full-time lawyer-slayer now." I explained to

her how sorry I was for lying to her, how it had all snuck up with one lie leading to another. I also explained what a good thing this could be, simultaneously helping other physicians and our financial situation.

She knew about the cuts we'd been seeing from Medicare. They had been having a serious impact on our practice. She also knew about the other changes, having heard me bitching about them for so many months. We had talked a few times about shutting things down and going to work for the hospital as an employed physician. It would mean being under the influence of people for whom we had no respect, but it made financial sense and was something we had to consider.

"So this is what you've been hiding from me all this time?"

I nodded, searching for some sign of where she might be going with my confession. Relief? Acceptance? A new partner? Or would it be divorce court and a lifetime in the single-ply tissue world of the state slammer, sharing stories with Hannibal Lechter or my favorite cellmate, Bubba? If she decided to turn me in, I would have little defense, though ambulance chasing lawyers are not the most well-loved of all the professions. Maybe I could play the martyr role and hope for a lighter sentence. I could see it now:

"Hero Physician Turned in by Ungrateful Wife" would be the above the fold headline. "Dr. Jack Hastings, healer of the lame and an awesome joke-teller, foolishly took his wife into his confidence, telling her that his healing hands had taken on an even nobler role: saving doctors from the ravages of greedy malpractice attorneys. His future appears to be a life of dismal incarceration, rather than pursuing his newly chosen career ..."

There would be public sympathy; women would be

lining up to my cell for visits. There would probably be so many pen pals that I couldn't answer them all, as they thanked me for my service. Still, it would be my preference to not travel down that road.

Aurora's shocked look started to fade to a slight smile. "Pest control for the medical profession, huh? Caduceus' Orkin-man?" She thought a moment longer. "Sort of a tort reform thing, too, I guess." Even after all these years together, it amazes me how we sometimes think so much alike.

She was putting things together now. "So the idea for the trip to New Orleans isn't for a romantic getaway, is it? Another lawyer on the way to a dirt bath?"

"I like to think of it more as an income-positive vaca-tion, *with* the most beautiful woman in the world at my side," I quickly added. "We take in some good jazz, a poorboy with those new improved BP gulf shrimp and there's one less leech on society's roles."

She smiled in anticipation.

"And then I was thinking maybe a little hop to Wiscon-sin? A weekend in Madison might just make the rest of our spring here seem a little more tolerable."

"Well," said Aurora, "it would leave Zach alone without parental input. That could be a little scary."

I waited expectantly.

"How much will they pay us?"

I breathed a huge sigh of relief. "The psychiatrist in Madison can only spare eight thousand bucks, and it will have to come in installments. The mental health profession has never paid that well. By the time I miss several days of work and then pay airline and hotel expenses, it may not even pencil out to much more than an even split."

"Sounds almost like a wash. Why did you agree to do it?"

"It's just the right thing to do," I explained. "The guy was giving up his free time, doing volunteer work for people who really needed his services. He shouldn't be getting sued for that." Aurora has always been there for the lost and the strays of the world, and now I was hoping we could put struggling doctors on her list of mercies. "Besides," I said, "it gives us a chance for a vacation in Madison!"

"The New Orleans job, however, is a different story. It's an orthopedic surgeon and he is willing to pay thirty grand. Apparently, the attorney embarrassed him in court, made him look like a fool. He desperately wants to even the score. A few cases like that, and we might live to retirement."

"Okay," she said. "You can stop pleading your case! You're like a damn lawyer yourself, sometimes. I'm in. Now what can I do to help?"

CHAPTER THIRTY-FOUR

For the New Orleans slaying, the client didn't care if it was a cleverly executed natural appearing death or a gruesome, splashed-across-the-tabloids *Godfather*-style assassination. He was best friends with the chief of police, and as was the case with so many others, this lawyer had a laundry list of people who would love to be at his planting ceremony. The payoff would come from the client's own offshore account, a simple confidential transfer, and again, there'd be no paper trail to connect us.

In Wisconsin, I'd have to be a little more circumspect. If the lawyer's death appeared to be intentional, the cops would look to see who had the most to gain. A psychiatrist with everything to lose in an active suit would be high on the list. Throw in the logistics of my never having been to Madison, and not knowing anything about the target and there was a lot of room for error. Aurora was happy to help with the brainstorming, but our ideas kept coming up wanting, and time was running short.

We were sitting at breakfast, beginning to fear that the time frame would pass before we had a concrete plan, when George stopped in with an excited grin. I had told him that Aurora had become part of the team.

"The Wisconsin client called. The plaintiff's lawyer, Feingold, asked to postpone the deposition. He's taking some time off for a legal conference, in New Orleans! Can you believe it? I'm seeing the makings for a truly happy ending here."

Aurora offered George a cup of coffee, which he gladly accepted, and a homemade sticky roll, light on the pecans. She comes from the camp that says nuts should never be mixed with food, while I'm more of a traditionalist; this compromise had worked well for years, except when family came to visit. The battle lines were drawn much more firmly there, and had led to serious friction. George, however, was happy to forgo his dry cereal bachelor breakfast and gratefully take whatever was put before him. The chef was pleased when he asked for seconds.

"Does this mean I'll be cheated out of my trip to the land of brats and cheese?" she asked, feigning disappointment.

George nodded. He was savoring the last bite of his gooey breakfast and was doing his best to avoid ending the experience. Aurora beamed and pushed another in his direction without waiting for him to ask. She looked at me and was about to make a suggestion, when I said, "I've got it!"

I had a professor in medical school who always struck me as being unusually bright. He had an impressive command of the language and knew how to say something and make the point stick. One of his favorite expressions had become one of mine: *augenblinck*—something so obvious that it could be discerned in the blink of an eye. I think it was German, though I had never checked to see if it was even a real word. I didn't want to spoil it, in case it was just something he had made up.

I had just had an augenblinck moment, so clear that I wondered why I hadn't thought of it sooner. It was so perfect that even the minor details were falling into place as I was leading my audience to the same conclusion.

"Honey," I said, "how do you trap a rat?"

She looked at me with a puzzled expression. "You put cheese in a trap. Mr. Rat can't avoid the temptation, sticks his face in, trap springs, case closed. Why?"

I was thinking back to the traveling Alaska woodpecker. "And what do lawyers love to do more than anything else?"

"I don't know," Aurora said. "Kick small dogs, steal candy from babies, stuff like that. I'm not a lawyer. How would I know?"

"No, they love to screw people, and what better opportunity for him to do that than when he's far from home at a conference. We lure him up to his room. He thinks he's going to get some action. The trap springs, case closed—just like you said!"

She frowned, not sure what I was leading up to.

"There's bound to be groupies and hookers hanging out," I said. "They're always there at these conferences." Seeing the concern on Aurora's face, I paused to assure her that that was not the case at medical conventions, only with the lawyers.

"We have a slightly different plan. We take him down, break his little Cupid's heart, and steal his wallet to make it look like a pimp setup. It couldn't be any more perfect!"

"So …," she said. "I'd have to play hooker? What if he tries to move forward with the transaction?"

"I'd have to kill him twice, if he actually touched you, but we'll plan it so that doesn't happen." My mind was racing.

"It would be great if you could talk him into a tie-up game. Remember how we almost threw away my neckties when I read that *New England Journal* article saying they spread germs in the ICU? And how glad you were the other day that we didn't?"

From her deep blush, I could tell that she did remember. George looked away, but I could see the smile, just before he did.

"He's a lawyer; he'll have lots of ties, maybe even silk. If he doesn't want to go that route, you could always get him drunk. Or if he's too impatient, we'll find a way for you to signal me. I pick the lock, sneak up from behind while you have him distracted, and we get what we want before he gets what he wants." I saw it unfold before my eyes. "Trust me. It really is perfect."

George was impressed, and the basics of the plan were set, final details to follow. To make it more spectacular, we decided to do both hits on the same day. The press would go nuts.

Chapter Thirty-five

Aurora traveled a few days ahead to scout things out and to gather a few necessities. She had no trouble finding a sleazy, "I'm-available-by-the-hour" ensemble. She had tried several service-oriented outfits, with my careful supervision through the miracle of the modern-day cell phone camera. Trying to help her pick the best one from fifteen hundred miles away was torture, though, and I suggested she buy them all, especially the champagne bust-enhancing semi-fishnet clubbing skirt. It practically screamed the message we were looking for. She considered it too trashy and opted for something tamer, and to be more frugal—with only a single purchase. The first time I've ever encouraged her to go crazy in a clothes shop, and she failed miserably.

The plan was to dump the outfit in a secure trash bin after the finale of her one act motel room drama. As much as I enjoyed the look, it would break my heart to do that, but it wouldn't do to be caught with it after the murder.

Aurora searched sidewalk vendors for the perfect blade. I needed something long and rigid enough for a reliable heart shot, but thin to minimize blood spray—knowledge I picked up in one of my self-help books. She was to stay away from pawn shops and major stores where they might have video cameras. I wasn't planning on leaving it behind, but such a blade leaves a definite signature. I didn't want my wife's pretty mug to show up on post office walls across the country, in case the police asked the public for assistance in trying to find who had recently purchased such a characteristic knife.

We'd also need a way for her to signal to me when the time was right for my grand entrance. She found a store that sold spy gear. It catered to voyeurs and jealous spouses shopping for hidden cameras, and to paranoids worried about government bugs in their homes. Business espionage specialists would also be regular clients, hoping to get a leg up on the competition. She found a wireless transmitter hidden in a fake diamond brooch, with a hearing aid sized long-distance receiver guaranteed for up to a half mile. "Real CIA stuff," according to the balding salesman who made it his personal mission to see that Aurora got all the help she needed.

When she got things ready in the room, Aurora would send a key word and I'd crash the party. The microphone would also allow me to monitor things, to make sure he didn't get too far.

I was impressed at how well the plan was falling into place when Aurora pointed out a small flaw—how was I going to pick my way in, when all the motels had gone to magnetic key card locks?

Damn! That would have been ugly. She had a solution, though—a taser. She could have it in her purse without arousing suspicion. If Feingold didn't want to play the necktie game, two high-voltage barbs would give her time to open the door. It would also make him much more receptive for the rest of our plan. She was really getting into the spirit of this.

CHAPTER THIRTY-SIX

We needed a coordinated plan if we were going to accomplish both attacks on the same day. The scene was set for the Madison lawyer. We'd kill him in the evening. That would leave the rest of the day for the local lawyer.

Millard Beauchamp was a legend in the southern legal community. He had risen from the nickel and dime cases—DUI's, trailer park divorces and petty civil suits when the case of a lifetime dropped into his lap. The newspapers thrilled over the charismatic, hard-biting attorney who won a million dollar product liability judgment against a company. It was made even better by the fact that the company was owned by a despised local politician.

Beauchamp had been taken under Harlan Carter's wings. Carter was old money, tracing back to the days of the slaves. He had a court room persona to fit any case, any jury that he came across. He could be serious and scholarly, discoursing on arcane aspects of the law, or light-hearted and humorous, if the case called for it. Carter and Beauchamp hit it off, the likable mentor and the talented student, and before long, Beauchamp had become a top-notch lawyer. He wouldn't look at a case, now, unless it had at least a six-figure payoff. He had also become a fixture in New Orleans' social circles, frequently entertaining judges at The Bilders, one of the South's most exclusive country clubs, and throwing extravagant balls reminiscent of those put on by his ancestors.

Aurora found the Starbucks across the street from Beauchamp's office to be a perfect stakeout. The picture window gave a good view, and no one would worry about a stranger spending a few hours there with a laptop and a cup of chai. The doughnut shop next door would have worked, but seemed a little too much of a stereotype. It would be an acceptable fall-back if a problem did come up at the coffee shop.

It only took two days for Aurora to get Beauchamp's routine down. Each morning, he parked his light-gray S-Class in the office's dedicated parking garage. No good options there, with a steady stream of colleagues and office employees, and only one possible escape route.

He took his lunch was on foot, with clients or others from the office. No real opportunity there, either, short of a mafia-style execution. Spectacular, but difficult to get away with, and with the added consideration of the emotional impact on the other lunch-goers, that wouldn't be an option. Aurora didn't want us to be responsible for a new wave of post-traumatic stress disorder cases.

After work, he headed straight home. Five o'clock sharp. It would be unseemly for a top partner to stay later than the underlings, one of the many privileges of seniority.

An upscale mansion in an upscale neighborhood was home, perched easily six or seven feet above sea level. It's amazing what insurance company money can buy. Fossil-containing slate slabs created a striking entry, winding through bougain-villea-lined trellises and elegant lawn statuaries, skirting past tiered goldfish ponds en route to elegant ten-foot bas-relief doors. Unembellished stone columns flanked the doors, and supported a second-floor conversation deck.

Aurora almost swooned. Many homes in this price range have an impersonal, showy feel that says, "look what I've got and you don't!" This one clearly rose above the neighbor's homes, but somehow came across as a place where friends and family would be welcome. Roast turkey on the holidays, croquet or badminton in the backyard on the Fourth—he probably even had a dog named Blue. The home didn't quite fit with the Southern décor of the neighborhood, but it complemented the area, rather than seeming out of place.

A keypad security system was prominently displayed by the front door, and the yard sign, discreetly placed outside the wrought-iron and stone fence promoted the exceptional service of A-1 Security Company: "Unsurpassed Home Protection since 1981."

Aurora called the day before I was set to join her.

"I can't believe it," she said. "I have everything all set up. It came together perfectly! Our best bet for the local guy, Beauchamp, will be first thing in the morning. He comes out for his paper, coffee in hand about six o'clock, probably already thinking about who he can screw for the day. It's still on the dark side, but barely. We'll be cutting it close, but it's a ways between houses, and we should be safe unless he sleeps in. I'll be there as your getaway driver. After that, I'll be ready to play hooker when the Wisconsin guy gets out of his conference.

We'll have all day in between to be tourists."

From now on, I was going to have to start calling Aurora the General. I should have brought her on board a lot sooner. "I'm impressed!" I said. "You've got it all covered."

"It's actually kind of exciting," she said. "You're coming in tomorrow, right?"

"I'm on the 4:30 from Denver. I'll let you know if there are any delays."

"Can't *wait* to see you."

CHAPTER THIRTY-SEVEN

It's a wonder how patients know to get sick just when a doctor is about to take a vacation. My only goal for the day was to get my work done, pack a bag and get a little sleep before my early morning flight. Unfortunately, the patients had a different idea. Maggie had to add a couple of patients at the end of the day—one was coughing up blood and another who was probably relapsing her sarcoidosis. Sarcoidosis is a relatively common "rare" disease. It makes up a fair part of a typical pulmonary practice. We have no idea what causes it, but it's usually curable.

I had gotten through the normally scheduled patients and was just getting to Rachel's add-ons when I got an emergency call from the ICU.

It seems silly to be on call the night before leaving town, but in order to get the time off, it's often necessary. The hope is always for a quiet evening; a single bad case can completely ruin things. This was going to be one of those nights. An acute case of alcoholic pancreatitis had come in, leading to one of the worst cases of diabetic ketoacidosis I had seen in years. His kidneys were failing, along with the rest of his chronically abused, malnourished body. A severe case of multi-organ system failure, a descriptive term for when organ systems start falling like lined-up dominoes, was unfolding before my eyes. Normally, this would be a dream come true. I love the challenge of these extremely ill patients; I just wish they would arrive at more convenient times.

I gave the nurses preliminary orders over the telephone, trying to stabilize things until I could get there. Ordinarily, when something like this shows up, I cancel my office and tell the patients to come back the next day. Unfortunately, there would be no next day this week, and the two Rachel had added in couldn't wait until my return from New Orleans. They would have to be dealt with before I could head to the hospital.

Presuming I survived the unfolding crisis in the ICU, and nothing else came up, the next step should be to head back to the office to address the perpetual paperwork nightmare. It defied nature, self-procreating whenever I had my back turned. It was worse today for my having ignored it earlier in the week. Stacks of charts rose in stalagmite formations, with phone messages, labs, and X-rays, plus numerous letters to write. Insurance companies demanding to know why Mrs. Jones needed that lung biopsy, or why Mr. Torres had to have that CAT scan—wouldn't an x-ray be just as good?

Then there were the usual bills involved in maintaining a business, and, oh look, another notice from the IRS. They felt that I hadn't sent the right amount of something for the last quarter of 2009. Pay now, or add interest at sixty-three cents a day, plus penalty, of course.

Somehow, I missed the accounting course in med school. Every time I thought I might be getting ahead, something like this would show up. Plus, I'm always paying a late fee on one monthly bill or another—organization had never been one of my strong suits. If I didn't get back from the hospital tonight, there would be more hell to pay when I returned.

Rachel saw the look on my face after I took the call from the ICU and didn't even ask. She went straight to what serves as a kitchen and made a fresh pot of coffee, grounds and all as was her habit, not being a user herself. Sleep was not going to be in the cards tonight, so I might as well try to stay alert.

Chapter Thirty-eight

Doctors have a language all to themselves. One of my patients joked that it was our way of looking smarter than we really are, and there may be some truth to that, but it actually has a legitimate purpose, like a verbal shorthand. A mind-numbing, suicide-inducing whole-body itch becomes diffuse pruritus. A call from an ER doc with a case of angioedema is a panicked plea to drop whatever you're doing, forget about traffic laws, and get there before the patient suffocates on their swollen tongue. Other times it can be even more important. A pus-filled sore is described as purulent—nobody wants his medical record to say they have a large 'pussy' lesion.

The add-on who was coughing up blood, hemoptysis, in doctor-speak, was a false alarm; it was a simple nosebleed. He left greatly relieved, but appreciative for our having gotten him in. The lady with the sarcoidosis really did seem to be relapsing, which was most unfortunate. The steroids we used to initially arrest her disease had worked, but at a terrible price. She took on the unmistakable "moon-face," and had gained nearly a hundred pounds. Her bone density tests were showing osteoporosis, the catastrophic bony decay that shrinks people, bending them until their spines run parallel to the ground. She also had terrible mood swings, another direct result of the medication. They led to at least one 911 call, and ultimately to her husband moving out and filing divorce papers.

She had just gotten the steroids down to a manageable dose when she started having joint pains, a cough, and shortness of breath, the hallmark symptoms of her original disease. She was devastated as I explained that she would have to go back to the original dose, and that it would be several months before we could try tapering her off again.

I would have liked to have had more time to spend with her, but the ICU couldn't be put off much longer. Increasingly panicked calls were coming, sometimes only a few minutes between them. Fortunately, she understood. I left her with a promise to return in a week and told her to call Rachel or Maggie if things got too bad.

The patient in the ICU was as bad as I had could have imagined. He was in severe shock and had to go on life support, even after an aggressive resuscitation. He kept two nurses running most of the night, but somehow he made it through and by morning, when I checked his care out to Dr. Gallows, he was reasonably stable. I was home in time to grab my suitcase and made it to the airport with easily twenty minutes to spare. The lady at the counter, a former nurse who got smart and left the hospital when the new administration started showing its colors, asked me what I was doing, getting there so early.

The flight went well, though with my recent preoccupation with death, I found myself wondering about the wisdom of traveling at half the speed of sound, miles above terra firma. When you really stop to think about it, an airplane is just a bunch of metal sheets held together by a few rivets, likely placed by someone fighting a hangover after a night fighting with his wife. There was not much between you and a spectacular, cratered death. Moribund thoughts aside, I was spent from the night and was unconscious for most of the flight, barely aware enough to make my connection in Denver.

When I first got out of training, red hot and ready to cure the world, a night like that would have only fired me up for another day, the excitement and adrenaline like a drug addict's fix. Two, or even three busy days in a row were no problem. These days, it's quite a different story. It can take those same two or three days to recover from a single bad night. If my endurance continues to decline, my new, non-traditional career will likely take on even more importance.

By the time I arrived at Louis Armstrong International, I had caught enough rest to be functional. Guess I have a few years left in me. I wrapped Aurora in my arms and reveled for a moment in her presence before heading to the parking garage and climbing into our trendy rental Hyundai.

"Remind me to avoid any kind of emergency getaway situation." My mind flashed to an image of a real-time newscast. Picture a line of police cruisers following Aurora and me as we cut between cars in a "high-speed" chase, sometimes pushing forty or even an astounding fifty miles an hour. The reporters in the traffic helicopter would have to struggle to keep from laughing as they beamed the images across the country.

The New Orleans temperature was already warming in preparation for the summer, but the humidity wasn't yet a factor; fortunate, as the rental's air conditioner wasn't working. If the stories I'd heard were true, stepping outside much later in the year was like dropping a steaming hot wool blanket over your shoulders. A simple walk to the car would be a marathon to an uninitiated tourist from our climate—arid as any southwestern desert, except for a few months in the late winter and in the spring months we were now escaping.

We made our way to the motel, where Aurora showed off her new outfit and we went over the plans she had made. I agreed that getting the local lawyer as he picked up his morning paper made sense. I had decided to let that wiseass kid at the gym live, so I had never actually tested my new martial arts skills away from the practice mat. This would be a good time to put Chu Me's instructions to the test. I was certain that I could quickly dispatch the lawyer and be long gone when his body was found.

The "General" had come up with a couple of escape routes, should a neighbor stumble along at the wrong time or should some other problem come up. She would have the car nearby, watching so she could pick me up in a hurry if need arose, ready to rev it up to full racing speed. She had secured walkie-talkies and had established a fallback rendezvous point, just in case we got separated, even drawing me a crude map. And I'd been worried to tell her about my new career path.

CHAPTER THIRTY-NINE

The actual event was almost anticlimactic. Well, maybe not for him. Just like Aurora had predicted, Beauchamp came out for his paper shortly after six o'clock, stubble-bearded face held over a steaming cup as he briefly surveyed the world from the lofty heights of his mansion. It was amazing he didn't have to wear an oxygen mask, living at that elevation.

He was not an impressive physical specimen, his financially privileged status apparently allowing a lifetime of fine dining and merriment. He actually grunted a little as he walked over and bent down to pick up his morning news. As he was doing so, I wandered up. I couldn't resist starting a casual, albeit one-sided conversation.

"Hey, scum-bucket lawyer! Yeah, you! Let's see you find a way to charge me six hundred bucks an hour for this!"

Okay, so it wasn't much of a conversation. As he looked

up, puzzled but not alarmed, I landed a lightning fast palm strike to his nose. The bone shattered beyond recognition. His scream was cut short by a round-house kick to his sternum, dropping him instantly. His coffee cup, fragmenting on the sidewalk, was the only sound of the assault.

Millard Beauchamp stared up in disbelief, his eyes widening in fear. My reflexes took over, and with a quick knife hand shot to his neck, it was over. Thirty seconds. Not bad with only a few months training.

He landed in the grass next to a thick tangle of juniper shrubs. Someone apparently felt they would be a nice complement to his front gate. Like scores of others at home, I had spent days removing every touch of those prickly nuisances from my yard and then salting the ground so they'd never come back. I had no idea that anyone anywhere else in the country ever put them in, nor any possible idea of why they would do so. Maybe the landscape schools got a subsidy from the juniper growers, or maybe some government program for planting underappreciated greenery was in effect. I'd heard of plenty of other equally worthwhile applications of our tax dollars, and it wouldn't surprise me in the least.

These things form huge, prickly masses of chaotic green. They vacuum up any windblown trash. Every fall leaf dropped from every tree in the neighborhood will magically find a juniper home, even if it has to travel twice around the block to find one. Before today's body disposal, I'd never seen a good use for the damn things.

I jogged up to where Aurora had the rental car. She was a little shaken, but I had expected that. She had been instrumental in the planning, but this was her first killing. I had her stay far enough back that she wouldn't get too much exposure, but she had been able to see how efficiently I had dealt with him.

"Remind me to never, ever make you mad," she said, dropping the gearshift into drive and taking us away from the scene of the crime. "I thought that stuff was just in the movies. Where did you learn to move like that?"

"The nurse's dorm," I said, "trying to protect my virtue."

I don't think she bought it.

We drove the streets for a few hours, enjoying the sunny weather and looking at houses. Aurora has a thing about front doors; she's in a perpetual search for the perfect one. The quest provided a perfect diversion for the afternoon, a chance to take the edge off before preparing for the evening.

We found an awesome lunch at a café on Frenchmen Street, listening to passable jazz in a nondescript bar while we ate. A mufaletta for her, with calorie-free French fries, and an appetizer-sized plate of deep-fried alligator tail for me, served with an exquisite aioli dipping sauce I would have expected to find in a gourmet restaurant. A bucket of mudbugs made the meal complete; for me—Aurora wouldn't touch them. In fact, she recoiled at the thought when I offered one to her.

The waiter was not shy about expressing his disappointment that he couldn't convince me to follow local tradition, and "suck they heads," but even with his displeasure, it was still a very nice meal. I will have to say, though, Louisiana craw-dads don't hold a candle to those we find in the clear mountain streams back home. Those are like miniature lobsters.

We had a few more hours, which we spent leisurely wandering, pretending to be average casual tourists, before heading back to our room, where I supervised Aurora getting into her new work outfit. She required way more supervision than she thought necessary, but I've always felt it was important to get a job done right.

The plan for the evening was reviewed one last time. We

studied the pictures of our mark, Russ Feingold, a soon to be ex-Wisconsin resident. A case of mistaken identity would be hard to live with, not to mention really bad press for our up-and-coming business. If our plan worked, Feingold would find himself set up with the voluptuous street talent "Charity," anticipating a night to remember. We had a workable contingency if that didn't work out, but it had a higher element of risk.

The conference got out at 5:00, and the weary participants did what conference-goers across the nation did. They headed for the bar to forget everything they had learned; except for Feingold. He didn't show. I was set up, waiting in the bar to the distress of the waitress. A guy ordering decaf just doesn't get the same respect as a bunch of boozers ordering Slow Sideways Sex on the Beach up Against the Walls, or double-shots of eighteen-year-old single malts, neat please.

When Feingold hadn't shown by 5:30, I gave up and decided to rendezvous with Aurora to see about plan B. I was just about to get up when he made his entrance, dressed to kill. He selected a table where he had a view of the dance floor and ordered something that made the cocktail girl smile. He sat, drinking and slowly drifting with the music, his own little rhythm matching the few early evening dancers.

I signaled Aurora, and she came into the lounge, walking seductively and earning the ire of every girl in the bar. She made her way over to Feingold's table, and that's where we found that we had failed to plan for another contingency.

She sat next to him, put a leg over his, and started a very nice conversation that could only go in one direction. But he chose the opposite. Instead of gently stroking that exquisite piece of soft female flesh, he gently slid her leg back to the floor and moved his chair back. I seriously doubt Aurora had ever been turned down before. I know I'd never do anything so dumb.

She got up and headed back the way she came in. The relief on every other woman's face showed in stark contrast to the disappointment of the men she ignored, each hoping to be Feingold's replacement. I met her near the bathrooms.

"What the hell was that?" I asked, "a sleazy malpractice whore suddenly becoming righteous and turning down the chance to get a little on the side?"

"That was my original thought," she said. "Then I noticed that his wedding ring was off. The imprint was there, but not the shine." She glanced over my shoulder to make sure none of her would be suitors had followed. "Did you notice how he kept looking over in your direction? He was definitely interested in finding something tonight, just not in what I had to offer."

Aurora did a lousy job of hiding her smile, as she turned me around and pushed me toward my destiny.

Shit! Damn! Shit, shit, shit, and more shit! This one was going to land in my court. That smirk on Aurora's face was definitely going to cost her, though at least there was one silver lining. Since everyone saw her leave the table without him, she couldn't be that "person of interest" the cops were always talking about in the wake of some newsworthy crime. That meant her new business suit could come home with us, risk-free.

I'm aware of the politically correct approach to modern life. I have gay friends, and my gay patients are treated just as well as the others, perhaps more so, as I strive to make sure they don't feel intimidated, but I have never been put in the position of having to play that I was on their team. Aurora could have gotten a thousand laughs out of this one, but thankfully, it was a story she could never tell, at least not with most of our friends. I'd just have to keep her away from Bicknell for a while.

"Good luck," she said with a smile, tilting her hips in that way women seem to instinctively know. "Hope you've got what it takes!"

I thought about going back to my booth for a moment before I made my approach, to have the waitress "freshen up" my decaf a bit; quite a bit, actually, before heading over to Brokeback table, but decided it would be better to get the game rolling. It would be bad if another captured his fancy before I got the chance. After being out of practice from twenty-five years of marriage, I wasn't confident I could win his heart over another. I'd better be there first.

I went down the two-step stairs from the bathroom hallway to the sunken bar, glanced over to make eye contact with Feingold, noted the slight nod of his head and wound my way over. As I passed through the tables, disapproving looks came from every direction. This was, still the South. I cast my eyes down and hurried past.

I leaned forward against the other chair when I got to Feingold's table, hoping that some of the lessons from my old high school acting days had been retained. "I noticed you sent that young thing off on her own," I said, resisting the temptation to try affecting a gay accent. "She was absolutely the most gorgeous thing." I hoped Aurora was getting good reception on her ear-bud receiver. "I sure hope her feelings weren't hurt."

He smiled and looked happier to see me than he had with the (in my opinion) much more desirable Charity. "I think she understood," he said.

"Mind if I sit down?"

He stood up with a gleam in his eye, extending his hand. "George DeLuca," he lied, "and I'd be most pleased if you would." Very formal, he probably knocked them dead in court.

"Hal Logan," I said, figuring our hospital CEO wouldn't

mind the loan of his name for such a worthy cause. We made small talk for an hour or so, getting nicely acquainted.

"I'm a lawyer," he mentioned. "Down from Green Bay for a conference and some fun in the sun."

Apparently for some fun in a place less familiar with the sun, as well.

"Wisconsin? That's why you don't sound like these people. I swear, half the time I have to make them repeat themselves so I know what they're trying to say. It's like a foreign language!"

When you're telling lies, it's best to maintain an element of truth, but telling him I was a physician probably wasn't my best bet. Sure, he loves to screw us professionally, but I didn't want to put something out there that might interfere with our fledgling relationship. If things fell apart, he could go look for someone else, but for me, this was a one-time opportunity.

"I'm not involved with anything that exciting," I deferred. "I do accounting for the firm that makes those plastic inserts you see in all the urinals in airports and such. We make the deodorizers too, but that's a different division. Pretty boring stuff, but there are a lot of toilets and there isn't much competition, so it's a volume business; we do pretty well."

He ordered a new Long Island iced tea. "These things are great," he exclaimed. "Someone once told me they were the most booze you can get in a single glass. I always have a few when I'm on the road." Turning to the waitress, he said, "Make it two, honey. My friend here needs something to help him relax."

I thought about saying no but felt he'd do better if he thought I was all in on this.

"I've been married for twenty-five years," I went on, "but it's never been what I wanted. I'm from a small town in Georgia. My dad was the Baptist minister. You can imagine what my childhood was like! My folks would have killed me if they knew. I married a high school classmate and hoped it would work, but it's been a torture of a life. Thank God for Viagra!

The kids are out of school, now, and I've been getting less and less happy as time goes by. I finally decided a few weeks ago to see what's out there, before I get any older. If I seem a little nervous, it's because I've been waiting for this for so long, but it's a little scary too. Still got some of that Baptist in me, I guess."

The small talk went on. Children, hobbies, movie stars and favorite musicals—he had seen *The Music Man* so many times that he practically had it memorized, and he couldn't help interspersing witticisms from *West Side Story*. He was actually a pretty interesting conversationalist.

"Do you work out?" he asked.

"Bench press a hundred twenty, and still going up," I bragged, stoking the fires a little. "Free weights," I added, "not those machines the lightweights use!" I'd almost said "girly men" but caught myself just in time. "But you want to talk about torture? Try working out with a bunch of sweaty farm boys and knowing you can't do anything about it!" Giggling in what I hoped was an appropriate manner, I said, "I usually have to wait to take my shower."

As the night went on, it became apparent that he was thinking of moving our relationship forward. He mentioned that his meetings started early in the morning, so maybe it wasn't smart to stay out too late. "Perhaps," he said, "we could go upstairs and get a little more … *well acquainted.*"

I didn't know people actually said that, but then again, I have been out of the dating scene for quite a while. I allowed that I had reached the same conclusion and accepted his suggestion that we repair to his room. Thankfully, there was someone else with us on the elevator to his eighteenth-floor love nest, or the ride would have been a much more unpleasant experience. From the look on her face, the lady going up had a pretty good idea of what was going on. Of course, if she really knew …

We got to his floor, spilled out of the elevator, and made our way to his room. I wasn't the only one a little nervous. I must be pretty good at this fake gay thing, because Feingold's hand was trembling as he fitted his magnetic key card in to the door slot. With the door open, he placed his hand on my sculpted, gym-hardened butt, way past what TSA is allowed, and helped me across the threshold.

He was ready to get going as soon as the door closed, but I begged for a minute to collect myself, making a show of pulling a selection of booze miniatures from his mini-bar. "Why don't you get in to something a little more comfortable?" I suggested. It was turning out to be a night of stereotypical dating phrases.

Russ slipped into the bathroom. I could hear him rustling out of his clothes, then another familiar sound—gargling. From the amount of time he spent at it, he should have the freshest breath in the morgue. I pulled the stiletto from its concealment, opened it, and waited outside the door.

He called out, hopeful—"everything okay out there?"

I replied with a nervous, "I think so."

With any plan, no matter how well thought out, there's a good chance that something will come up during the execution. My forgetting about the universal change over to magnetic card locks, for example. I thought about the poor maid who'd have to clean up the mess after Feingold/"DeLuca" did his early checkout. I could have just gone ahead when he came out of the bathroom, as I had planned, and just leave a nicer than usual tip, but I figured the police would just put the cash in the evidence file, leaving the maid high and dry and still having to do the cleanup.

I considered putting the knife away and doing another kung fu exhibition. The potential for noise alerting an accompanying resident was a downside, though, and in the enclosed space, my still novice moves would be restricted, not to mention the obvious commonality with the earlier murder, a fact that wouldn't escape the police, spoiling the intended 'randomness' of his death. No, it would have to be the blade.

Most motel bathrooms have a tile or similar blood-resistant floor. They probably weren't designed with that in mind, but it worked. Between the low signature of my chosen blade and the good floor, the bathroom would be a much more considerate place for Feingold to come to his end.

I closed the knife, as silently as possible, and then checked the door. I found it unlocked and slipped in behind my target. When he looked up in the mirror where he was doing his final preparations, I locked my eyes on the reflections of his. In retrospect, it seemed like a good diversion to keep him occupied, but it was actually one of those self-defense things. Briefly letting my gaze take in my surroundings as I entered the bathroom, I had been treated to one of those 'seeing something that can't be unseen' scenarios. You just can't scrub your eyeballs clean when they've been confronted with something like that.

Someday, in a fair and just world, there will be a law preventing certain people from owning Speedos, but so far, apparently not. And where the hell do you find heart patterned Care Bears in a size forty-four? It's just not right.

Russ Feingold, aka George DeLuca, seemed to find them

appealing though, and I was just going to have to deal with it. The marble countertop had an array of alarming looking items, the real purpose of which went way beyond anything I've ever dreamed of (or wanted to). Some of his toys looked like they would have had to come with a detailed instruction manual; one possibly would need a legal waiver. I think the idea of Aurora tying him hand and foot to the bed with silk neckties might have been a touch on the pedestrian side—he'd gone way beyond that a long time ago.

Perhaps after my work was done, a few of these items could find a new home in Oregon—that is, if anyone markets a super strength industrial grade Clorox.

I put my hands on his shoulders, as if for a warm-up back rub. I refuse to say foreplay; no way, no how. Let him think what he wanted, which apparently he did, as was evident when he turned around to face me, exposing the second of the days can't-be-unseen sights. He reached out for a tender caress, and substantially more. I stepped back to create a safe distance, flicked the stiletto back open and plunged it fully into his heart. It was a slight modification of a pericardiocentesis, a rarely needed but lifesaving procedure. This was only the second time I had ever employed it, but with a decidedly different objective than the first.

His eager look turned briefly to confusion, and then to fear and anger. He started to scream, but my hand closed fast enough on his throat to keep it in check. I left the knife in place to minimize the blood show and slowly lowered him to the floor.

He glanced up, a plaintive look on his face. "Why do you people hate us so?"

He thought it was a hate crime, which I guess it sort of was, just not for the reason he had assumed. I thought I owed it to him to tell him the real reason, but his eyes rolled up, and he was gone before I got to tell the whole story. He might have gotten the important part.

When it was obvious that the American Bar Association was down a second notch for the day, I put on some latex gloves I had borrowed from my office and did a preliminary crime scene cleanup. I didn't want to leave a big mess for the local law enforcement to deal with, or for the maid. The knife made an unusual, and rather discomposing sucking sound as I extracted it from Feingold's chest. It retained a small amount of gore as it pulled free. The knife would be headed for a watery grave soon, so I didn't waste much time cleaning it, just a rudimentary wipe down.

I hadn't touched much in the room; the wet bar, the bathroom doorknob, and of course, the liquor bottles, all easily cleaned. A motel must be the worst placed in the world for a CSI team to do an investigation, so even if I had forgotten a few places I wouldn't worry too much. Multiple visitors having left trace evidence over the previous several days would likely obscure anything worthwhile, plus I had no fingerprint record of my own, having always been a law abiding citizen. Still, it seemed prudent to do a little strategic touch-up.

That finished, I pegged the A/C to the bottom, hoping to keep the late protector of the medically wronged from warming too soon, and spoiling the rest of our trip. I had some sightseeing to do with Aurora and I didn't want him attracting undue attention by decomposing too quickly. Feingold and I had spent quite a bit of time in the bar and had obviously attracted quite a lot of attention. I had no interest in sharing bad vending machine coffee with the police, in a room lined with one-way mirrors if any of the other bar go-ers could do a better job ID'ing me than the shocked people in Redding had been able to do.

Plus, there was some consideration for the other motel guests, who wouldn't want their morning room service tainted with the smell of a decaying lawyer. The Do Not Disturb sign artfully placed on the door completed the picture, though I don't think there was much that could have disturbed him at this point. Still, it never hurt to be polite.

I made my way to the lounge where a nervous Aurora was waiting. "All went well?" she asked. "You were up there quite a while. I was beginning to wonder if I was going to have to start getting jealous. The two of you looked so good together that I thought maybe you had had a change of heart."

"It was like a like a choreographed scene from Broadway," I bragged. "Things couldn't have gone more smoothly and I managed to get by without doing anything to make me feel like I'd have to run back to our room for an hour long scalding shower. I cooled the room to give us an extra day or two, but the less time we spend here, the less chance someone will remember us. You seem to think he and I made such a cute couple; others might have noticed too."

"You really were," Aurora teased, looking back over her shoulder as she led the way out.

"Also," I said, "we've got to get rid of that knife. It was perfect for the job, you did great by the way, but it's not something I want to hang onto any longer than necessary."

The knife's disposal site had been selected in advance, thanks again to my favorite general. Audubon Park, in the western part of town, had a quaint little pond where lovers sparked and the depressed sat to watch the carefree ducks that had long ago forgotten to be alarmed at the sight of man. I suspect that they had also forgotten the part about relocating with the changing seasons. Why leave a happy home where there were no dangers and where complete strangers fed you and expected nothing in return? It's an interesting corollary to the modern welfare system.

A duck pond is the perfect place to hide a murder weapon. After having sunk to my knees several times, and almost losing my life once while waterfowl hunting, I have nightmares about what a few decades of duck crap can do to the bottom of a pond. You could hide an M1 Abrams tank there, and no one would ever find it.

That knife would never again see the light of day. If it did, by some miracle, it would be in a La Brea-type archeological dig, in a far distant future, when there would hopefully not even be any more lawyers, nor anyone caring about one who had disappeared on a bad date in Louisiana.

Aurora and I meandered barefoot among the magnificent spreading oaks, with soft grass spreading up between our toes—two engaged lovers, lost in each other's presence, until we were certain we had complete privacy. There could be no romancing couples or nocturnal joggers to see us toss the knife to its final resting place. Assured we were alone, Aurora sent it spinning end over bloody end toward its grave in the organic depths. When the knife hit the water, it sounded like a depth charge, but other than a few ducks who indignantly paddled away, it got no notice.

With that done, the rest of the trip would be spent in vacation mode. Aurora had never been to the Big Easy and was thrilled by all there was to offer. She was somewhat intimidated, too. Growing up in a small town and now living in a rural, conservative part of Oregon, the endless display in New Orleans left her in a near constant state of open-mouthed wonder.

A neon tattooed woman, shaved completely bald, was leading her equally tattooed man around on a spiked dog collar, growling commands at him and whipping him when he didn't obey fast enough. We crossed paths with another interesting young lady—her clothes were painted on. I was sincerely admiring the artistic talent involved in creating such a masterpiece, to her amusement. Aurora was not pleased by the amount of attention I gave her, though, and I only made the situation worse when I tried defending myself, mentioning that surface anatomy had always been one of my favorite studies, "and after all," I said, "I am a chest doctor."

That's when she nudged me midstride into the pole of a fake turn-of-the-century gas light. My cat-like reflexes failed to bring me back from my reverie in time for an artful dodge, earning me a black eye and a few snickers from other passers-by.

"Tourists!" said one man to his wife, smiling and shaking his head.

Aurora mentioned that I hadn't paid that much attention to the works of the great masters when we toured the Louvre. A braver man might have replied, but I'd learned my lesson for the evening.

Pedestrians were walking about with open containers of alcohol, barker's lured tourists in for on-stage sex shows and transvestite reviews, all interspersed with simple cafés and shops, the kind you'd find on any main street in America. Aurora was a little out of her league, finding something new and sometimes alarming with every block. Someday, I'd have to take her to West Miami Beach. That was where things really got interesting.

We walked to Barlow's, a five-star steak and seafood legend. It was the Southern waterside dining establishment of the infamous '1 per centers.' Our lack of a reservation and my recently blackened eye, courtesy of the lamp pole, earned us a cool reception. A generous "gratuity" for the maître d' served as a good substitute, though, and we were rewarded with a nice table overlooking the river. The advantages of my new specialty were beginning to show—we could afford to eat with the best.

Our table was also relatively secluded. It might have been my generosity up front, but more likely it was a way to have us be a little less conspicuous in our pedestrian, off-the-rack clothes. At least Aurora had changed from her rent-me-by-the-hour outfit. That might have caused a stir, though it would have fit right in on the street.

I offered a toast as we waited for our meals. "Five and oh, and not a whisper of suspicion."

She nodded contentedly.

"Really," I went on, "except for the running into the peeing neighbor, which didn't turn out to be such a bad thing, and letting the cop in Redding see my face, things have gone pretty smoothly. And our portfolio is expanding nicely. We'll be back to where we were before the housing crash. Maybe we can start having a little fun."

Our meal arrived, perfectly prepared and presented; delicate sturgeon for me. I wondered why I had traveled half-way across the country, only to order a dinner from my home state, but all reservations disappeared with the first bite.

A well-aged corn-fed Midwestern filet caught my gorgeous dinner partner's eye. It was complimented by a wild mushroom medley and a garlic-cilantro dipping sauce. "Perfection," was Aurora's declaration. "Absolute perfection!"

Pelicans fished on the river, dipping their heads periodically into its swirling currents. The waiters were attentive, but not over-bearing, and the evening unfolded in utter tranquility. I was wondering if things could ever get any better when Aurora leaned forward across the table, her eyes catching mine in a promising fashion. The look left me searching for my next breath, and wondering what the rest of the night might have in store, but she was just distracting me. She took advantage of my helpless state to grab the last piece of bread, before retreating to a safe distance.

"I'll remember that," I promised. "You'll never see it coming, but I *will* have my revenge."

Aurora quaked in imagined fear. "Should I up my life insurance?"

I reached across the table, taking her hand.

"I used to be in such fear of ever reaching the retirement mark," I admitted, "that I never made plans for any kind of life after work. It was to be toil until I dropped and then let some latecomer step in, marry my beautiful widow and enjoy the fruits. It struck me as being kind of pointless, but it seemed to be the life I was locked into."

"Look at us now, though. Not only are we making the world a better place, we are actually moving forward toward a day when I can tell the powers that be to take their regulations, roll them up and stuff them up their collective asses. You and I will sail off in to the sunset while those with less imagination carry on like they always have."

"And look at the great working vacations we get," Aurora said, smiling proudly across the table. "We should have started doing this years ago; think how many of your colleagues must have lain awake at night, stressed all to here," holding her hands together under her chin, "and waiting month after month to see what would happened with their lawsuit, all the while wishing they had the guts to do something about it, but then chickening out and sitting idly by while their futures were wrested from them and they were made to look like fools. Think of the countless millions of dollars squandered on malpractice premiums and on unnecessary tests, done only to keep society's nonfunctioning masses from winning the 'medical lottery.' No one else had the guts to actually take that first step, Jack. You are a pioneer." Now she really was making favorable eye contact. "And you're so good at it, too!"

Was she still talking about the hit-man thing?

"Whoever said that thing about not teaching an old dog new tricks," she proffered, "never met this sexy old dog."

CHAPTER FORTY

After dinner, we wandered Bourbon Street, watching the parade of human wildlife. They say Vegas never sleeps, the same could be said for the Big Easy. After wandering around until our feet were about to go on strike, we took a break at an upstairs café. On a balcony enclosed in an ornate railing of intricate cast iron, we ate the best beignets in town—at least, according to the owner. He must have had several shops in town, because I'd seen at least three others hyping the same claim.

The waiter asked if a cup of coffee would go well with 'the best beignets in town,' and I thought that sounded like a winning plan. Ordinarily, I'd go with decaf at such a late hour, but I was in New Orleans, with a million things to celebrate, so I went for the gold. *Laissez lez bons temps rouler!* There would be plenty of time to sleep on the plane.

After that, we walked around for a few more hours, generally without talking, just holding hands and connecting on a rare plane. It was one of the nicest evenings. We searched the stores still open so late at night, and collected a few souvenirs. Almost without realizing it, we had looped back to our hotel, pleasantly exhausted, and feeling every one of our advancing years, but both delighted with the evening.

Sleep came surprisingly easily and lasted until the alarm signaled the start of our final day. While Aurora kicked off the last vestiges, I grabbed the television remote, temporarily forgetting the disturbing conclusions of a motel-room hygiene study I'd read a few years ago, and called up the morning news. I wanted to see if Feingold had been discovered.

Our staying in town the extra day had been a calculated gamble. We had thought about catching yesterday evening's red-eye but decided it was worth the risk to have one nice night on the town. We had felt we should be okay, unless Feingold's wife tried to call him to see how the conference was going. She might eventually become alarmed enough to call the police when she couldn't reach him, and our surprise would be out. I was counting on the fact that things probably weren't that smooth back home in Wisconsin, and that she wouldn't be spending too much time trying to keep up on her husband's day.

If our secret was out, the police would be taking statements, and since Feingold and I had been in the lounge for so long and had left practically arm in arm, they might have a dangerously good description of me. Good enough to make boarding an airplane a risk. I could make a few minor cosmetic changes, but a true disguise would never get past TSA. I might have to give up my flight and take a rental car home. With over two thousand miles, I'd never make it back to the office in time to see my Monday morning patients, and with Aurora along, I'd be cooling my heels outside every rest stop toilet between here and the West Coast, turning a three day trip in to a marathon.

I was relieved to see that the television news morning edition, while going into great detail and speculation about the first victim of our lawyer safari, had not yet found Feingold to be newsworthy. That was bound to change in the near future, but if we could make the connecting flight in Denver before it happened we'd be home free.

Getting through security was no problem, at least no more so than being forced to halfway disrobe, pass through the electronic voyeur, and have our carry-ons searched for weapons of mass-transit destruction. It occurred to me that airport security could be an opportunity to wreak havoc against a malpractice attorney, if a client chose not to go all the way to a final termination. Sneak in a dangerous contraband item, a box-cutter or blackjack, throw in a well-worn copy of the Koran, and watch the fun begin.

"Sir, is this your luggage?" the TSA agent would ask.

"Yes."

"Did you pack it yourself, sir?" he'd ask, as the rest of the TSA closed a circle around them. The idea was definitely worth further consideration.

Aurora and I breathed a sigh of relief after gaining our seats. We tolerated the familiar discussion on floating seat cushions and non-inflating oxygen masks with a smile. Aurora kept looking out the window, waiting for the law to come running up like a lost lover in a romantic movie, but we were soon above the clouds, heading home from our first joint mission. By the time we had wheels up, she was able to loosen her death grip from my now bloodless hand, though she left an imprint of her mother's ring so deeply in my flesh that a skin graft might be in my future.

Head lolled against the window, oblivious with her Sharper Image airplane earmuffs, Aurora fell into a peaceful sleep. I tried to maintain a polite flow of conversation with the young lady in the aisle seat. She apparently didn't appreciate my theory of what would happen if someone forgot to tighten one of the wing fasteners, though, and asked to be transferred to another seat. No sense of curiosity, I guess, but the extra space was nice—it was like a free upgrade.

It's a good thing I was able to get some rest the night before we left, because it wasn't going to happen on this flight. All had been going well, until we hit midair turbulence, the worst I've ever been through. Things deteriorated rapidly; my cross-aisle seatmate was just getting up for a much needed trip to the back of the plane, when it felt like the airplane was going to be wrenched from the sky. My neighbor was briefly airborne, before landing crosswise over my lap in a most unladylike manner. Her coffee spilled, and she was so rattled that the original reason for getting up from her seat would no longer be an issue. Thank you, Mother Nature.

The baby immediately behind me was catapulted from a peaceful slumber into an ear-splitting state of full alarm panic. How such a small package can produce such an Olympic caliber wail is beyond my understanding. I wouldn't even make it thirty seconds, but it appeared the baby was in it for the duration. Equally mysterious was the parents' indifference to the suffering visited upon the rest of us. If the next flight went in a similar fashion, I was going to need another vacation to recover from this one.

An interesting thought occurred to me. Would these circumstances rise to the standard of justifiable homicide? (For the *parents*; I'm not an animal.) Perhaps I could take the earphone cables from their iPad, or Zbox, or whatever the hell they called those things that so effectively insulated them from the auditory torture of their baby's screaming and jury-rig a functional garrote. Judging from the pained looks of the other passengers, I'd receive an enthusiastic ovation as I was being carted off to jail.

We deplaned in Denver, with no extra attention from the law. I hadn't mentioned it to Aurora, but I had been concerned that there might be scrutiny of passengers on outbound flights from Louis Armstrong, one final chance for them to catch us.

We were soon on our final leg. There was no turbulence and no need for the earplugs I purchased at an airport kiosk. It had been an eventful vacation, but flawlessly performed, and Aurora and I arrived home, tired but smiling.

As we pulled into our garage, the mythical beast Zach drove up in his beater, yet another new girlfriend at his side. (Takes after his dad on that one, I guess.) Aurora had been worried about leaving him on his own, though I had persuaded her that he'd be fine. We'd left him a few bucks for meals, and it seemed he had gotten through the experience without permanent damage.

"Hi, Mom. Hi, Dad. Been out shopping? Did you have a nice day?"

I sighed. "Yes, son. Yes, we did."

Chapter Forty-one

A new and unexpected problem came up after the New Orleans trip. The challenge and anticipation I used to feel at work started to fade. Medicine become mundane compared to the excitement of roaming the country, eliminating lawyers and outwitting the police. The day to day sameness of my practice started to chafe, and the impending government mandated emersion into electronic record keeping further downgraded my work satisfaction. Years of working in patient care, with skills sharpened on the field of battle, were being usurped by geeky computer freaks whose entire work experience came from an Xbox.

I still enjoyed listening to my patients' stories and of course, the personal interactions. A host of patients with incredible experiences have come through over the years. Movie stars, combat veterans and people with all kinds of interesting hobbies and family histories. I've had foreign patients who had fled the oppression of their government, (many of these were from 'The People's Republic' of California), and others whose families had homesteaded here. Sharing their stories and seeing them through their difficult times continued to enrich me.

There was room for humor with some patients, too. I had a patient who became a good friend. He desperately needed a lung transplant but was reluctant to have it done. I tried everything to convince him, but he wouldn't come around until I got him laughing about it.

"What's the worst part of getting a lung transplant, Jim?" I asked in my most professorial physician tone.

"The pills?" he guessed. "Rejection?"

I shook my head.

"No more seafood buffets?" They were on the strict no-fly list.

"Nope. It's the part where one day you realize that you're coughing up someone else's sputum!"

My first office patient after my return from New Orleans was of special interest, a wildlife biologist. The first day back from vacation is typically similar to the day before—too much stuff for the available time. I knew it would put me behind if we spent much time talking, but I love the outdoors and couldn't resist.

"Tell me about your work," I said, before getting to the problem that brought him in.

"Fisheries biology, forestry, law enforcement, you name it," he said, "and I do it. I'm just finishing a fascinating and very expensive research project. It took most of the past year and we had to petition twice for expansions of our budget."

"What were you studying?" I asked.

"It was huge. You know we're in a major waterfowl flyway, right?"

"The Pacific fly zone."

"Well," he went on, "you know how every time you see a flight of geese, one side of the V is longer than the other?"

"Yeah, I've often wondered what advantage they get from that. Some kind of aerodynamic or navigation trick, I suppose?"

"Nope. Like I said, it took a while, but we finally got it figured out."

I waited.

"The V is lopsided because ... one side has more geese!"

Okay, I guess it goes both ways. I almost fell out of my chair.

"Should I be looking in the next issue of *Nature*?" I asked.

I do still love medicine; it's just not quite as exciting as my new specialty. Work at the hospital was more stimulating than the office, despite the horror of the new computer system. True adrenaline-pumping, heart-racing emergencies occur, and I love it when they do, though they tend to happen at hours that I'm getting too old for. It takes me a while to get my land legs back after a bad night of call. Perhaps I am starting to get a little old for the ICU game.

I was told this would happen. Near the end of my fellowship, a senior attending physician, probably a venerable fifty or so by the look of his graying, receding hair had tried to get me to give up clinical medicine and stay on at the university doing academic research.

As usual, I didn't listen. "I love the ICU," I told him. "The lab is nice, but I want to go where I can be a full-time intensivist. It's why I spent all these years training."

"Everyone wants to be the hero," he said. "Saving lives and earning the adoration of the nurses. But after a few years, you'll start to get tired of that beeper and the long nights spent in the unit. You'll start to think of a different life, one where you can sleep, and where you can have the freedom to see your kids grow up, to work on your handicap or seven-ten split or whatever you love. No more getting up from your wife's warm side and trudging through the snow at three in the morning for yet another crisis or answering pages during your daughter's recital. I've seen it a million times. I did it myself. I know."

Of course, I knew better. The ICU was where it was happening, and I wanted a piece of it. And what did he say about those nurses? I'd work until I hit my mid-fifties and then semi-retire to a relaxed office practice and spend the rest of my days enjoying my abundant savings. I'd reflect back on my days as the "Caped Crusader" of the ICU as my grandchildren chased fireflies through a well-manicured yard, the envy of the neighborhood. Aurora would be smiling, nestled beside me on our front porch swing, holding hands and watching them go. Maybe I'd even go for the white picket fence.

Working in the hospital gave me some of the charge that I had grown used to, but it still wasn't quite the same, and I began to wonder again if I could build up enough of a client base to make a full-time career of debriding the country of those pederastic, down-dragging lawyers. I'd have to be fairly busy for a while. I don't have one of those taxpayer paid, income-for-life retirement plans waiting in the larder, the kind that lets so many of my patients retire from their public service jobs while still in their mid-fifties, but it could probably be done. I'd talk it over with George, to see if he thought we could build it up to that level. I needed to check in with him anyway, to see if we had gotten any more requests.

Aurora and I decided to have George over for dinner. She'd work up some of her kitchen magic, the kind we could share with company, and we could discuss how to expand our new medical outreach program. George asked if he could bring his new girlfriend, but I explained that this would be a business meeting—no extra ears allowed. We set a date for the next evening we both had free from call.

Chapter Forty-two

The news had a flash about two lawyers killed on the same day in New Orleans. I had turned the radio on as I drove to the gym for a lunch hour weight lifting session. Both lawyers specialized in malpractice. The question came up as to whether or not the homicides were related. One was suspected to be a targeted murder; the other, possibly just a coincidence—an extramarital hook-up at a fancy hotel gone badly. Still, there was a lot of speculation. Was there a rogue physician exacting revenge from the lawyer community? Radio talk shows would be full of this for a while, and I was curious what the callers' sentiments would be, so I grabbed a sandwich and tuned in to Bill Hunter, an up and coming host who was trying to make the break from a regional to a syndicated audience.

"Hi, this is Gunther, from Idaho. It's about time someone started getting on those damn pinko bastard lawyers and gave them what they deserve. I hope they made them suffer like the pigs they are. Now we need to start in on those Muslims and border runners ruining our country. Where do I sign up?"

"Bill? Hi, this is Joey, from Boston? This is just another consequence of that horrible right-wing conspiracy. We need to get all that hateful stuff off the air. Everyone should tune in to NPR."

It would go one like that for a week or two, until it was replaced by another story, and the country would move on to the next topic du jour. There was always a politician or actor or other famous somebody doing something stupid to gain the limelight, but if we got good press for a while, the idea would be out there. Doctors might no longer be fair game. If things settled down too much, it would be easy to re-stoke the fires with another couple of hits or maybe a Unabomber-style letter, warning lawyers of the consequences if they didn't end their evil ways.

CHAPTER FORTY-THREE

A small problem came up while we were waiting for our dinner with George. Channel 3, our local part-time news, part-time entertainment channel called. Harvey Nash was our very own homegrown version of a flamboyant newscaster. I personally would have preferred tuning in to Glenn Fry's famous bubble-headed bleach blond, but our town has a serious shortage of those.

Harvey sported three-piece suits in a town of ranchers and lumberjacks, and talked like Ted Baxter from the old *Mary Tyler Moore* show, thinking the affectation gave him more credibility. He was rumored to spend more time on his makeup than on his material, but he managed to get by. He would have never made it in the big city, but the competition here was manageable.

Harvey seemed to have decided that I was the local source of knowledge for all things medical. He wanted to interview me for a piece on the string of malpractice lawyer deaths.

"Some enterprising FOX reporter has started digging around," Harvey said, "and came across a story about that lawyer who got knifed in Redding a while back. He coupled that with the two in New Orleans, and the story suddenly got wings. We need to get on board this one early, Jack. Three murders would definitely raise conspiracy theories, but a fourth has surfaced to really make it interesting. The major networks are going to be all over this one."

My gut clenched; a fourth victim? Was he talking about Moon? "Where was that one, Harvey?"

"Pensacola," he responded, to my relief. "A lawyer got skydiving lessons from his wife as a birthday present a few weeks ago. His chute failed on his solo attempt. The forensic squad thinks that it was sabotaged, though it's apparently taking some time to sort things out, with all the mess. Everyone was focused on the wife, but now they are looking at the doctors he has been suing. This is way too good to pass up. Can you help me get in front of it?"

I was wondering if maybe I was up against some competition. Not that it was a worry. There was plenty of room in the field, but still, it *was* my idea.

I have been Harvey's on-air guest before, for various health-related topics. A few years ago we had quite a panic when whooping cough surged through our elementary and middle schools. Being a pulmonologist, they clued in on me. They must have liked my performance, as when AIDS came on the national scene Channel 3 had me on for a two-part series, cluing the public in on the little we knew.

A few times, when news was slow, they'd call me for something to fill the minutes. Harvey said I had camera presence. I actually enjoyed doing the interviews, my fifteen minutes of fame, and the hospital nurses often remarked that I looked cute and scholarly at the same time, "like that doctor on prime time."

Harvey probably chose me for the interview because I was in his speed-dial, but I wondered if the motivation might be more sinister. Even though it never hit the papers, it was reasonably well known that I had been named in a suit. If they understood that it went to the circular file after the unexpected death of the prosecuting attorney, uncomfortable questions might come up in the interview.

A *natural death*, I would have to emphasize, if I took the invitation and the topic of Moon's death came up. If I didn't take the invitation, though, it might look like I was trying to hide something.

"I would love to, Harvey. Thanks so very much for asking."

"Tomorrow evening's edition work for you? I'd like to get this going before everyone else jumps on board. We could tape at noon, or we could go live, if you'd rather."

I chose the taped interview. With more time to consider my answers, there would be less chance of getting trapped in a bad situation. I tried to decline the makeup session but was told that it was an absolute. The consequences of going on air without it were too terrible to comprehend.

"Can you make me look like Daniel Craig?" I asked.

Okay, no humor in the makeup department. Maybe I'd hit them with some of my better stuff later, when the pressure of the show was off, and see if it was just a bad day for them. I have some great traveling salesman material, and there's always that one about the priest on the golf course.

For previous interviews, I'd always shot live, so there had to be an introduction to the taping process; where to look, how to sit, enunciation, be sure not to touch there. Good thing I'm a fast learner. They could edit those out since it was being taped, but preferred it if they didn't have to.

Harvey was going to do a live lead in before the taped session. He read through it once, for my benefit, and to give me an idea of the gist of the story before he began the interrogation—I mean, interview.

"This is Harvey Nash," he said, as if everyone in the viewing area didn't already know, "with a developing story of national importance." Cue the music. "Lawyers across the country are being hunted down for suing doctors. Are we seeing the actions of a single homicidal physician who thinks he has a self-prescribed license to kill, or is this the vanguard of an army of disgruntled healers, striking back against the nation's litigators? Will more be hitting the ground soon? Today, I interviewed a local practitioner to get his views on the situation, Dr. Jack Hastings, board certified critical care specialist and pulmonologist from Intermountain Regional Medical Center." He turned to smile in my direction. "Dr. Hastings, welcome and thanks for coming."

"Thank you, Harvey. It's always a pleasure to be here at Channel 3."

"Dr. Hastings, what's your take on this situation. Do you think there is a doctor out there killing off malpractice attorneys?"

"Well, I just finished the *New York Times* nonfiction best-seller, *The Emotional and Financial Joys of Killing Attorneys*, and found it to be a fascinating insight into this new hobby." I let the shocked look settle a few moments, and then

let him off the hook. "Seriously, Harvey, physicians are healers, not raging, lynching lunatics. If it is the case that a doctor
is doing this, which I *seriously* doubt"—I turned my eyes to
the camera, "let me say in my clearest possible tone, the medical community as a whole would never stand for such a thing.
It would be the action of a deeply disturbed individual, someone who had fallen completely off the rails and not acting on
behalf of his colleagues. I, and all the others in our field, are
dedicated to saving lives. We would unequivocally condemn
any such actions."

Thoughtful, inquisitive, his favorite profile toward the
camera, Harvey turned back to me. "There has been a major
push by medical groups over the last few years to get tort
reform measures passed, both on state and national levels.
Without exception, every effort has been a failure. This has
got to be a frustration for the medical field. It stands to reason
that someone might decide to take matters into his own hands
and bypass the legislative route. These homicides would seem
to suggest that that might be the case, yet you say you don't
think so. If you think it isn't about doctors sanctioning attorneys, do you have any other ideas?"

"Yes, Harvey, I do, but first, let me compliment you on
being aware of the malpractice crisis in this country. If more
had your kind of knowledge, perhaps we could get something
done."

Harvey beamed in the spotlight.

"Now, as far as this lawyer killing conspiracy idea goes,
I think it's just made up news designed to fill the twenty-four
hour cycle, a coincidence. There are four hundred million
people in this country, and many die every day despite our
physicians' heroic efforts." I paused for effect. "It's part of
life. Some deaths are natural, some involve tragic accidents,

and yes, some are homicides, but people die all the time, and lawyers are not immune to the phenomenon."

Harvey was loving it.

"The guy in New Orleans—Feingold, I think was his name? It looks like he was killed by a lover, or in a vicious hate crime, nothing at all to do with his being a lawyer. The other one there I haven't heard enough to know about, but it could have been random, or he could have had any number of enemies. It will probably turn out to be a personal or matrimonial issue. That's the way these things usually wind up.

"I remember the lawyer in Redding and the speculation even then that it might be related to his malpractice career. As it turned out, he had gambling debts, and I understand he had death threats after his product liability victory with that ridiculous automobile sunscreen suit. It's irresponsible to try to pin those deaths on our nation's dedicated physicians, people who selflessly give their lives to their field.

"Plus," I said, "these deaths have occurred thousands of miles apart. Even more, if you include the one in Florida. How do you put that on one guy? Murder over all those state lines would get the FBI involved, which no one in his right mind would want. The doctors I work with are far too smart to go up against those odds."

Then, I couldn't resist. Doctors are no different than others; we all have egos and other foibles. "*If* these were the actions of an individual, though, he would have to be pretty clever. Disturbed, to be sure, but extremely clever."

"What about the fourth case, the one in Pensacola?"

I caught myself just as I was about to say that I didn't have anything to do with that one—big mistake avoided. "I haven't heard enough detail to even comment on that one, Harvey, but I'm sure something will turn up. On first look, it does appear that it might have been a homicide, but the cops these days are good. Just watch a few episodes of CSI. They'll get it solved. In a week or so, you'll see this supposed conspiracy is not even a story anymore. The lawyers will breathe a sigh of relief, and go right back to chasing ambulances and getting rich off the backs of competent physicians, and the world will go on in its natural fashion."

So far, no mention of my short circuited lawsuit, and I wasn't about to bring it up. No point in ruining a perfectly good interview. If it had hit the newspaper, as happened with Gwen's suit, there was no way it wouldn't have ended up on today's center stage. Nash would have done his best investigative reporter interpretation. Problem is, he might have come up with something.

As it was, I'd gotten through without a visible sweat and even managed to get in a little anti-malpractice speech, without coming across as being sympathetic to the thought of killing the lawyers. Not a bad performance.

Harvey finished up.

"Well, there you have it, folks. Thank you, Dr. Hastings, for sharing your insight into these unfortunate deaths." Looking back to the camera and resurrecting his would be national host-of-importance voice, which had faded slightly during the course of the segment, he pointed at the camera in his signature move—"you make the call!"

I smiled as I got up to shake his hand. There wasn't much worry that he'd be snatched up by one of the major networks, but he'd done his best.

CHAPTER FORTY-FOUR

In Redding, a few hundred miles to the south, Enrico Rodriquez, Rick, to his friends, was finishing up another rotten day in a series of steadily more rotten weeks. He met up with Jim Parker, an old friend from the police academy for a few after patrol beers. Jim had migrated out of the state before the financial crunch, and it was clear that he had made the better choice. He would have been well on the way to a decent retirement but earned permanent disability when a third-time drunk driver ran him over during a routine traffic stop. Multiple surgeries and weeks in the hospital were followed by months in rehab.

Each morning, his orange juice was accompanied by a couple Vicodin tablets; three on a bad day, but he could walk again. He managed to hold a job doing low risk building secu-rity but there would never be a chance to reclaim a spot on the force.

"Jim," Rick said. "I've just about had it. I'm burned out and half bankrupt. I almost ate a bullet last night, but it would have killed my poor Catholic mom. Almost did it anyway but decided not to give that bitch of an ex-wife the satisfaction. She already has me broke, and her fancy lawyer is dragging me back to court next week to try to get an even bigger slice. She says the kids need it, but I think her retainer at the plastic surgeon is running out.

Meanwhile, the whole state of California is going broke. It's only a matter of time before they start cutting the force, or reducing our *extravagant* salaries. I tell ya, man, the smart ones are doing like you did and getting out while they can."

Jim gestured to Rick's glass, got a negative response, and then held up his own empty, indicating to the waitress that a refill was in order. "I heard," he said, "that they are thinking about making the guys in LA buy their own bullets and flak jackets. If that's true, I can't blame them for leaving."

"Yeah," Rick said, changing his mind and waiving the waitress back over. "I really can't even afford a couple of decent beers at the end of the day, but I guess if I don't spend the money it will just go to Sheila, or those damned attorneys. Sometimes I think the two sides work together to keep the case going. This thing should have been over a year ago. They're bleeding me dry."

"Sounds like it's time for a change," Jim said. "Why not get away? There's nothing holding you here. Come to Nevada. We could go fishing, head to Vegas once in a while to give the girls hell. You could easily get in ten years and spend your time arresting people for more than border crossing violations and tagging bridges."

"You're probably right," said Rick. "Things have gotten so bad around here, you wouldn't believe it. A few weeks ago,

I clocked a brand new top-of-the-line Beamer doing over a hundred. The guy was freakin' twenty years old—acted like he was doing me a favor by pulling over. Stem-sucking bastard! His watch probably cost more than my oldest son's Cal State tuition."

"I popped him for half a key of coke. It was in plain sight … sort of. Son of a bitch pulls out an inch-thick pile of hundred dollar bills and starts counting them off—says to me, 'how would you like to be my friend in blue?' I actually thought about it for a minute. Probably should have taken him up on it, instead of calling him a worthless piece of living shit as I dragged him out on to the street. His lawyer had him out by nightfall, and I got a reprimand and a black mark on my record for being 'rude to our clients.' I couldn't even make the moving violation stick."

Rick looked up when the waitress came by with their refills, and then glanced past her meth-afflicted face to the flat screen. It was the only updated item in the bar. Most of the mismatched furniture looked like refugee items from a depression-era attic. The bar countertop was flaking Formica, with who knows what living in the cracks. It looked like it used to be red, but even that was debatable in the poor lighting. Most didn't notice, though, and those who did weren't here for the décor, anyway.

For the first time since Rick been coming in, which had been a lot lately, there was something showing besides the mind-numbing sportscast of the day. Was there ever a time when some season wasn't underway? The state, even the country was falling apart, and the only thing people seemed to care about was settled after nine innings on a grassy field or with a spectacular fourth quarter touchdown drive.

Tonight, though, Rick was getting a break. A syndicated

interview was showing. Rick thought he recognized the guest through the fog of beer and the chasers that Jim had fronted him, but he couldn't figure out why. A mug shot maybe, or a special alert BOLO—be on the lookout— passed around on morning report? That didn't seem right. This was someone he had actually seen, not just a recollection from a face head had seen in a photo. After years on the force, he knew to pay attention when his instincts clamored, and they were starting to light up like a Christmas tree.

"…to keep me here forever," said the waitress. "You called me over." She stood a moment longer, which was hard for her to do, as she looked like she was tweaking on meth. "Hello?"

Rick waved her off, his attention now fully on the TV.

Muttering something that wouldn't raise customer satisfaction, the waitress drifted off to find a more attentive customer.

The interview was just coming to its end. The host was an idiot, but it all came together when he thanked his guest. It was Dr. Hastings, the fisherman from the day that asshole lawyer got toasted at the courthouse. He had been interviewed about dying malpractice lawyers, talking down the idea that they were being killed by revenge-minded doctors. What had he been doing, walking around that part of downtown on a fishing trip anyway? It was a long way from the river, and why had he been so sweaty? It was time, Rick thought, to have a serious conversation with a certain doctor from up north. He might have just found the solution to his problems.

"Rick? Hey, buddy, you okay?" asked Jim. "I thought I'd lost you for a moment."

"What? No. No problem, Jim. Sorry. I got distracted there for a moment. The host on the boob tube was mention-ing that there have been a lot of lawyers killed lately, bunch of fucking malpractice leeches. He was asking that doctor if there was some kind of conspiracy going on. The doctor said no way, that it was just a coincidence. A few lawyers got whacked in a short time frame but that it didn't mean anyone was targeting the profession. I'm convinced."

"Too bad," said Jim. "I could give them a few names, if they ran out of prospects."

"No kidding. Wonder if someone might ever get the idea to do that? Maybe I could talk them in to expanding their horizons to include ex-wives and divorce attorneys!"

"Amen to that!" said Jim, raising his glass. He'd never married, having seen the turmoil his friends had gone through. At times, he wished he would have taken the chance, but then he'd always end up back in the same situation, holding a friend up as their life fell apart. "Amen to that."

Chapter Forty-five

There were no more obvious lawyer killings over the next few weeks, and the story did indeed fade. Dinner with George came, our first real corporate meeting since Aurora got on board. As we sat around the table eating and discussing past homicides, I mentally flashed to a similar scene from *The Godfather* or one of the other mafia movies that had been popular at the time. I wonder who they'd get to play me, if the story every came out?

"George," I began, deciding it was time to get to the important part of the meeting. "With all the crap going on in medicine these days, I've been thinking about expanding our operation to full time. Aurora agrees, but we thought we'd better run it past you. Do you think we could get enough business to stay afloat?"

"Well, it's something to think about," George replied. "Our customers have all been happy, and a few more referrals have come in since we talked. Not enough to replace your practice income but enough to be a good starting point. Depends, too, on how much risk you're willing to take. I turned one down without even discussing it with you. It was in a little town in Kansas. You'd be spotted as an outsider the moment you arrived, and the attorney also served as the pastor of the local church. There's no way you'd get away with it. Plus, the case appears to be legitimate—it does happen once in a while."

"No way," I said. "I'd never have tried that one. Might as well play Russian roulette with a semi-auto; the result would be just as predictable. You're welcome to turn those down every time."

"I figured. Before you even see an opportunity, I've done a preliminary screening. Remember, I've got a stake in this too. The next one is more promising, though it's a little different."

"What's the story?"

"It's local, just over the mountains, and it's perfect for us. The suit is a money grab all the way. The patient had a bad result from a breast enhancement. She's a two pack a day smoker and failed to follow the pre-op rules to quit at least a month before surgery. The surgeon is tired of having smokers lie to him, so he routinely tests them with a cotinine level in the pre-op ward; hers came back positive. He told her he wouldn't do the procedure until she came up clean and was about to cancel it and send her home, but she talked him into it, claimed it was second hand smoke from a party."

"Ah, the old 'I didn't inhale' defense! Worked well the first time it was tried."

"Right! Anyway, Dr. Singh felt the patient had one of the

best outcomes he'd seen in ages and was going to discount his fee if she'd model for a before-and-after shoot. Unfortunately, she got a post-op infection, the exact reason he won't operate until patients are off the cigarettes. It was that flesh-eating strep; she had to have most of her soft tissues debrided, all the way down to the ribs, in places."

"Damn," I said, imaging the final result.

"The breast was history; they were lucky to have even saved her life. The infection left a mess you wouldn't believe. They did salvage the other breast, but I've got to wonder why. It's so disfigured that it is not even recognizable. Dr. Singh showed me a set of photos. She looks like a display from that traveling anatomy show, the one where they have cadavers in various degrees of dissection. I told him he should he should offer to pay her to use the photos, but as props to convince people to follow the pre-operative rules.

"Anyway, the patient feels that she is entitled to 'financial compensation' sufficient to offset the loss of self-esteem, future companionship, and wages. She worked as an exotic dancer at Josie's Tender Trap and says she was going to audition for a spot in Vegas in a few months. Even though the infection was caused by her lying and noncompliance, the lawyer claims the surgeon should have followed through with his original refusal to operate and sent her home."

"Sounds perfect, George. And a plastic surgeon! That's even better than orthopedics. We should see a pretty good return. You mentioned that it was different, somehow, but it looks pretty straightforward to me. What's the unusual part?"

"The client wants the lawyer out of the way, but not completely expatriated from the land of the living—that's actually the way he said it! He is Indian, but did his training in England, and has a very formal manner. He wouldn't sign on unless we agreed to his terms. I think Jiminy Cricket has been whispering in his ear, reminding him of that "Thou shalt not kill" commandment we were all taught in Sunday school."

I laughed. "I used to have one of those consciences, but got rid of it. The thing kept getting in the way."

"Anyway, he just wants the lawyer put out of service. He'd be ecstatic if we could get him disbarred, but anything would be acceptable. Anything that would provide some satisfaction and get him out of circulation long enough to forget about the suit."

I love a challenge, and was already planning. It would be perfect if he would be flying anytime soon. TSA, at your service! A stint in the federal penitentiary would cool his 'punitive damage' jets for a while.

"Sign me up. That bastard will be sorry he ever woke up to face the twenty first century. He may not want to be, when I'm done, but he'll still be very much among the living."

George smiled, "From the look on your face, Jack, I am glad I'm not in his shoes. I'll get the details to you tomorrow."

CHAPTER FORTY-SIX

It's an interesting thing, planning the destruction of another person's life. There are so many avenues of attack—personal, professional, financial, and legal aspects jump out. Violence could be an option as well. With a couple of broken arms and a neck in traction, it would be hard to get much done in the courtroom. It would also beg the question of who his true friends were, when it came time for routine personal hygiene. If there was no one willing to help he'd be put in a nursing home for at least six weeks.

It was hard to know where to begin; I wanted to truly lower the boom on this guy. Take him out of play for a while and possibly open further opportunities. There had to be lots of physicians willing to use less lethal means, and our risk would be much lower. This could open up a whole new spectrum of employment if it went well.

Our new target would be put in a position where the lawsuit would become a back burner issue. He'd be busy fighting for his own survival and would get a taste of what it was like to have your life ripped out from under you, a little poetic justice. Putting him on the defensive would give a tremendous satisfaction, and without the guilt.

A few years ago, a patient was brought to my office in handcuffs. Two guards watched his every move. It's not unusual for prisoners to come for a pulmonary consult. They always had handcuffs, but nothing like this elevated level of scrutiny. Usually, it was just one guard, and he was happy to remove the cuffs while I interviewed and examined the patient, sometimes even stepping out of the room. Not with this patient. It was two guards and both kept a constant eye on him.

He wasn't an imposing specimen, not someone you would expect to overpower the guards and bust a hole through the wall, scattering bodies in his wake as he made a dash for freedom. With his bookish glasses and slightly bulging belly, he looked like he'd be more of a danger to a tray of Aurora's cinnamon rolls than to society.

The guards also seemed to be watching the surroundings, and I wondered if they were worried that an accomplice might be waiting to help him off The Rock. What was I dealing with?—a mob kingpin, an international drug lord or terrorist mastermind?

The reason he was seeing me in consultation was hemoptysis, coughing up blood. It was a common complaint in a pulmonary office. The list of potential causes was huge, everything from a nose bleed or simple bronchitis to life threatening conditions like cancer or vasculitis, an overwhelming auto-immune condition. In a prison population, though, where alcoholics, drug addicts and the homeless are forced to live in close confines, tuberculosis was a major player.

This guy, however, had only been in for a couple days. Not nearly long enough to be growing 'Red Snappers,' as we in the know call the little disease-causing mycobacterium, and he wasn't, "coughing up pieces of his broken lungs," as Jethro Tull immortalized in their classic "Aqualung," an all-time favorite song in pulmonary circles.

I introduced myself. His name was Derek. Last names were not permitted. He seemed pleasant enough, making me wonder again why such an intense level of security.

"Tell me about the blood?"

"It started my second night in," he had said in a painful, raspy voice, made worse from talking around his broken teeth. At first, I had thought he had a bad case of meth-mouth, but further inspection showed this was all from trauma. "It's worse today," he murmured, looking surreptitiously over at the guards. They maintained a level of enthusiastic nonchalance, if that's possible. I figured there was more to that story.

We did an extensive interview, questions probing for signs of cancer, infection, kidney diseases, and blood-clotting disorders, the usual litany of questions, and then went to the examination. The problem was solved when he raised his orange prison shirt. Derek was covered with deep purple and yellow bruises. One of his ribs was misshapen, and placing my hand over it, I could feel the ends clicking with every breath, indication of a particularly brutal fracture. The distinct shape of a footprint over-laid the break, and I wondered how it would compare to the nonskid soles of the guards' boots.

"We call this repeated blunt force trauma," I said. "It's a doctor's way of saying you got the hell beat out of you."

No response.

I pointed to the shattered rib. "That one must have hurt."

He looked at the floor, nodding slightly.

It turns out, he was a child pornographer. His appearance readily confirmed what I had always heard, that they were not well received in the slammer. His first night was free, probably because his reason for incarceration wasn't known, but the next two nights he was treated to enthusiastic welcoming parties. He was reluctant to discuss things in detail, with the guards in the room, but what he described I wouldn't have wished on anyone. Well, maybe a few front line hospital administrators, but not on any normal human beings.

The guards were watching as much for attempts on Derek's life as they were to keep him in custody. He had been relocated from California, but there was still the risk that one of his victim's parents would have tracked him down. My big question, then, was how aggressively would the guards work to protect him if it did hit the fan? In the movies, the Secret Service is always ready to take a bullet for POTUS, but here, I wasn't so sure.

The hemoptysis was clearly coming from his beatings, and I feared that another would be one too many. I got him moved to safer quarters. I wasn't looking for his gratitude, I was just saving him from further brutal beatings and from other nightly activities we don't need to go into, but he was very happy with my services. He told me that he would love to do something to return the favor someday—I just hoped he didn't spread the good word to all his buddies. They weren't the clients I wanted filling my waiting room.

Derek ended up turning state's evidence and got an early release. He sweetened the pot by starting an internet program to help the police route out others like himself. He was quite successful—it was the old 'set a thief to catch a thief' strategy. Child pornographers tend to be a close knit community; Derek was able to make it so that many of his friends became acquainted with the prison rituals he had suffered. He would be a great resource for what I had in mind for my new victim.

I called him the next day. "Derek, this is Dr. Hastings."

"Doctor! Doctor! It is so good to hear from you!"

I had never quite placed his origins, but I suspect somewhere in Eastern Europe. "Derek, how are you these days. You haven't been by the office in forever."

"Aw, Doc, you know how it is. Busy this and busy that. A man never knows which way to turn some days." He always had weird sayings that I couldn't make much sense of. I'm sure in his country they meant something, and that it was simply lost in the translation to English.

"I know what you mean," I allowed.

"What can I do for you?"

"I need a favor, Derek."

"Doctor, for you, anything you ask! I owe my miserable life to you. Say it, and she is yours." He did owe me, hugely, though I'm still not sure how I feel about that.

"I'll buy you lunch," I said. "Meet you at the park in half an hour."

Treating someone to a hot dog lunch from a park vendor doesn't seem like much of a way to curry favor, but these weren't just hot dogs. Marley's started as a temporary stand just inside Harmony Park. It had escaped the city zoning ordinances for so long that it was actually a 'permanent' temporary stand. No city official had the guts to try to displace him, at least not since Jacob Havens tried. It was the first and last act in his short career as zoning coordinator.

When word got out that he was trying to shut Marley

down, his stock went rapidly to zero. Street corner lampposts had signs asking for his expulsion from the city. Some were graffiti-modified to suggest less dignified punishments. Channel 3 did a live special on the protests outside Havens' home. Harvey Nash was in fine form, and when his segment hit the air, the crowd grew to an enormous scale. If the city hadn't caved, they'd have had to install porta-potties on his block and institute traffic control measures.

The public employees union had somehow intervened to help him arrange a transfer, so he could keep a city job, though it was in animal disposal. This wasn't as a dog catcher, mind you, or nuisance wildlife relocation, like the TV show— it was clearing the maggot-laden offal from our local streets and highways. Not a great job but better than he might have expected. Many felt the animal carcasses he picked up were more deserving of compassion than he was. You just don't mess with certain regional institutions.

Marley's stand was home to the best dog known to man—a massive kosher beef frank of dreams, erupting in an essence of divine flavor as it slowly cooked over a secret blend of smoking chips, known only to Marley, himself, and used in extremely conservative amounts-enough to add the final unique touch, but not enough to overwhelm the nuances of his custom butchered meat.

Chicago had nothing finer. New York? Fuggettaboutit! I've heard six-figure executives speculating about Marley's mystical process, but it's guarded more closely than the recipe for the Colonel's secret "herbs and spices." The Chinese would be decades behind if the Pentagon could learn to keep things so well hidden. So far, he had refused all offers at franchisement, or to sell the secret, even with the promise that it wouldn't be opened until after his death, and it was sadly recognized that Marley's stand would die with him.

If you want to sink your teeth into one of these delights, you better show up well before the noon opener, or be prepared for an agonizing wait—a wait with the tantalizing scent of heaven drifting by, churning your gastric juices into a fluid rage, your desperate stomach crying out for relief. It was a sadistic tradition for the early birds to drift back past the line, transcendent looks upon their faces as they savored their treasures, juices drifting down their chins, triumphant as they passed by the suffering masses. There was no fear of retribution; it was the safest place in town, with half the city's policemen in line, waiting for their turn in front of the master.

If you wanted to make an impression, Marley's was the place. The other advantage for today was that the park provided the opportunity for a private conversation. I was looking for a very private conversation.

Derek showed up just as I was paying for our dogs. There was no need to wait for friends to show up before ordering, there was only one way to enjoy these dogs and that was with everything. Once, when my heartburn was acting up, I ordered one without the sautéed jalapeno strips. The sun stopped in the sky. If someone had dropped a pin, its reverberating cascade would have deafened everyone in the line. The scorn that was directed at me almost made me slink home without my sausage. A snapshot of my face took a place on the wall of shame—it was weeks before I dared stand in that line again.

The park benches were full, and when a vacancy came up, it didn't last. Finally, Derek and I scored a spot with a scenic overlook of the parking lot. We sat down and got the portable banquet out of the way. When you've been waiting in that line and then finally get your hands around one of Marley's dogs, even serious matters of state are put on hold.

Short and squat, Derek looked a lot like he did the last time I'd seen him. His double chin would have made a tom turkey jealous and he hadn't lost the annoying tic under his left eye. The only obvious change was that his remaining fringes of hair were engaged in a battle against time, and loosing. He actually looked like a stereotypical child pornography pervert. Nobody was ever going to comment that, "he was just the nicest neighbor. Who would have ever known?"

Whenever I saw Derek, it was an effort to hide my revulsion. I had to remind myself that he'd come over to the good side, even if he was late getting there.

"I need some information, Derek, and you're my best shot." Lowering my voice, I added, "It's the type of thing that would be best staying just with us."

"I got no interest in getting back in to any kind of trouble, Doc. I owe you everything, but I am not going back into that life."

"Just some info, Derek, and it can't get you into any kind of issue. I need the names of some places where a guy could go online to see some young kids doing adult things."

Looking over his shoulder, as if I was trying to set him up, he responded, "I can't do that, Doc. I'm on the clean now. You can't ask me to get into that again." He shifted uncomfortably on the bench. "You have no idea of the torture I went through, knowing what I was doing was wrong but unable to stop. I don't want to go back. I won't, and I can't believe you want to risk giving up your practice and going to jail. Now I can see why you helped me before, and I'm still grateful, but get some counseling. Get out while you can."

"Derek, it's not for me. I'm doing a project, but it has to be completely on the hush. I can't say much about it, but I need you to trust me."

He stonewalled a little longer, but finally gave up a few sites that "might" still be active. "I haven't been there in years," he said, "but you can try."

"I also wonder about how to get to one of your trap sites, where you talk to the bad guys. Then, I need you to forget that we had this conversation."

My target was across the mountains, and I hoped that when my attack came to light, it would stay with the local papers and never make it over here. Derek could probably be trusted, but I didn't want to run the risk of his connecting me in any way to the misfortune of a soon to be disgraced malpractice lawyer.

CHAPTER FORTY-SEVEN

My preliminary research on my new object of destruction, Jonas Wildebrand, suggested that he was a cut above my normal target. He went to church, did a variety of civic projects, and even did some volunteer work. I actually felt good about not killing him. He was also having some personal troubles, which would give credence to my plans for his destruction. His wife was divorcing him and had already left for warmer climes. His sudden exploration of child pornography would fit in with his new lonely lifestyle and his major life stresses.

I would spend a few weeks accessing illicit web sites on his computer, establishing a track record, and then later engage in a live chat with an imaginary teenager on Derek's entrapment site. "Widebrand" would invite her to a friendly get together. The charges would eventually be proven false, but he'd be off the malpractice circuit for a while, and my client's case would hopefully go away. It's even possible that after it was shown to be a frame, he might figure it was a response to his doctor-persecuting lifestyle and think about finding a new dodge before something like that happened again. We would head to Medford my next free evening, and start the process of further destroying his life.

My new onboard computer, a birthday present from Aurora who constantly made such a big deal of a few bad shortcuts, made the hour and a half trip easy. I had named my computer Hugh, in honor of my favorite mountain man, Hugh Glass. His legendary exploits through the mountainous West had thrilled me as a kid, and his incredible perseverance and refusal to give in to adversity had served as an inspiration in my adulthood. Who better to be my guide?

That worked as a name until the first course adjustment, when a nagging computerized female voice demanded that I "turn left on Ash and proceed point seven miles. . ." Hugh was definitely not going to work. Before the trip was over, the computer had gone from being a friend to my worst enemy—the directions were wonderful, but the voice that delivered them prompted me to come up with a new nickname, one I'll keep to myself.

I needed to get access to Wildebrand's computer, which meant grabbing his password. It would be best if I could have some time when he wasn't home. I'd have to find his computer and hide my key logger. Hopefully, the computer would be away from his bedroom, which would allow me to use it in the future when he was home. The frame would be hard to sell if he was at some charity event when I was accessing pedi-porn sites.

A key logger would give up his pass code, but they are so widely known now that the first thing in Wildebrand's defense would be to see if anyone had installed one on his computer. I would have to be more sophisticated than the average spouse spying on spouse game. I bought a remote device, an electro-magnetic emission monitor that would require no physical interface with his computer. Hidden nearby, it would track the unique signature impulse of each keystroke. When the data was run through a frequency analyzer, it would show what each keystroke image looked like, and the password would be easily obtained, along with any other keyboard activity.

Wildebrand lived in a fairly average neighborhood, a little nicer than some but not the upscale, in-your-face, I'm-a-rich-bastard-lawyer quarters like some of our earlier targets had left behind. He worked long hours at the office and seemed dedicated to his profession. Probably someone I could have liked, had he chosen a different career path. Tonight, like most evenings, he was at the office late. I should have plenty of time. We parked a few houses away, where Aurora would have a clear line of sight to his driveway.

"If he shows up while I'm in there," I said, "buzz me on the walkie-talkie, and I'll blaze a trail out the back door. We'll meet at the playground." There was a grade school visible out his back window—I couldn't have scripted this any better.

"Good luck, my little home-breaker" Aurora said as I slipped out the door. "I hope he doesn't have a hungry pit bull wondering why his owner is late with dinner."

"Thanks, dear. Love you, too."

His front door was easily picked. It was a simple lock and had been in place so long that it was well worn. A first timer would have no problems with this one. Only three pins to position, and almost no pressure needed with my tension wrench to put them in place. There would be no sign of my having been there and, with the few seconds' involved, small chance of someone walking by to admire my breaking-and-entering skills.

There was no alarm system, and no liver eating dog lying in ambush, but the surprise of the day was that I had just broken into a hoarder's house. And he was very good at it, as near as I could tell. Finding his computer would be a challenge, and though it didn't have anything to do with my game plan, I had to have a quick look around to see what was in his house of treasures.

There are different kinds of hoarders, actually, and some are highly intelligent, accomplished individuals, even professionals. Some hoard trash, psychologically unable to throw anything out. Their homes are sanitary disasters, sometimes beyond repair, with new life forms developing on a daily basis. Others keep random items accumulated through the years. I was thankful that he was largely one of these and not an animal hoarder, with geologic stratums of decaying feces and soggy dead cats underfoot. Going through his house was kind of like going to a neighbor's real estate open house when you have no intention of buying, or looking through a friend's medicine cabinet—pure, absolute nosiness.

His kitchen was a bachelor's scree of dirty dishes. Empty Ramen noodle packages were crumpled and randomly scattered on the counter and floor. One even floated in the scum of un-drained dishwater festering in his sink. His bedroom was a catacomb of rumpled clothes in haphazard piles. The bed, an unmade tangled mess I wouldn't touch without a full series of vaccinations and a hazmat suit. It's no wonder his wife took off. I just wondered why it took so long.

The overall effect of a recently divorced, hoarding bachelor's pad gave a distinctly depressing feel. If I lived here, I'd probably work late too, unless he kept his office in a similar state. Jonas Wildebrand, attorney at law, seemed to have a tough life. I was about to make it tougher.

In a heart-grabbing moment, my walkie-talkie suddenly came to life. "Jack," Aurora whispered, "what's taking so long? You've been in there ten minutes. He could come back at any time."

"You won't believe what I found! I'm on my way to search for his computer now and then I'll be right out." I snapped a few pictures on my phone—Aurora had to see this.

I found his study, and fortunately, it was relatively uncluttered. Even though it was better than the rest of the house, there was no shortage of places to conceal the key logger. It had an eight-foot range, but the closer to the keyboard, the better the data collection. I found a spot, and then checked with Aurora, who confirmed the coast to be clear. I stepped out Wildebrand's front door after locking it from the inside, and Aurora and I were on the way home in time for *The Late Show*.

I was on call for the next week and figured that would give Wildebrand plenty of opportunity to transmit adequate data to the logger. The frequency analyzer needed a few thousand data points to get a firm conclusion on which signature went with a given key. It would be a waste of time to pick it up too early, and with gas at usury prices, an extra road trip was to be avoided.

Our second trip to Medford went as smoothly as the first. We cruised past his office to make sure we were in the clear, went to his house, and removed the logger. I would have loved to have shown the house to Aurora; she was intrigued by the photos, but we didn't dare go in blind. The only negative of the journey was when Aurora insisted we go by the mall on a peanut butter cookie run. Apparently, those specific peanut butter cookies are infused with some magical powers, because she can't be dissuaded once the thought hits her. It doesn't matter if she is ninety miles away over the mountains. When a fix is called for, there will be no peace until it happens.

I was happy to help, but convinced her it would be best to fulfill her sugary needs after visiting Wildebrand's place. It would be unfortunate if he came home in the middle of our keyboard logger retrieval party. We got to the mall shortly before closing, and. . . *they were out!* Hell hath no fury. For a moment, I thought the poor girl manning the cookie shop was going to be turned in to a salt pillar. In all the years we've been married and with all the things I've done to disappoint Aurora, I've never been subjected to anything so intense or hateful as the gaze she fixed on the cookie lady.

Trying to defuse the moment, I made my second mistake of the night. I suggested that it wasn't all bad. "It's a great sign that they sold their inventory. It means they do enough business to stay open for other times you want to come over, and they must make them in small batches, so you know they'll always be fresh." Then, it happened.

"And don't you think your thighs will appreciate the break?"

You'd think I'd know better. I was an accomplished doctor whose people skills had gotten him through some seriously difficult situations, not to mention a 'veteran' husband of more than twenty years, and yet here I was, pulling the biggest rookie mistake in all of history. Maybe I could blame the cold medicine. It was going to be a long drive home, though I felt fortunate to be doing it without grievous physical injury. Still, tomorrow would be a Ben Gay day. The couch in my office is sadly lacking in the neck support department.

I downloaded the data from the key logger into my PC and started the analyzer program, working to decipher Wildebrand's password. It was late, but I figured I might as well stay on task. There wasn't going to be anything else going on. I'm not quite sure how it was my fault that the mall confectioner had run out of her peanut butter Prozac, but the editorial comment about her thighs, intended to be a light hearted comment, was probably not wise.

It took a few minutes to get the results. I'm not one of those computer guys with the latest, greatest systems. Zach's computer did games that required enough power and speed to give NASA's computers an inferiority complex, but I had just recently said good-bye to my old 486. It had been replaced by a Pentium-something, already out of date according to the computer store geek, who shook his head in bewilderment as I insisted that it was all I would ever need.

With Wildebrand's password secured, I looked at his recent Internet activity. If my good fortune got any better, I'd give up my medical career and invest my life savings in lottery tickets. I may have found the real reason his wife left. My original plan had been to take a few weeks of traveling back and forth, logging several times into kiddie porn sites, and then to get him caught in the law enforcement chat room. I was greatly surprised to see that he had already been going to one of the sites Derek had selected, along with a number of other suspicious addresses—even the names made my skin crawl. I had accidentally stumbled across a real child pornography degenerate.

All the sympathy I felt earlier was gone, replaced by a jubilant sense of triumph. Talk about killing two birds with one stone. Wildebrand would go down hard, along with his lawsuit, and a pervert would be off the streets. As an added benefit, there would be no eventual discovery that this had been a setup. He'd be taken out of the loop as permanently as my earlier marks had been.

I'd sleep well when this assignment came to closure. Dr. Singh would be impressed, thinking the arrest was the result of my clever frame-up. He would become a source for further referrals, and a full-time career in lawyer reduction would be one step closer.

CHAPTER FORTY-EIGHT

Aurora and I traveled over the mountains the next night to begin the final steps to assure Wildebrand's destruction. For tonight's operation, we needed him to be home, which would ordinarily mean getting a later start, but tonight, I needed to do some relationship repairs.

"Why don't we go over early," I suggested, "and have a nice dinner and maybe see if that shop in the mall has any peanut butter cookies?"

She glared at me, the memories from the last attempt still fresh in her mind. She accepted the peace offering, but her 'if it will make you feel better' comment made sure I knew she was still sore, and that this wasn't even close to the end of my punishment.

Women! I'd be serving the full sentence for that mistake.

With her confections gathered, and dinner out of the

way, we set up our stakeout. Wildebrand came home about 8:30, probably to a gourmet Ramen dinner in front of the television. He took his damn time getting to bed, probably poring through his hoarded treasures or indulging in his hidden fantasy.

I was getting a little impatient. I had to be at work in the morning and didn't want to be up all night. The longer he made me wait, the nastier I was likely to be when I went online as "Magnum421," his screen name. I was just about to suggest to Aurora that we climb into the backseat and pretend to be teenagers when the lights finally went out, giving me one more reason to bring him down.

I gave him a few minutes to get well into the deeper stages of sleep. With all the obstacles I had to negotiate, I wanted him dead to the world before I made my entrance. The lock picked as easily as before, and I once more made my way into his study.

I sat at his desk, rehearsing the keyboard slang I'd learned one more time. Wildebrand's desk chair was the most comfortable I've ever tried. Soft leather with perfect weight distribution and no pressure points, and almost unbelievably, it was even made in America. I could sit in it for hours. I would have to keep an eye on the local classifieds in case he had a yard sale to raise funds for his defense.

It felt creepy, using his keyboard, knowing what he did with it. I brought rubber gloves, and they helped, but the idea was still there. The mental distraction nearly did me in. Like I said, I'm not a computer person. I fired up Wildebrand's portal to pedophilia, forgetting about the obnoxious Windows log-on chime. It sounded like an air raid siren, reverberating through the quiet of the house, and it seemed to go on forever. I should have thought to close his study door, but it was a little late for that now. There was no masking the sound, and I waited anxiously for the cautious sounds of him approaching through the maze of his living room, doubtlessly with a baseball bat or machete or a large-caliber handgun. Hearing nothing, I got up and quietly approached his bedroom, using my patented elk-hunting stalk. He was deep in an undisturbed sleep.

Returning to the computer, I signed on to the talk room set up by Derek's undercover task force.

Magnum421: "Anyone out there?"

Starstruck-girl3: "Hey. Don't talk so loud. Don't want u waking up my parents! LOL!"

Magnum421: "Know what u mean. Mine would kill me if they saw me online so late. They got so many rules. They don't understand. Sometime I think I should just kill myself. Then they'd be sorry."

Starstruck-girl3: "I know. I almost joined a cult last year. They would have freaked"

Magnum421: "I asked mine if I could get a learner's permit so I can drive. I want it so bad. I could be free. They keep me tied up like a dog. Do you have your homework done? Make your bed. Go to school. Always some kind of shit like that."

Starstruck-girl3: "What's up w/them anyway?"

Magnum421: "It's a freakin' power trip. If I have kids, I'll never treat them this way."

Starstruck-girl3: "No way!"

Magnun421: "They are gone this weekend, some kind of convention or sum thing, so I can do what I want. I took some money dad had hidden under his Playboys. Party train!"

Starstruck-girl3: "Jealous. Wish mine would take off."

Magnum421: "Where do you live? I'm in Oregon. Medford."

Starstruck-girl3: "Hey, me, too!"

Magnum421: "You sound cute. Maybe come over when the gestapo is gone. We have the whole place to ourselves."

Starstruck-girl3: "How would I get away?"

Magnum421: "Tell your parents u going to a girlfriend's for the night."

Starstruck-girl3: "Awesome! See you Friday night!"

Friday was going to be most interesting for Mr. Wildebrand.

Chapter Forty-nine

They kept the arrest out of the news. His hard drive revealed a spider web of deviants for the forensic computer specialists, an intertwined network of the worst of the worst that society has to offer. They were able to identify a number of them and set up one of the biggest busts in years, including a local politician who had run on a strong 'family values' platform. The magistrates would be busy.

Wildebrand's practice closed, his cases falling off the face of the earth. The other attorneys in town made a big show of distancing themselves from him—none were willing to take on his cases and run the risk of appearing to have any association with the center of an international ring of child pornographers. Our client was more than impressed and threw in a nice bonus.

After the new fees were deposited, I did an online check of the Channel Islands balance and was happy to see the interest was well above that of my traditional bank. It was even better than my money market, and did I mention, tax free? If I had started this new life a few years earlier, a retirement on a tropical island would be in my near future. It would be day after day of umbrella shaded drinks, enjoyed on the beach after a day of wading the shallow flats for permit, one of the greatest challenges in fly-fishing. Scantily clad young ladies would be frolicking in the gentle waves, laughing at my witty bon-mots and one-liners—my wife beating the life out of me for drooling into my umbrella shaded drink. Everyone needs something to look forward to.

CHAPTER FIFTY

Unfortunately, with improved financial status comes the temptation to upgrade one's standard of living. Aurora brought home a stack of glossy new car brochures and, much to my surprise, none of them featured the latest models from Kia or Hyundi. Daiwoo was somehow left out, as well. She started talking about taking nonworking vacations and adding a new sewing room. What she was contemplating would require a significant escalation of violence against the legal profession. It was time to see George again.

"Beer?" he asked, ushering me in.

With my negative reply, he grabbed one for himself, and I followed him to his study. "What's on your mind?" he asked, settling behind his desk. His trashcan was heavily laden with empties, and the condensation ring from his last was still evident on his desk's glass top. Not the best behavior for a partner in my new business. I might need to have a word with him.

"We've got a decision to make," I said. "Originally, we were going to try to make a point with the lawyers and see if we could get them to think twice about filing unnecessary claims, do something good for our colleagues."

He looked up from his desk.

"I think we may be letting the financial aspects get in the way of that." I circled around to see what had George's attention. It was a catalog of luxury hot tubs and gazebos. Frolicking bikini models fawned over the baby boomer smart enough to have purchased the company's product. The other page was set in an obviously private backyard, with just the suggestion that the ladies were clad in nothing more than their birthday suits. The grin on the owner's face reminded me of the smug confidence depicted in the old "Lucky Bob" commercials, in my opinion, one of the better products Madison Avenue has ever turned out. No one in their right mind would believe that a simple pill could increase the size of their manhood, but...

I needed to steer George back to the original intent of our mission.

"Aurora's getting used to the extra income and wants to keep the hits quiet, off the radar, but I've been thinking of working more on the social aspect. Let the lawyers see that they are on notice. Up the ante a little with a few high-visibility hits, and see if we could start making some progress on the litigation front. Get us back in the press. Change some history."

He looked concerned.

"It's time we make a final decision on which way we want to go," I said.

He thought for a minute, carefully considering his reply. "Jack, you're beginning to sound like a domestic terrorist—

it's not a good look for you. I think we should just keep on as we're doing, quietly polishing them off, one lawyer at a time. If someone wants to make assumptions about their diminishing numbers, they're welcome to do so, but I don't think we should push the issue."

He was obviously happy to be receiving his steady stream of finder's fees. It looked like a corporate decision had been made. "What have you got lined up?" I asked.

Pushing back in his chair and lovingly cherishing a fragrant new Cuban smoke to life, George was ready. "The consults are rolling in now, faster than we can possibly handle. I think we're really onto something. Everyone we've helped has put us onto at least one other case—we're well into our second generation, getting new referrals from previous referrals. If you're still interested, Jack, I think we have enough to go full time."

We went over what he had in the queue, and he was right. Our side practice was growing exponentially. We'd have to either start being more selective about the cases we accepted, or make the decision to give up completely on the more traditional, healing-based medicine. It was tempting.

No more malpractice, no more nighttime ICU trips or rising from comfortable slumber to plow lonely furrows to the hospital, long before the snowplows made their first passes. No more meetings with smarmy administrators, appealing insurance denials, or dealing with controlled medications somehow flushed down the toilet, needing to be refilled "a few days early."

A pretty good life awaited me, if I wanted it, and there were so many referrals pouring in that I could focus on the worst of the worst, giving me at least a sense that I was fighting the good fight.

"Looks like we'll be putting that old *Primum, non nocere* adage, "First, do no harm," to permanent rest, George."

The first one in his stack was a request to off a hospital administrator, with the special provision that unusual pain and suffering be involved. Several specific suggestions were offered, and if the tone was a reflection of the opinion of a majority of local doctors, they might be even worse off than we were.

"I guess we're not the only place with problems in that department," I told George. "That's going to be worth serious consideration, might even do it as a pro bono. Think of the morale boost for doctors and nurses across the country if we expanded to remove a few of those soul-sucking administrative parasites!"

Time wouldn't be a factor there. Those guys never go away. It was a definite yes, but there were likely to be other cases that needed doing in a more timely fashion. I'd just wait 'til something else came up in the area and then take care of both.

George had acquired a small dossier on each of the nominations, after weeding out those he knew I wouldn't consider. Those, along with a brief synopsis of the case gave me a chance to decide which ones to go forward with. I reached over and pulled up a barstool and looked through what he had gathered. Some were easily weeded out from the start. There was no way I was going to travel to New Jersey, at any time of year. They had plenty of hitmen already; maybe not malpractice specialists, but certainly people who could get the job done. Likewise, two other cases were ruled out, just because of the distance involved. Another, in Seattle, was easy to reject. I'd love the chance to hang out at Pike Place, and Aurora has been begging me to take her whale watching, but it looked like a completely legitimate case, and the attorney was well regarded in the community.

I asked George why he didn't rule that one out.

"I almost dropped it," he said, "but it's so close, and its near enough to where those hospital administrators are, so I thought I'd at least let you look at it."

"Shred it," I said. "We have plenty of more deserving candidates."

Memphis looked interesting. It was another high-value orthopedic surgeon. Aurora would love to see Graceland. She might even give up on that ridiculous idea of a nonworking vacation if I could find a few more good cases like that. It had appeal for me, as well. I've often wondered what it would be like to have a truly carefree evening, sipping mint juleps on the front porch of an elegant Southern mansion, the sun gently settling into the humid western sky and the crackle of the bug-zapper providing a steady summer melody. And wasn't there a Dolly Parton museum somewhere around there? I could spend all day admiring her—ahh—vocal cords.

There was another opportunity that also caught my interest. It was in Kansas City. I've never been there but hear remarkable things about their barbeque. They also have a legendary Christmas light display at the Plaza, but that would require a more seasonally adjusted sanction. This case stood out for several reasons. Financially, it would be our biggest to date. It was a high visibility case, at least regionally, and it easily met my new "justifiability" clause. All the ingredients were there. I wish now that I had sent it to the shredder, but second guesses don't count in real life.

Its high-profile nature was easy to understand. I could only imagine what it might do in the way of national head-lines, if I was successful. The plaintiff had engaged the figure-head services of a major-league attorney, Dallas "Herschel" Jackson. He ordinarily didn't do malpractice, but was along for name recognition. Jackson was an exceptionally talented attorney. He had turned an open-and-shut murder case against "Sammy" Berlioni into a route, sending the federal prosecutor to finish his career punishing traffic offenders some place where he'd never embarrass his supervisors again. The judge, who had authorized the condemning wiretap, had a sudden change of heart and testified that he had been misled by the FBI. He recanted his consent for the tap, just before taking early retirement and moving to an expensive villa in the Bahamas with his new "trophy" wife.

A seasoned malpractice litigator, Joshua Belkamp, was taking the lead. He, too, was one of the best in the country, specializing in highly lucrative obstetrics cases. He was famous for his jury selection, always seating a few who were baffled by even the simplest of scientific arguments, and who were easily led down the emotional path to a favorable verdict. He came out of a very comfortable retirement for one last chance at making the headlines.

The newspaper articles that George had accumulated showed that the case had become a local media sensation, with the potential drama of a classic John Grisham story. The attorneys each side picked were from the *Who's Who* list, promising to make this courtroom battle the most watched legal event of the year. It was already being tried in the public eye, months before it was set to enter the courtroom, and was a perfect opportunity; there was no need to go any further through the list.

"I'll take it."

George smiled—"I had you pegged for that one."

Dr. Geoffrey H. Edward, III was a regional star; an esteemed cardiothoracic surgeon, the son of an equally respected neurosurgeon, and grandson of one of the principles who helped turn the Northeast into the cutting edge of medical training. He chose to make a home in the Midwest—fly over country to the more sophisticated people he grew up with, but he saw it as an opportunity to make a difference. A long-standing tendency of philanthropy and a record of taking care of some of the biggest names in the region had earned him the unfortunate honor of being called in as a consultant for the vacationing son of Sheik Banwhar al'Ashidi, a despot whose brutality stood out even among the worst of the Mideast dictators.

The young "Sheik-to-be" had developed bacterial endocarditis, a heart infection almost always caused by injection drug abuse. This did not go over well with his father, who fired the original physician who had the nerve to establish the diagnosis, and to uncover the cocaine addiction that had caused it. By the time Dr. Edward was called in, the patient had taken a predictable downhill turn. A Christmas Eve emergency surgery was his only hope.

In Dr. Edward's skillful hands, the Sheiks' son survived, but an intra-operative stroke left him with a devastating brain injury. It was almost certainly from the delay his father had caused by changing physicians, and though he lived, he was too compromised to return home and assert control over his oil-rich kingdom. A dictator dribbling rice pudding down his chin didn't inspire the fear necessary to keep a population in line. To make matters worse, he was the sheik's only son. The al' Ashidi empire, raising terror in the Mideast for generations, was down to its last.

The regional media was abuzz over the prospect of one of the world's wealthiest men suing one of the most respected, influential doctors in the Midwest. It provided an interesting diversion from the steady stream of dismal economic news and the even more depressing weather. *People* magazine had done a three page feature, and it was rumored that the legal battle would be replayed in a major Hollywood production.

Dr. Edward had also engaged an outstanding attorney, Stan Ariel. His name was widely known for the year he quarterbacked his team to the Big Eight championship. His professional career had been anticipated to be brilliant, but it was cut short by a cancer diagnosis. He hadn't been expected to survive, but with the skill of a team of doctors, he had beaten the odds. His once imposing frame had been changed forever, and his hair, once the Adonis look that women swooned over, had been replaced by an unruly mess that could never be tamed. He turned down a coaching position, instead dedicating himself to a life in law, defending doctors from people like Joshua Belkamp.

Still, the defense was outshined by the spectacular team put together for the plaintiff. When Hollywood heartthrob Brad Dirkson was involved in a fatal early morning accident, his career looked like it was over. The high school cheerleader he had met at the party died at the scene. She somehow wasn't wearing a seatbelt while Dirkson drove erratically down Rodeo Drive. A rookie patrol cop, relegated to the midnight shift, saw the whole thing. He described the horror as if it had happened days ago, not the year and a half from the defendant's delaying tactics. Jackson finally convinced twelve jurors that it was the fault of a combination of prescription medications and fatigue from a late night of filming his next blockbuster, saving him from at least five to ten in minimum security and ensuring years of further hits for the masses.

That success put Jackson in the national headlines, and paved the way for his most notorious case—basketball legend "Jumping" Joe Barker. He'd been found standing over his estranged wife's bleeding body, murder knife in hand. By the time the case was resolved, the prosecutor was forced to make a humiliating public apology to the superstar, basically begging him not to sue for wrongful prosecution. (He is finishing his career doing divorce cases in Waterloo, Iowa.) Having "Herschel" Jackson at your table was as close to a guaranteed not-guilty verdict as money could buy.

The case was made even more interesting by the fact that it wasn't the surgeon asking for our services. He'd be as surprised as the rest when news of the double homicide hit. It was being bankrolled by an interested, anonymous third party. From the size of the offer, it appeared to be a *very* interested third party. With the case already being watched across the country, and with the substantial fee involved, the case was tailor-made. The press would have a field day, and if lawyers like Jackson and his Belkamp could be taken down, every attorney in the country would think before filing that marginal case or attempting to extort guiltless doctors.

Aurora was thrilled to have such a good client. She was tied up with charity events for the next several weeks and wouldn't be able to come with me, but she already had plans for the extra income.

"Come to the garage for a second, honey," she said. "I have a car on loan for the weekend." She oozed against me. "Maybe we could take it for a quick trip down the coast."

Opening the garage door, I was greeted by a fire-apple red two door European import. It had imprinted leather seats and aggressive bug-eye headlamps. Wind-tunnel inspired glass sloped at a seductive angle, as if begging for the rush of wind. With its four inch ground clearance, the car would be a fixture in the garage for a good portion of the year, but it was so sleek that it was almost irresistible. It appeared to be racing, even while sitting still—this was the kind of car that transformed over-the-hill, toupee-wearing executives into bad-ass swinging bachelors, ready to take on all comers in the dating world.

I was impressed and mentally put myself in the cockpit. Catapult-like acceleration would crush me as I blasted down the coastal highway, giant redwoods whizzing by like fence posts, and the wind whipping through my hair. And yes, it is *my* own hair—a little on the gray side of youth, but not a store bought piece or a cheesy comb over implant. I've always felt that any woman impressed by such speciousness wasn't worth impressing, though a whole industry has been set up to disagree with that, so perhaps I'm a little off on that one.

If we could get absolute top dollar trade for her mini-van, we could swing it, and if I could book a high-quality hit for every month or so, and keep the car out of Zach's teenage hands, we might be able to pay the insurance, though even then, it would be a strain. I started to explain the implausibility, but Aurora looked at me with those damnably irresistible "you can do anything" eyes. I hadn't seen those in years and was forced to reconsider. A second look at the sticker had me doing the math. If we eliminated some of the accessories, like the steering wheel, it just might be possible.

CHAPTER FIFTY-ONE

After months of planning inconspicuous hits, it was refreshing to contemplate something more straightforward. It would be spectacular if I could get both attorneys at the same time—avoiding collateral damage, of course. No suicide vests here, but one idea from the terrorists occurred to me, something to magnify the publicity effect. I'd send them a letter, my own version of a billet-doux. It wasn't exactly what my partners wanted, but if I was going to be serious about the political aspect of our campaign, it was time I take the gloves off. End the speculation and put the bad guys on notice.

"I like the idea," George said, when I put it past him, "but what's it going to do to our business if suddenly everyone knows we are targeting these guys. I'd hate to get shut down just as we are starting to succeed."

Didn't we just have this discussion?

"George, I have it all figured out. The increased notoriety will actually help our business," I argued, successfully. "That phone will be ringing off the wall—I guarantee it. We could even raise our rates."

"I have an old typewriter gathering dust in the attic," George said. "It belonged to Joyce's grandfather. I suggested selling it at a pawn shop once, but she got incredibly mad—said it was the only memento she had to remember her favorite Grampa, that she used to sit on his lap while he typed. Since he died when she was three, I suspected her recollections were as about as genuine as Bill Clinton's 'vivid recollections' of watching black churches burn in Arkansas, but my arguments went nowhere; it should be perfect. Then, after the letter is typed, we can throw that damn thing in a pond. I feel so good every time I get rid of another piece of that bitch's life."

We composed the letter. It wasn't great, but it got the idea across:

> *Dear Messrs. Jackson and Belkamp,*
>
> *We are notifying you that people of righteous indignation have taken exception to your practice of profiting from raping good doctors. Please be aware that we plan to end your miserable lives. The world will be a better place without you. Enjoy the few days you have left, spend your ill-gotten gains and make peace with your God, if you have one. We are striking a blow for freedom.*
>
> *Sincerely yours,*
> *The Righteous Justice League*

We typed a second copy, put them in envelopes, double-checked the addresses, and wiped our fingerprints off to prepare them for the mail. It was time to add two more attorneys to the endangered species list.

Rounding the last corner on my way home, I noticed a dilapidated pickup sitting in my driveway, the driver clearly waiting my return. It took a moment to place him. His face seemed familiar, but his name escaped me. Just as I was walking up to ask, it hit me, stopping me dead in my tracks. Officer Rodriguez, the cop from Redding! I tried to hide my shock, feigning surprise as if I didn't understand why he had showed up on my doorstep, but I quickly realized there was no point. If he had traveled all the way from Redding, he must have pieced things together. The fact that he was alone and not in uniform registered, and gave me a bit of hope.

"Hello, Officer," I said, "didn't expect to see you again. Would you like to come inside?"

"I think it would be best," he replied, cautiously slipping out of his truck. He was eyeing me like a professional, keeping a safe distance. The bulge under his jacket was further proof that he was a cautious man.

"It's okay," I offered, holding the front door. "I'm not prone to violence; not normally, anyhow."

He declined my offer, indicating that I should go in first. The house was empty. Zach had gone wherever a teenager tends to go, and Aurora was involved with the annual cancer center fund-raiser. I think it was going to be a seven-card hold'em tournament this year. With Joyce Bicknell's sudden departure, Aurora had inherited the task of securing donations. She was trying to make it the best year ever, spending long hours canvassing the neighborhood. There wasn't a jewelry store or shoe shop that had escaped her attention—

she had even approached my favorite sporting goods shop, acquiring a high-end waterfowl shotgun. Joyce would have never attempted a feat like that. It became clear to me that this was a case of one-upmanship over a dead rival. Women definitely live in a different world than we men do.

I motioned the officer to our new suede couch and offered him a cold beer, which he accepted gratefully after the long drive. I handed it to him unopened, to allay any suspicion he might have, and sat down in my easy chair. I'd let him start.

He waited a few moments, purling the cold brew around his mouth, eyes briefly closing as he enjoyed George's new summer ale. "I imagine you have an idea of why I'm here," he said.

"I have a few thoughts."

"I saw your interview a while back," he said. "Some cable network executive thought it was good enough to syndicate. I'll probably never make detective, but I was quite impressed by your knowledge of the lawyer murders. And the way you explained things, talking the host out of the idea that there was a campaign against them—that was magnificent. You should run for office."

I'd been undone by my foolish ego.

He took another swig of beer. "This is pretty good stuff," he said, studying the label and trying to place the brand. "I'm going to have to look it up when I get home." I could see he was starting to get past his initial suspicion and into the flow of what he had come to say. "Things haven't been going too well for me lately." He looked around my living room, appreciating Aurora's home décor talents, his finger absently tracing the mouth of the beer bottle. "Looks like you're doing all right, though. I hear all kinds of stuff about doctors' incomes dropping and stuff. You must have found a way to get past that."

Silence seemed to be my best strategy. Rodriquez had the upper hand; I'd let him run the show.

"I was thinking you might be able to help a guy out. Maybe come up with a 'donation,'" he said, fingers giving quotation marks. "Enough to stake me so I can get out of California before it goes completely tits up. I've been looking around, and I think a new start in Nevada might be just the thing."

"How much would this 'donation' involve?"

He finished his beer and raised an eyebrow, prompting me to fetch another. After much hemming and hawing, bringing me up-to-date on his ex-wife's burgeoning demands and his no-good lawyer who couldn't seem to get things finished, he mentioned a number well into the five figure range. He clearly felt the lawyer killing business was more lucrative than I did.

"That's a little generous," I countered, "but I have a proposition. From time to time things come up that are a little problematic. I could use a part-time employee, but haven't been recruiting, for obvious reasons." I leaned forward. "Help me out, Rick. I'll throw in a nice sign on bonus, of course, and the work would be easy and low risk."

"Doc, there is probably *one group* that hates lawyers even more than you do, and I've got fifteen years in the heart of it. Try spending weeks busting a child molester, only to have some coke-snorting lawyer set him free on a technicality. Or arrest the same dope dealer half a dozen times and still see him on the streets a week later. Lawyers will look a jury in the eye and lie with complete sincerity. I gotta tell you, once we got past the indignation of having someone off a victim right in our front yard, most of the force didn't feel all that upset about it when Blackman bought it. We'd prefer defense lawyers over malpractice, of course. Those guys undo half the good work we do, but anything is still progress."

"Shakespeare."

He looked at me, puzzled, for a moment and then lit up with a smile, remembering his high school English class. "First, we kill all the lawyers!"

"Henry VI," I said, "one of my favorites." It wasn't an exact rendition of the master's work, but I was certain that it was a quote recited frequently among frustrated cops. "Wonderful, but not quite what I was thinking. It was another appropriate passage that was on my mind: 'The devil can cite Scripture for his purpose.'"

He nodded his head. "It's kind of funny back home now. The attorneys are all looking over their shoulders. I almost needed a diaper the other day, I laughed so hard. I came up behind the attorney who was representing a perp my partner had arrested. When I touched him on the shoulder to get his attention, he completely passed out! Dropped like a ton of bricks. You'd have sworn that his bones had dissolved. His briefcase flew open, papers scattered all over, and his foamy frappe Starbucks metrosexual coffee sprayed over everything, including his paralegal. He woke up right away, all red-faced and mad as hell."

"Cataplexy," I said, "a classic case."

"Right, I've heard of that. Anyway, he came right around and started to scream at me. He got a few words into his tirade and then suddenly looked around and shut up. He apologized, and told me not to worry about it, that it had been no problem. There's never been a cop in Redding history who could have done something like that to that asshole and not get reamed up one side and down the other. That guy is the most caustic mouthpiece in town, and all of a sudden, he's as polite as a whore at Easter services. I think it almost killed him, but he smiled, shook off his papers, and headed off to the can. You are a genius, man!"

"So what do you think?"

Rick smiled and held out his hand. "You probably won't be needing a W-4?"

"Welcome on board," I laughed. "We actually have something to start you with. I have a couple of letters that need to be mailed, but they need to be postmarked somewhere else, for obvious reasons. My partner, George, and I were just wondering how to do that when you showed up."

We spent the rest of the afternoon getting to know each other. Rick was actually a great guy, and we had a lot of similar interests. I felt sorry for what he was going through at home, and it felt good to be helping him out. George would need to meet him, of course. He was a little taken aback when I called to tell him I was coming over with a new employee, until I explained that he had figured out what we were up to, and there hadn't been much choice. I did throw in how much he enjoyed George's home-brewed beer as a sweetener.

"I've never seen anyone savor a brew with such joy," I said. I might have embellished a little, telling George that Rick said it was the best beer he'd ever tasted, but it worked—Rick was welcomed with open arms when we arrived at the bachelor pad.

There was no need to go over our operation in detail. Rick wasn't going to be a partner, just part-time help. Mainly, it was another get to know each other session and a little about how to communicate with us and arrange payment for when he did a job. He was very reasonable in discussing rates, and I think he was energized to be a part of this; a little forbidden excitement, a few extra bucks to stick in his pocket and the chance to live a cop's forbidden dream. He was right when he said the police hate lawyers as much as doctors do, telling us story after unbelievable story where lawyers had undone good police work.

He also kept us going with tales of revenge. Broken taillights were a favorite, but more creative stunts were called up for a few favorite lawyers. We laughed until we were in pain when Rick threw out the best they had ever come up with.

His partner had a brother who filmed for Channel 13. They convinced the station chief to do a series modeled after the exposé where internet child molesters are filmed while they are being arrested. The police kicked down the front door while a particularly despised lawyer was having a quick nooner with his mistress, film crew recording his frantic efforts to hide himself. Rick's pantomime was priceless.

When the lawyer finally got his speech back, he swore that he would have all the cops' badges and sue them until he owned City Hall. Rick pointed out that they would be happy to provide the tape as evidence and that it would be an open-and-shut case, should he decide to go through with it. The story is a legend on the force, and the attorney has been much more selective about the clients he represents.

With the ice broken and the business basics done, George had to show off his beer production. With Joyce out of the way, he'd taken over a whole room. If I remembered correctly, it had been her yoga suite. Now it was a carefully organized chaos of tubes, beakers and vats in various stages of fermenting. A delightful fragrance filled the room, the result of weeks of experimenting with grains and hops from all over the globe.

Rick was enthralled. He had found a beer lover's paradise on earth. It was obvious that if I didn't intervene, the day would disappear, and Rick had a few hundred mile trip in front of him.

"George, how about getting Rick a few bottles of some of your new varieties so he can take them home? He's got a long drive ahead."

"I hate to do it, George," Rick said, "but Jack's right. I better be heading home, or what's left of it. Lieutenant Hardass wouldn't understand if I missed work from staying out all night, buddying with a couple of serial killers."

He'd mail the letters in the next few days, to give the lawyers in Kansas City time to get them before I made my move. They needed to see them and report them to the police if we were going to achieve the maximum effect from their deaths. The police would question Dr. Edward when the letter came out.

"Officers, if I was going to kill those guys," he'd say—not such a bad idea, if you really think about it, there is no way I'd warn them or draw attention to myself by sending a letter. You guys must think I'm an idiot!"

That, coupled with the California postmark, should deflect much of the suspicion, and with any luck, word of the letter would leak out to the press.

CHAPTER FIFTY-TWO

I arrived in Kansas City in late June, just as our weather was moving into that perfect phase of warm days and cool nights. I had to drive, as I was traveling with a few items that might have been hard to explain to TSA. The lock-picking tools might get through in checked luggage and maybe the KA-BAR, but the garrote and the .308 with its homemade silencer would be tough to explain. I expected the lawyers would have added extra security, and had planned accordingly.

I had monitored the websites of the Kansas City newspapers and was surprised there had been no mention of the letter. Looking back, that should have been a warning, but I was too caught up in the challenge. I was even dreaming this might be my ticket into the hitman Hall of Fame.

Herschel Jackson would be the first to go. Google Earth had come through, showing me enough details for my initial reconnaissance, but there was still a need for direct eyes-on-the-ground intelligence. The humidity was oppressive. Dripping sweat blurred my vision as I crept through the low brush outside Jackson's country home—"estate" would be a better description. I'd been in place since the previous evening, positioned to review his security, and getting personally acquainted with several new species of man-eating insects. I had thought I'd planned for everything—night-vision binoculars, ghillie suit to be decorated with local flora, plus food, water and even a snipers best friend, a Traveling Man's bladder, but the insect repellant had slipped my mind. I'd have to make a note of that if this was going to be a common practice.

I couldn't slap at them or even scratch, for fear of giving myself away—that is, until something very large crept its way to my private parts. At that point, there was no longer a choice. Self-discipline and willpower only go so far. I was afraid to see what the Satan-sent creature was, but it was big enough to give an audible crunch when my exploring fingers finally trapped it and ended its miserable life.

I'd read stories where army snipers sat motionless for days behind enemy lines, gathering intelligence and waiting for that perfect shot. I hope they are well paid.

There were no motion sensors and, thank God, no dogs. A guard stood at the front door, and another made randomly timed rounds, changing course and occasionally reversing directions, always taking in his surroundings. This was not a minimum wage rental guard—he clearly knew what he was doing.

I slowly positioned myself to be ready for my assault, but he changed his pattern again, leading to one of the most intense moments of my new career. He passed behind me, where I couldn't see him. His measured pace stopped just behind me, so close I could hear his breathing. He stopped like that at times, to take in the surroundings more carefully. I was hoping this was one of those, but when he didn't move on, I prepared myself to spring into action, taking my chances against his skill. That's when I heard a familiar sound.

One of the nice things about being a guy is that the whole world is a bathroom. I've heard there are customers who pay for the "golden shower" but I have to say, it's not that great. The guy must have been a little older than he looked; his prostate was drawing the experience out far longer than I felt was necessary. He better enjoy the shake—it would be his last.

He would be target number one. The KA-BAR would be put to use the next time he passed by. From then on, things would have to go swiftly. The guards maintained radio contact. If the stationary guard noticed it had been interrupted, I would lose the element of surprise. In the movies, that doesn't change things, but I left home without my prewritten, good guy always wins at the last-moment Hollywood script to back me up.

The guard at the front door would be next, taking a round from the .308. There would be some muzzle flash, but the silencer my friend made would keep the report down to a level where it shouldn't be a concern, and Jackson should be sleeping, as I had chosen two o'clock as "G-hour."

The interior of the home might be guarded, but I hadn't seen any sign of that after a day of watching.

I rose to a standing position after the guard finished and had moved out of sight. My camouflage melded with the ragged shadow of a ragged hackberry tree. When he came by again, I didn't want to tip him off by creating a lot of noise while coming out of my ground concealment. I felt bad that I'd have to kill the two sentries. I hoped once more that they weren't simple rent-a-cops, hired for the occasion and looking forward to returning to their families at the end of their shifts. That concern was put to final rest when the perimeter guard checked in with his throat mike. He couldn't have affected a better wise-guy accent if he'd been trying out for the next episode of *The Sopranos*. His presence should have been an alarm; looking back, there were a lot of those I chose to gloss over; what would a mob goon be doing on patrol outside a Kansas City lawyer's house?

He had stopped no more than five feet in front of me, a fireplug of solid muscle, and from the way he moved, this wasn't a brainless, steroid-enhanced thug whose intimidation factor was worse than his abilities. This was a guy who appeared to have serious martial arts training.

I had cleared the ground in front of me of as many dried twigs as I could, but in the dark I had missed a few. One snapped under my foot just as I slipped out from behind my tree. His response was immediate. If he had settled into a fighting stance, it would have been all over, but he foolishly went for his gun instead. My razor-sharp knife drew across his throat, severing structures I had treated so differently in cadaver class. The knife was back in its sheath almost before he had a chance to register that anything was wrong. He sank to his knees, and I was able to lower him quietly to the ground, no alarm raised.

My rifle was outfitted with a 3-9X variable power night vision scope, but my high-tech investment wasn't needed. The second guard had failed to disable the hallway night light, silhouetting him every time he walked in front of the side lights, and he was smoking a cigarette. I'm guessing door watching hadn't been part of his normal responsibilities, with him making two rookie mistakes like that. With a whispered cough, a heavy 190-grain hollow-point bullet, loaded to subsonic velocities, was on its way. The transfer of ballistic energy was spectacular. I'd have to be careful to watch my feet going into the house—there was no point giving the police bloody footprints to help their investigation.

I stripped off the ghillie suit and made my way past the gore. The door was locked, but picking it was a simple matter. I was inside in less than three minutes. Glock in hand, I did a quick search of the ground floor. There were no additional guards. Upstairs, I found that Jackson and his wife had separate bedrooms. I've heard of that but have never understood it. You choose to spend your life with someone and then go about spending as little time together as possible. I cherish every moment I get to spend with my wife. It was his choice, I suppose, and not nearly as bad as his choice of careers was about to become, but still—

There are lots of ways to kill a person, but some methods have more impact than others. Poisoning was a relatively gentrified method, a historical favorite of female killers. A shooting or knife attack could look random or simply efficient, but a garroting sends a clear message: you fucked with the wrong guy!

The piano wire found Jackson deeply in slumber and worked its magic with amazing efficiency. I had practiced on mannequins but was still surprised by how well it worked. He thrashed a little, enough to make a mess of his bed but not enough to mount any kind of effective response or to raise an alarm.

The plan had been to move on to Belkamp early the next day, before Jackson was missed, and then to be on the road home. I had given up on the idea of a simultaneous public execution. It would have been newsworthy, but there were too many memories from the episode in Redding.

Google Earth had come through again, showing a Kansas City equivalent of the famous grassy knoll a few hundred yards away from Belkamp's front door. It would have been the perfect spot to set up for a long-distance assassination. When Belkamp left his home, my silenced Gunsite Scout Rifle would be put to use once more, and I'd be on the way home to my loving wife and expanding bank account. Unfortunately, my plans were up for a change.

I couldn't resist taking a look through Jackson's desk. He must have done a lot of work at home, as there were case files from several clients and a number of medical references on his ornate antique desk. He was doing a crash course in cardiology—make that, *had* been doing a crash course. Now, he was just decomposing.

Despite the volume of work he must have done here, the desk was compulsively neat, except for a few abstract doodles on his desktop planner. They were actually pretty good. A gold-embossed frame held a picture of his wife. A whimsical appearing fountain pen caught my eye. "David Oscarson" it said, in an impressive engraved script. I had never heard of him but there was something about the pen that led me to scoop it up as a souvenir. Maybe it was the almost reverent way it was positioned, all by itself, just to the right of center, or maybe just it was the unique look. Either way, I decided it would find a new home in Oregon.

The desk was locked, which increased my curiosity. Studying it, I realized I'd never seen anything even remotely similar. It was a thing of rare beauty, lovingly created by a long-deceased craftsman. I didn't want to damage the desk, but I wasn't about to leave without at least an attempt to see what was hidden inside. I was just about to insert my pick when I took one last look around its top. Jackson must have had great confidence in his home security, the key was in a small and intensely ornate oriental bowl, next to the picture of his wife.

The drawer opened soundlessly, another sign of this being a supremely well-made piece of furniture. A quick surveillance through the drawers showed all the comforts of home—a well-worn stack of rather unconventional porn magazines, a bottle of eighteen year old Macallan, only marginally dented, and an engraved matched tumbler and shot glass from his alma mater, proudly proclaiming his year of graduation.

A small derringer was set in a position where it would be ready for use on short notice, both .25 caliber barrels loaded. A few loose extra rounds were in a shallow partition. Wonder who he thought he was going to stop with that, a mildly agitated meter reader?

The deep lower drawer on the right had a thick organizer log, which on quick inspection changed my plans for the evening. A detailed ledger of criminal activities and names stared up at me—several of them were familiar.

I had just killed the Mafia's lawyer. Thoughts of holing up for the night and ambushing his partner in the morning, as had been my original plan, were replaced by an intense desire for self-preservation. This was a dangerous beat I was walking, and the sooner I was on the road, the better chance I'd have of seeing another Oregon sunrise.

Stacks of large-denomination bills filled the last drawer. A money laundering operation, or perhaps an insurance policy, ready for a quick escape if it became necessary. There were too many bills to fit into my bag. The logical step would have been to drop what I was doing and blaze a trail out of

Dodge, never looking back, but the potential value of the log was not lost on me. It has been a long time since anyone made the mistake of accusing Dr. Jack Hastings of having good judgment. The folder and as much of the cash as would fit disappeared into my knapsack, along with the funky ballpoint. (The pen, when I finally had the opportunity to check on it, turned out to be worth more than Aurora's engagement ring. That's a piece of trivia that will go with me to the grave.)

I set out for Belkamp's house after stopping at a twenty-four-hour box store. With the change in plans, I was in need of several items. Things were going to heat up in a few hours, and I needed to have Belkamp on ice and to be well on the road out of the state when that happened.

Belkamp must not have taken things as seriously as Jackson had. There was no sign of extra security. In fact, there was no security at all. The remote-controlled gate separating his neighborhood from the unwashed masses might count for something, but in reality, it was only enough to stop tourists, and perhaps the last of the Fuller brush men. It posed no problem for a determined hitman. I wrapped a bicycle chain lock across the opening; I needed to make sure that the last half of my evening's activities wouldn't be interrupted.

Belkamp lived alone, a common thread with malpractice lawyers in my limited research. His home was a beautiful two story colonial. It was a shame, but the safest plan would be to torch the place while he slept. I hoped there were no pets or valuable antiques or other things the world might miss.

A brief glance inside his window put me somewhat at rest. His tastes seemed to go for the modern stuff, more designed to impress other sophisticates than to reflect any real taste. Most of what I'd seen in that category wouldn't turn the world upside down if it was lost. I still laugh about the "intense, emotion-packed display of the artist's tortured life" a colleague saw in the framed self-portrait my son did in second grade. "I had no idea such emotions could come from simple paints," he had said, "and the artistic *brilliance* of not signing it reflects his sense of worthlessness! Where did you ever find this treasure?"

I placed wedges under Belkamp's doors and then lit several small fires, strategically placed around his house. The dense junipers became raging torches, sending sheets of flames clawing violently up his walls and past his roof. The bushes burned with such intensity that they created their own wind. I had planned to cover any attempt he might make at escaping out the windows, but there was no need. His security bars, positioned internally I'm sure, to comply with the neighborhood covenants, conditions and restrictions-the dreaded CC&R's we all must live by, were as effective at preventing his exit as they were at keeping intruders out. I briefly saw his panicked face as he rattled the bars inside his bedroom window, just before he was driven back by the heat. I raised my Glock, in hopes of ending his suffering, but my reactions were too slow and he disappeared just as I was pulling the trigger.

When the frustrated fire crews finally crashed through the locked gates, they were just in time to see the house collapse, crackling sparks reaching for the heavens. It was far too late for Belkamp, and I was soon on I-70 with the early morning sun shining in my rearview mirrors and *The Best of the Talking Heads* playing at a volume Zach would have approved of. It was a favorite album from my medical school days. "Psycho Killer" was up; it had never made more sense than it did today, and I grinned as I turned it up even louder.

CHAPTER FIFTY-THREE

The malpractice case itself had not gotten any real attention back home, nothing like the sensation it stirred in the Midwest, but the spectacular murder of the two prosecuting attorneys was front page material, a starving news commentator's wet-dream come to life.

The cover was indeed off. There would be no more pretenses about actuarial tables and coincidental lawyer deaths. A full-scale war was on, and the attorneys were losing. Perhaps I should schedule a repeat television interview.

"Well, Harvey, it's hard for me to admit it, but you were right." I'd look up from the floor and stare directly into the camera, white knuckles gripping the chair, anguish on my face. *"Some horribly misguided soul is out there killing malpractice lawyers and thinking he's making the world a better place.*

That's why I asked for the chance to come back. I appreciate your letting me use your show to appeal to him, to appeal to him to stop before anyone else gets hurt. Turn yourself in," I would plead, *"and get the help you desperately need."*

I wondered if I could pull it off.

CHAPTER FIFTY-FOUR

With the proceeds from Kansas City nestled in the bank and potential referrals from our secret and well-financed sponsor pouring in, I mentioned to Aurora that it might be possible to look into that sweet, low-slung ride she had been dreaming of. Coupled with the culinary treat I had planned for the evening, my stock on the home front should be rising.

It was cheesecake night, an occasional tradition that gave me great delight. I loved dessert, but my dainty wife had an aversion to 'empty' calories, so I seldom indulged my baking fantasies. Cheesecake was one exception, and of course she could demolish an entire plate of peanut butter cookies, but I was generally under strict orders to curtail the dessert portion of my cooking hobby.

I had been dreaming of a new cheesecake recipe, actually a modification of someone else's recipe, for a traditional

New York I had seen in a gourmet magazine. I planned to add a thin base layer of white chocolate ganache with coarsely chopped hazelnuts, and to modify the crust with half chocolate and half traditional grahams, swirled together to give a marbled appearance. I'd toss a dusting of freeze-dried espresso powder into the chocolate half of the crust, to give it one more personal touch.

The cream cheese was whipped, and I was frothing up the egg whites, a trick I picked up a few years back that gives the cake that fluffy, restaurant-quality loft, when I was frozen in front of the television. A Redding policeman had been brutally murdered. The chief of police was being typically closed mouthed, spouting the usual diatribe about how the guilty party would be brought to the full attention of the law …, but failing to answer any questions. An on-scene reporter, though, suggested that there had been torture. She wondered if it might be a hate crime, since the victim was Hispanic. They weren't releasing his name, pending family notification, but I could see Rick's battered pickup in the driveway.

I dropped my egg beaters in a panic. Where the hell was my cell phone? I had to warn George. Why is it that the more you need something, the harder it is to find? I hollered for Aurora, but got no response. The house was silent, save for the pounding in my chest. I crashed down the hall, half expecting to find my wife's bloodied corpse. The door to her "sanctuary" room was shut; I almost broke it off its hinges.

Aurora startled, her headphones coming off in alarm. She had been working out with a Suzanne Somers tape. Every night spent in cheesecake heaven carried a debt. There was always a week or two of self-recrimination. It looked like she was trying to get an early start.

"Rick was murdered," I said, before she had a chance to ask what was going on. "They tortured him and killed him. I need to call George but can't find my cell phone. Then we have to get out of here."

"It's in the drawer where you keep your keys and wallet; I had to do a little cleaning." She paused—"Jack, Gill is coming over to introduce his girlfriend tonight. They should be here any minute!"

Gill, our oldest son, was living in Portland, the heart of the liberal "Left Coast." He'd been talking about his new girlfriend, Amy, for months. She was as politically conservative as he was, and from his description, she practically walked on water. She had come to his attention when he saw the one bumper sticker displayed on her SUV. It was a simple: "Objectivism," a tribute to her heroine, Ayn Rand.

Amy got her elk every year, a fact Gill never seemed tired of reminding me of, and could outshoot most of his buddies. She would definitely come in handy during the zombie apocalypse, and my son was totally smitten.

"Damn!" I said. "Call him and tell him to stay away."

Aurora was clearly overwhelmed. A minute ago, she was contemplating dinner with her son and possibly the mother of her first grandchild, plus the anticipation of a new, decadent cheesecake recipe. Now I was telling her it was time to run for our lives.

"Grab a few things as fast as you can and meet me at the car. Don't waste a lot of time trying to think of everything; we'll buy the rest. We just have to get out of here."

The cell phone was right where she said it would be. I dialed George on the run to my den where I keep my Colt 1911, a beautiful piece of World War I history. It is one of the highlights of my firearms collection, and I couldn't bear the thought of losing it. Plus, even after ninety years, it still worked perfectly. The Glock 19 was in my car already, with two magazines loaded with seventeen +P hollow-points.

Hopefully, Aurora would think to grab her gun from the bedside stand. I hadn't mentioned it, but then, I wasn't certain that it would be worth taking the time. It was just a .380 and would be more likely to anger an adversary than to cause life-threatening injuries. I had little confidence in it, but she liked it because it fit her hand and had very little recoil.

The phone kept ringing, and I was about to give up when George answered. "Jack," he said breathlessly, "what's going on?"

"Get out of your house, George! You've got to go now!"

"Whoa!" he said, "can't do that."

"Someone got to Rick. I just saw it on the news!"

"Come on, Jack. It's probably some gang-bangers out to settle a score, or some—"

I interrupted his protest. "They *tortured* him, George. And it's only a few hours' drive from Redding. They could be here any minute. I don't know where we went wrong, but right now, the important thing is to find someplace safe and get holed up. Make sure no one follows you. I'll meet you behind the bowling alley, and we'll figure this out."

"Jack, are you sure this is necessary? Leesa just came over, you know, and it's been a while since I've seen her. We were just—"

"Get the hell out of there, George. Grab that .357, if you can. Get her clothes and drop her off somewhere. Promise her whatever you have to, but do it. I don't think these guys are going to be in a talking mood when they get here."

"Don't you think you're overreacting? Rick was a stand-up guy. He wouldn't have given us up."

"George, you stupid son of a bitch, you're not listening! These guys are pros. They tracked him down from halfway across the country. I don't know how, they must have some serious resources, but they did it. They *tortured* him, and they wouldn't have killed him if he hadn't given them what they were looking for."

"All right, all right." I could hear him moving about. "Leesa! Leesa! Grab your stuff. We have to get out." He was interrupted by the sound of his front door crashing in, followed moments later by Leesa's terrified scream. A sickening crash cut the scream off before its natural end.

"Oh, shit! Jack. Get over here!"

I heard his phone hit the ground and then agitated but unintelligible shouting. The boom of George's Smith & Wesson, familiar after taking him to the range, was followed by the rattle of many smaller caliber rounds.

I yelled at Aurora as I raced to my truck. It took several tries to get the key into the ignition. It was like one of those nightmares where you run and run, but never get anywhere. Finally, I hit the slot, and it started right away. Good old American engineering. I hammered the gas, not bothering to wait for the door to finish opening. Shattered pieces trailed behind me as I spun around and raced down the block. Normally, it takes a little over fifteen minutes to make the trip. I made it in half that, but it wasn't enough.

George's front door had been smashed in. Neighbors, with no sense of self-preservation, were starting to fill the street to see what the shooting was all about, providing yet another good argument against evolution.

Thick black smoke was pouring out George's upper floor windows as I leaped out of my truck, racking a round into my 1911. Three dark-suited goons raced out the front door, one supported by the others. He was holding his red-stained side and not looking very good. George must have connected at least once. Not bad against professionals like these, but if they were on the way out, he would have ultimately gotten the worst of it.

The driver reached the Crown Vic while I was still taking everything in, and I had no good line on him without putting the bystanders at risk. The others were slower, with one clearly failing, but they made it to the back door in time to get him dumped in.

The last muscle made a huge mistake. Instead of diving into the car himself, he reached for his gun. I emptied my magazine at him and then slammed home another. At the range, I'm as good as the next guy, probably better, but under stress, nothing counts more than experience, and I had none. I didn't see where most of those rounds went, probably somewhere in the backseat, but at least one squared my target, spinning him around and dropping him. The Crown Vic spun out, one tire ripping shards of flesh as it passed over his torso, spinning him around like a dog's chew toy.

The back door opened fully as they fishtailed around the corner, offering a momentary glimpse at a second form, sprawled face down on the floor, with legs elevated on the blood-stained seat. The door slammed shut as the driver snapped the car back to a straight line. They disappeared around the corner as emergency sirens started to light up the night. I fired a few more shots at its fleeing taillights and then held up, worried again about the neighbors. When the car was found the next day in an irrigation ditch outside of town, it was filled with bullet holes. Bad guy number two was found, sporting a contact wound to the forehead. Like the one left at the scene, he had no form of identification; definitely professionals.

The strobes of the first patrol car were dancing off the windows a block away, and I could hear its engine racing as I jumped in my truck and made a panicked exit. I risked a look back as I corrected out of my turn onto Washington and saw its headlights coming into view. I punched the accelerator to the floor and slid around the next corner, wiping out a fire hydrant with my rear end. Glancing in my mirrors, I expected to see the police bearing down, but somehow the street was empty. Either they hadn't seen me or they were focused on the burning house and the mutilated body on the lawn. I dropped to a safe and nearly legal residential speed and headed home to get Aurora.

The fire grew beyond all efforts. It was total incineration. The firefighters couldn't even get close enough to mount a real fight. Heat damage to neighbor's houses was limited only by the wide yards mandated by the CC&R's. I'm sure the killers had planned to torture George in hopes of finding the records I had stolen from Kansas City, but with the shooting, they'd had to settle for the next best thing and burned his place to the ground.

They'd be coming for me next and would want to discuss their missing property, just in case it hadn't disappeared in the fire. I might get a short break, as they were down two players, but with the resources they had available and the importance of what was at stake I wasn't going to count on it. I called Gill and told him to forget about the visit and to not go back to his apartment until I got in touch to tell him it was okay.

"Mom called too. What's going on?"

"You still have your concealed carry, don't you, son?"

"Yeah, Dad, I'm set. Amy is, too, but you still haven't told me what this is all about."

"It's complicated, son. I made the wrong people mad, and they want something back enough to kill for it. I'll clue you in when I can, but there are some really bad dudes out there." Did I really just say dudes? "They'll do anything to get to me, even going through you kids. I'd rather you didn't give them the chance."

"You're freaking me out, Dad, but I'll watch my back. I can stay at Amy's ranch. Her dad is one of those privacy guys. He says he'll shoot down any of those government drones that fly anywhere near his place and I'm pretty sure he has the stuff to do it. Nobody gets on his ranch without his say-so. You watch your back too, okay dad?"

"Will do. I need to meet up with Mom now and make some plans. If things don't work out, know that we both love you." I hung up before he could respond, and called Aurora.

She answered before the first ring had finished. "Jack, where are you?"

"George is dead, honey, and we've got to get going or we'll be next. I'll be home in five minutes. Be ready when I get there. I don't want to spend any more time there than we have to."

"Don't go there," she said. "I went out the back when you drove off. I grabbed my gun and ran to the Wilcox's. They're nervous about having me here but said I could stay until you arrived. Someone is going through our house. I can see them looking around. There are at least two of them, maybe more. I'm afraid to call the cops. What are we going to do?"

"Watch out the front door. I'll be right there. I'll drive by, and if it's clear, I'll call you and swing by a second time. What about Zach? Do you know where he is?"

"He's with his buddies. I called him and told him not to come home and not to talk to strangers. He accused me of treating him like a kid, but I made my point clear. He didn't know I could speak teenager."

When I picked Aurora up, I explained about the Pandora's Box I had opened. The file I stole had enough information to put away the boss and half the members of the Berlioni crime family, along with a handful of their soldiers—page after page of detailed records: murder, drug distribution, prostitutes, and bribery. It was also full of crooked cops, judges, and politicians who would be happy to do anything to help them get the records back and to keep their names out of the news. I think the file was Jackson's insurance policy. Either that, or he might have been about to double-cross them, though I doubt he was that stupid. Anyway, it was a special prosecutor's Holy Grail, and when I took the time to look more thoroughly, there were detailed banking records, including account numbers and passwords. I had killed the Cosa Nostra's lawyer and made off with their family secrets, and now they wanted an up close and personal visit.

Our world had indeed become a much smaller and more dangerous place. They would not only want their records back but revenge, something I wasn't in the least looking forward to. I had also used the information in the file to help myself to a small portion of their bankroll, adding thievery to my expanding list of sins. I wasn't greedy with my withdrawal, but retirement would no longer be a concern, and the Salvation Army will be able to help a lot more people at Christmas this year, thanks to the Berlioni's generosity.

I had counted on the Bank of Clarkenshyre's commitment to confidentiality to protect my identity when the Berlioni's went looking for their money, but with mob enforcers redecorating my living room and two of my partners dead, that probably wouldn't be an issue.

It was getting late enough in the day to be thinking of

finding a place to sleep, but in a town this size, it would be hard to get off the radar. There were only so many motels, and it wouldn't be hard for a set of determined pursuers to get through them. I've spent a lifetime here, and a busy career; half the people in town know me, not an ideal situation for a guy on the lam. The goons would also know my cars by now, and might even have my credit cards on tracer, perhaps even my cellphone. Looking at the list of high-profile contacts in the files, the advantage was definitely on their side.

"Honey," I said to Aurora, thinking of another avenue they might pursue. "Call the kids. Tell them to turn off their phones. Those things all have GPS. If they have to get in touch, have them borrow someone else's, or use a Trek phone. Tell them to send a text instead of calling. We'll check periodically, and tell them when we'll be getting our own Trek phone so we can talk more freely."

"If they get in trouble, have them give us an alert phrase. Tell them if they are being threatened or coerced to tell us how much they miss Scooter and want to see him again. If we initiate a call, it will mean we are in trouble, and they are to do the exact opposite of what we tell them to do."

I thought a minute longer. "And tell them not to use their credit or debit cards. Get as much cash as they can from an ATM, well away from where they are hiding, and then don't use them again, for anything."

We pulled into a gas station, filled the tank, and followed our own advice, maxing out our cash limit. I thought about trading cars with Maggie. She had the new "sporterized" Ford Focus. It would be a great combination—speed and handling, but still inconspicuous. Unfortunately, the trade-off could put her in danger and that was not an option I was willing to consider.

Changing license tags would be a stop-gap measure, but better than nothing. I asked Aurora to help me keep an eye out for a dimly lit alley where we could try to find one and make the switch. Her scream brought me back. A car was coming from the left, bearing down on a bull's-eye course. I had been so distracted that they would have dead-centered us if she hadn't seen it. I mashed the accelerator as I instinctively turned into their direction, partially deflecting the blow and avoiding the worst of the impact. A second later and we would have been pinned on the concrete lion guarding the library steps.

My head slammed into the window, hard enough to blur my vision and almost guarantee a headache that would make the aftermath of last year's Super Bowl party whimper in defeat, but we had survived. I regained control and sped out onto the street, pushing my engine to its extreme and wishing I had given in to my wife's sports car desires.

Greasing through red lights at full speed and dodging surprised drivers, while watching our pursuers draw up for another shot, was nothing any aspect of life could have prepared me for, not even helping Zach qualify for his driver's license. The next time I read a novel where they talk about life slowing down to a snail's pace in times of crisis, or watch a movie where the hero is making wisecracks to the beautiful heroine, deftly avoiding one disaster after another while his life is spinning out of control in a high speed death ballet, I'm going to have to call bullshit! This was going down at light speed. Reaction trumped any thoughtful planning, and there was no time for anything but survival.

There was no way we were going to outrace them, pickup trucks have their uses, but high speed evasive pursuits aren't on the list. The black Crown Vic's grill appeared as a grinning menace in my rearview mirror, Grendel salivating over his next hapless meal. The mobsters must have gotten a fleet deal on the damn things; my poor truck was seriously mismatched against their powerful sedan. They would be on our bumper in moments, set to send us into a fatal spinout.

My heart was pounding, far faster than anything my cardiology friends would have advised, and I had no idea of how I was going to get us out of this in one piece. Every corner or evasive action cost us speed—the situation was hopelessly deteriorating.

The police station was close, but even if it was possible to reach it, we'd have to crash through the window and hope for the best. The guys on our tail would never let us park in the visitor section and walk in the front door. And even if we did make it, there would be the issue of those dead lawyers. Still, a lifetime in jail sounded a better than what these guys had in store for us; I took a two-wheel sliding turn onto Anderson Boulevard. It wasn't far to Main. One more left turn there, and it would be a straight shot to the station. I hoped we could make it.

Unfortunately, as I straightened and faced Anderson, I was faced with a new nightmare—a turnabout. It had been put in place a few months ago and I had forgotten all about it.

We were done. There was no way we could stay ahead through that. I started to apologize to Aurora, when the rear window exploded in a deafening volley of gunfire. I reflexively swung into a tire-screeching series of turns, weaving lane to lane in hopes of throwing off their aim, all the while yelling for Aurora to get down out of the line of fire.

I straightened out long enough to risk a quick look to the passenger side to see if she was okay. Instead of cowering on the floor, as I had expected, Aurora was furiously trying to reload my forty-five.

"Stop doing that!" she yelled. "I'll never get them if you keep knocking me on my ass!"

Aurora had also realized how much trouble we were in. She had grabbed my 1911 and had fired out through the rear window, spidering the Crown Vic's windshield. Unfortunately, in my hurry to get away from the disaster at George's, I had failed to top off the magazine, cutting her off in mid-barrage. Have I mentioned that I loved my wife?

The unexpected bullets slowed our pursuers down enough for me to gain several car lengths. I screamed a fish-tailing left turn through a red light, just missing a Suburban with a wide-eyed housewife, and creasing an import sedan and causing it to crash into another. The bad guys were left stuck behind the chaos, unable to get through the intersection.

I made several random turns, paying no attention to where I was going, and pulled into the darkest alley I could find. My truck seemed relieved when I shut it off, protesting noises coming from under its steaming hood. The driver wasn't much better off, trembling with an adrenaline overdose of massive proportions.

We sat in silence for a few minutes, decompressing.

"We need a plan," Aurora mentioned, a deadpan look on her face as if this was an everyday occurrence.

I couldn't keep myself from laughing. "Honey, you have the most incredible grasp of the obvious."

We couldn't stay with the truck, the police or the mob would be all over us the moment we hit the streets, but we couldn't stay here for long either. One 911 call from a Good Samaritan concerned about the shot up truck and the desperate strangers inside, and it would be all over.

The solid ground felt good under our feet, providing a

moment of reassurance in an evening of chaos. I gave Aurora a brief but heartfelt hug. There was a real chance it could be our last, and I allowed it to go on a few extra moments, fully aware of the danger, but savoring it even more fully for it. Sirens screamed through the night. In the narrow confines of the alley, they seemed to be coming from all directions. One moment they would sound as if they were racing off into the night and the next, like they were coming around our corner, officers ready to pounce. Aurora and I were providing the local law enforcement with the biggest evening they'd had in years, though I doubt there would be any gratitude expressed if they managed to catch us.

The F-150's trade-in value was rapidly declining, between the shot out window, mangled rear end, and the extreme abuse I had inflicted on its engine. I think an alignment might be in order too, as I had largely disregarded the rules about curbs and potholes in my rush to get to George's house. Sadly, it was time to say good-bye.

It had been my first-ever brand new off the lot car, and had been my pride and joy. It was always parked at the vacant end of the lot, away from others who might be too careless with their doors, and was never, ever subjected to a mechanical car wash; nothing but hands-on care for my baby. She had custom fitted floor mats, and only the finest buffing chamois were allowed to touch her. Fountain drinks were strictly forbidden, despite top to bottom Armor All protection—it only lacked one thing. There were no "Dodge Sucks" or "Piss on Chevy" window stickers. I kept meaning to get one, to dress it up for the doctor's parking lot, but never seemed to get around to it. Actually, the truck lacked two things, now that I think about it, but the second wasn't going to happen as long as it was my truck.

There's something seriously wrong with a guy who saddles his vehicles with pet names. B-1 Bomber, or Love Machine, or my all-time favorite, "the Passion Wagon." Right! These would be the guys enjoying romantic Saturday evenings—with their cars.

The backseat was a maelstrom of scattered possessions, tossed with broken safety glass and a few spent .45 cases that would never make it to my reloader. I grabbed what seemed most important, the ledger and Aurora's overnight makeup bag, of course. Several boxes of ammunition went into my pockets, and then it was time to pat my truck on the bumper and wish it well for the future.

Gesturing for quiet, I signaled for Aurora to follow me out into the cooling evening. Hearing only one set of footsteps, I spun around and found myself alone. There was no sign of Aurora.

I looked around in a panic, calling out softly with no result. We'd landed in the Bermuda Triangle. There was no way she would have left without me, and the mob would never have taken her and left me alive and in possession of their file. It made no sense.

House lights were starting to come on, creating ghostly shadows, and it wouldn't be long before nervous homeowners would be looking out to see what was going on. The police wouldn't be far behind. Panic started in, again. We had come so close.

I dove behind a rusted trash can, the best cover I could find, as a car coughed to life down the alley. From the smell coming from my refuge, someone must have had a really good day fishing... last week. It was all I could do to hide there, but I couldn't bring myself to run off without looking one more time for Aurora.

With no headlights, the car headed in my direction. I shrank back as far as I could behind my foul refuge, Glock out and ready. I had no interest in shooting an innocent bystander, and hoped that simply brandishing it should keep the questions and answers to a minimum, giving me a little more time to try to figure out what to do.

The car eased around my truck and stopped in front of me. The driver's window rolled down and a beautiful face appeared out of the shadows.

"Care for a ride, sailor?"

It was the best proposition I'd had in ages, and I wasted no time in taking her up on the offer. "How did you do that?" I asked, pointing to the tangle of wires under the dash.

She seemed uncomfortable. "It's just something someone showed me a long time ago." She paused, looking into nothingness—"a very long time ago."

CHAPTER FIFTY-FIVE

The adrenaline roller coaster had taken a toll. Physically, we were spent, our bodies crying out for rest, but mentally we were in a hyper-vigilant state of alertness, functioning in pure survival mode. We were focused entirely on escape; there was no capacity for anything else. The chances of making a mistake were growing exponentially—we had to get off the streets.

Headlights came around the corner a few blocks ahead, just after we had pulled out. They were closing on our position, traveling much faster than a family coming back from an evening ice cream run would be expected to do. As the car drove under a street lamp, the only one left working on the block, it was revealed as a plainclothes police car, running silent. The two officers inside gave us the once-over as they passed. Another set of lights appeared behind us, also coming up fast.

Aurora took the next turn, giving me a brief glimpse back as the cops pulled into the alley, doors flying open as they slid to a stop. In moments, they would see that the alley was empty, and a single neuron snap would be enough to have them wondering about the car they passed—the low-rider with the two nervous looking middle-aged gringos.

"Not to appear ungrateful," I said, "but do you think you could come up with something a little faster next time you steal a car, and maybe a little less conspicuous? We really don't fit the low-rider stereotype."

Aurora was a little testy, as she came off her own adrenaline high. "You want me to take it back?" She glared over at me, only to see that I had been kidding. It took a moment, but she finally smiled. "Besides, it was a little dark in there. I couldn't see the cool paint job or the fuzzy dice until I was already in. And I kind of like it. Someone spent a lot of time loving this baby. I bet they even gave it a cute name. I've always loved that in a guy."

"Really?" I asked. "I didn't want you to think I was weird, but it almost killed me to leave my poor old Silver Beauty behind in that alley, all broken up like that and headed for the impound lot with all those criminal cars. It's just not right." I tried my best piteous look. "And to see me driving off in a Pinto with flake metal flames and a welded chain steering wheel—that must have been so hard."

I reached out, taking Aurora's hand. "If only I had known the last time I waxed her would be my last. I'd have used my best chamois. Do you think she'll ever forgive me?"

"I had no idea you were such a sentimental softy," she said, eyeing me coyly and gently placing a reassuring hand on my leg. "I would have thought all those long nights with dying patients in the ICU had hardened you, but I can see how deeply this has affected you!"

Now who was being shit-shined?

"All right, you win. Can we find someplace to ditch this thing? Every cop hoping for a promotion will be looking for it. I don't want to be their ticket up the ladder."

Neither of us knew this part of town well enough to take a chance driving around. I was about to suggest we simply abandon it, when Aurora made a hard stop, backed up, and moved into an alley by a rundown mini-mart. She pulled up beside a man sleeping next to his "Why lie? I need a beer" sign. She left the car running while she rousted him from his cereal malt slumber. A fifty-dollar bill was stuffed into his hand.

"There's another one of these for you if you'll take our car and drive it to the train station," Aurora promised, raising him to his feet. I was moving to help, but as he stood, it was obvious that the man was a shell inside his baggy clothes. They wouldn't be needing any assistance.

The wino's eyes peered eagerly out from the caves of his sunken sockets, the deep classic pumpkin-yellow jaundice made even more alarming in the car's headlights. His protuberant belly confirmed the advance of end-stage liver disease. He grasped his new treasure, doubtlessly anticipating his departure into another day of mindless bliss. Perhaps he would even buy some of the good stuff.

Ordinarily, I'm dead set against drunk drivers, having seen too often the tragic results of their bad judgment, but this might be the one exception. I didn't expect he'd get very far. He'd either pass out again or, more likely, the police would recognize the car and put an end to his journey. They could do the world's most enthusiastic body cavity search, but he'd never be able to tell them anything more than "that nice lady gave me fifty bucks." And who knows? Perhaps the police could get him dried out and give him one last chance.

With a little help from his new lady friend, our drunken friend fell in behind the wheel, gave a last smiling wave, and set out on his journey.

We wasted no time saying good-bye before setting off on our own. Foot travel wouldn't do for long. We were physically spent, and in this neighborhood, we would be easily spotted. We cut between buildings, twice having to backtrack to avoid patrols, before stumbling across a used car lot. A selection of generic sedans awaited Aurora's touch, and it didn't take long for her skills to shine again, liberating a late model Ford from a dark corner. I always like to use American products.

We drove downtown to where I could find an all-night coffee kiosk. It was a risk, but falling asleep at the wheel and dying in a fiery crash would also ruin our day. With a sixteen ounce cup of courage in hand, Aurora and I were on our way to find a No-Tell Motel in Medford, where we'd cash in our chips for the evening. That was about as far into the future as either of us could think until we got some quality sleep.

CHAPTER FIFTY-SIX

◆

There's an old saying: "You get what you pay for." We had pulled into motel where we were about to put that saying to the test. The naïve small-town doctor asked the tattooed clerk if it would be okay to pay for the room in cash, instead of a credit card. Glancing at our wedding rings, his reply was pointedly sarcastic. "I'll make a special exception to motel policy, since you seem like such a nice couple. How many *hours* would you like?"

Thirty bucks provided a room for the two of us, along with a handful of our closest friends from the insect world. After our long day, though, we weren't in the mood for conversation.

"I hope they don't mind if we just turn in early," I said to Aurora. "We can always catch up on things in the morning." I thought it was a pretty good one, but her dismayed look never wavered. She had lost her sense of humor the moment we had stepped into the room.

With the absence of a functioning lock, a chair was placed under the doorknob. We double-checked to make sure that our magazines were full, more concerned with the local environment than our organized crime enemies, and we were soon dead to the world.

I had been worried that the caffeine, the adrenaline, and the uncomfortable bed would make it hard to fall asleep. The couple next door didn't help. They were getting the most from their thirty bucks, and their enthusiastic sounds weren't muffled by the poorly constructed walls, but exhaustion won. The next thing I knew, the sun was pouring in, and a new day had begun.

We awakened to sweltering bites, having provided a convenient midnight snack for our roommates. They probably weren't used to having people stay for the whole night and had taken full advantage of the situation. Either that or they really were upset at our lack of civility the night before.

Aurora had some unidentifiable science fiction creature locked in her hair. It's hooked feet were almost impossible to get untangled, and its vicious looking pinchers were doing their best to make an impression on my ring finger. As I was working to get this fresh creation from Hell out of her hair, Aurora was intensely scratching herself in a most unladylike manner.

"The best way to be sure you're rid of all the creepy-crawlies would be for me to help you in the shower," I said. "You know, for a detailed cleaning and inspection."

"You are so generous," she responded. "Always thinking of someone else, aren't you? It's like living with Albert Schweitzer and Mother Teresa at the same time!"

"Empathy is an important part of being a doctor," I replied, happy that she had gotten back at least some of her wit. "I'm only thinking about your wellbeing."

"Thanks for the kind consideration, but I'm perfectly capable of handling this on my own—been doing it for a lot of years. Why don't you check in with the boys?"

She called me back a moment later, but my hopeful anticipation faded when I saw the concerned look on her face.

"What is that?" she asked, pointing to a stain on the ceiling.

It looked like someone had used the shower for their final solution. The forensic clean-up crew had been less than thorough, with what looked like small bits of tissue still in the corners.

"Looks like mold staining," I replied. "You know how much more moisture is on this side of the mountains."

"Thanks," she said. "You don't want to know what I thought it was."

I glanced one more time back into the shower. The soap had been left partially used by the last guest (or guests?), and there was an unpleasant smell coming up from the drain.

"I don't think I'll be very long," she said. "Why don't you check with the boys?

Zach was staying with his friend Ben. I'd never hit it off with him, though I'm not sure why. There was just something indefinable there that made me wonder. His folks were okay, so no worries there. Their politics were a little off, and there was a rumor that they had turned vegetarian, but there were no human sacrifices or anything. I was grateful they were letting Zack stay.

"Hey, Ben, it's Jack. How's it going? Can I speak to Zach?"

"Hey, Doc. Zach's not here. He went to the house this morning to get *Warzone III*. I've wanted to try it forever, but he hasn't gotten back. I did just get a weird text, though. Said to tell you he really misses Scooter. Didn't he die, like, a long time ago?" but I was already hanging up before he could finish the question.

I barged into the bathroom to find an indignant wife. "Didn't I tell you I could handle this alone? She saw my face and stopped. "What's wrong? What happened?"

"They got Zach," I said.

The color drained from her face. Her knees buckled, and I had to catch her to keep her from hitting the floor.

There was a moment's pause, then a shrill "you bastard!" She slapped my face, but there was no strength in it. "None of this would be happening if you hadn't started killing those damn lawyers!"

I pulled her in close. "They won't hurt him as long as we have what they want." I hoped that I projected more confidence than I felt.

I turned on my cell phone and found a text from Zach, timed earlier this morning. "Dad, my car broke down and I need a ride. Can you pick me up at the house? I left a message with Ben, too. Did you get it?"

Message received, loud and clear. "Sorry, son," I texted, "I can't come get you. Your mom and I went out of town and may not be back for a while. Can you get a ride with someone else?"

The reply came as a phone call, almost immediately. "Hey, asshole, I'm gonna kill your boy. He'll be glad for it by the time I'm done with him. You'll get to see the video just before I cut your balls off and stuff them down your throat!"

Apparently, they didn't teach the up-and-coming mobsters new insults. I'd been threatened with that one a dozen times since junior high, though now was probably not the best time to be trading insults.

"I think I know what you want," I said. "Let's see if we can work something out so we all go home happy."

"Bring it by your house and you get the boy back. I might even let you live, but don't try nuthin'. We can tell if you photocopy the file. If you do, I'll kill you and your wife and your kids and every fucking Hastings I can find in the phone book. We clear on that, asshole?"

This guy must have had a terribly unhappy childhood.

"Gotcha. No photocopies, no funny stuff."

"Just be there in half an hour, and bring the money you stole."

I'd be willing to bet the money would never make it back to his boss. "Whose name should I put on the check? There's no way I'll get my hands on that kind of cash on short notice, and I'm not even in town—thought it might be safer to spend the night in a different ZIP code. I can be back and have the money by tomorrow afternoon, Wednesday at the latest, and you can have it all. I just want my son back."

"We need to meet some place a little more private than my house, though. The cops are looking all over for me, and neither one of us wants me sitting in a chair downtown having doughnuts with southern Oregon's finest. Pick a spot out in the country, somewhere I can see that you didn't bring an army, and we'll get this done."

I could imagine the wheels turning in his mind. He wouldn't know the area, and there was no way he'd be able to pick a suitable location. "You name the spot," he finally said, "but remember, I don't mess around. You get one chance."

"There's a good place where I used to pick mushrooms, half way to Giles." Giles was a 'close the shops by nine' spot in the road, one of those towns where you have to wonder why it was ever founded. No Starbucks, not even a place to get a Big Mac. The post office was a window in the back of the grocery store, and the only recent development I'm aware of was the super sidewalk paralleling the highway, generously funded by federal "stimulus" dollars to ensure 'economic prosperity' for the nation. It was easily six feet wide, the nicest sidewalk I'd ever seen, and connected two empty lots at opposite ends of town. Construction kept a crew of workers employed for almost a week. The regional economy is still waiting for the promised ripple effect, though I'm sure it's coming.

"There's a graffiti-covered rock on the right side of the 56 highway. It's about fifteen miles east toward Giles. There's a road going north from there up to an old gravel pit. Meet me there tomorrow evening at five, just you and Zach."

"Bring that beautiful wife, but if I see anyone else, your kid dies."

"Yeah, I get it. Let's just get this thing done so we can have our lives back."

Demanding that Aurora come along was an obvious tell. There could only be one reason to have her there, and it had nothing to do with her radiant beauty. The time had come to go on the offensive. It was time to play "Who Wants to Survive the Mob," and I was about to use my phone-a-friend option.

My fishing buddy Brad is a good person to have on your side. We used to hunt elk together, but he switched from rifles to bows to up the challenge. He'd lived his life in the woods, and thought like the animals. Even after changing to archery, a much more difficult sport, there was an elk in his freezer every year. I managed to carry hundreds of pounds of his venison out of the hills, but like most hunters, I never filled my own tag.

His archery prowess was legendary. Every year, he dominated the national and even international competitions. In some sports, when an athlete rises to the top, his jersey is retired. With Brad, they retired his event. No one was willing to compete if he was on the roster.

Put a shotgun or a rifle in his hands, and the results were similar. We hunted ground squirrels together, eliminating tens of thousands of the crop-eating vermin. The first time we got together for a squeak shoot, I gave him a ration, not realizing just how seriously he took the sport. His CZ .204, a beautiful piece of finely fitted walnut art, had been painted over in camo. He had paid the necessary federal fees to attach a silencer and had a ridiculously high power scope, something I'd have expected to see on a military sniper rifle, not on the edge of an Oregon alfalfa field on a cloudy April morning.

I brought a few hundred rounds for my .17 HMR, a rim fire caliber of fairly recent development. I was terribly proud of the rifle; it had devastating effects and accuracy out to about a hundred fifty yards, a huge advantage over the .22s most squirrel hunters used. Brad brought a thousand hand loaded hollow point .204 rounds, dialed in for pinpoint accuracy out to three or four hundred yards, and another five hundred rounds, loaded differently for his back up rifle.

"What?" I asked. "Are you going to declare war on the damn things?"

He smiled and set to work. At the end of the day, his body count was easily triple mine—the squirrels never knew what hit them. He even had two coyotes and a badger.

"So, dude," I said, pointing to his rifle as we were packing up for the trip home. "Where do you get one of those?"

I had another friend I could call if Brad wasn't around. Actually, there were several others, all who would be happy to help, and all most capable of getting the job done. One, in fact, was the type who could fit that old cliché about being your worst nightmare, easily topping the two-eighty mark and as steadfast a friend as could be found, but the long-range marksmanship Brad could provide seemed like the best resource for what I had in mind. I held my breath as his phone rang.

"Hello?"

"Brad, its Jack. How's it hangin'?"

"Hey, Doc, low and a little to the left. I'm hearing a lot of things these days; you're the man of the hour. The cops were chilling everyone at work last night, trying to get a line on where you might be hiding. They've driven past my house every half hour or so, in cleverly unmarked cars—it's adorable. Someone must have let on that you and I hang out once in a while. What's going on?"

"I'm in some deep shit, my friend, deeper than anything you can imagine. I could really use a hand. Are you going to be around this afternoon?"

"Whatever you need, Jack. Meet me where we used to chase the girls, back in high school. I'll be there in an hour."

I'd forgotten about those days, and treated myself to a moment of reminiscing.

"Make it an hour and a half. Aurora and I holed up out of town last night, and it will take a while to get back."

CHAPTER FIFTY-SEVEN

A natural hot spring lay nestled in a box canyon on his grand-father's ranch, secluded and known to only a few of Brad's closest friends. Many a winter evening was spent watching snowflakes commit suicide in the gently steaming water. The natural spa had amazing aphrodisiac properties, especially that unforgettable evening when the aurora borealis treated us to an incredible light show. While the other high school hope-fuls pumped iron and spent their money on expensive cars, Brad and a few of his select friends, me included, had only to get a date to the water and the rest was taken care of. It was as close to a sure thing as can be had without resorting to illicit chemicals.

Even after all the years since my last pilgrimage, the gate lock combination flew off my fingers. Muscle memory—it never forgets. My mind was a different story, however. Had I ever taken Aurora on a hot-spring date? This could get a little awkward if Brad said the wrong thing. I'd just have to hope he had the brains to not spend the evening reminiscing about our old aquatic adventures.

He was minutes behind us. He didn't ask questions, but I felt obligated to give him a short summary. I didn't have to ask if he would help; he would have been insulted if I had. Instead, I went to work going over my plan. There was no way these animals were going to let us live, and I expected they were at the site now, planning their ambush.

There was a perfect vantage point about a football field away from the rendezvous sight, just to the west. There was a shallow dip in the basalt, polished by generations of amorous teenagers who weren't lucky enough to have a friend with a natural hot spring. Racy petroglyphs suggested that modern day high school students weren't the first to recognize the spot's potential. It was a perfect lover's lane, with great views, but stacks of boulders conveniently isolating it from outside eyes. It also offered perfect concealment for a Mafia sniper, with a good elevation advantage and a clear line of fire to where we would be meeting.

They wouldn't realize that I knew the area well and would be expecting them to use it. Another couple hundred yards farther out, there was a rocky ridge line where friends and I used to play paintball and hunt mule deer. It offered a bird's-eye view of the basin and was an ideal counter-sniper position. Brad would be set up hours before the meeting, ready to back me up when things started going south. With the early evening hour, the sun would be immediately behind him and there would be little chance of his being spotted, and at that range, his rifle was still shooting on a vertical zero. With a target substantially bigger than a ground squirrel, he would consider this a chip shot.

I asked him if he saw any holes in the plan or had other suggestions, but he had none.

"There won't be any opportunity for communication," I told him. "No wires or mikes. You'll have to use your own discretion. If you see a threat developing, take it out. If I get the chance, I'll drop to the ground, but if I don't, take the shot anyway. There's no way I'm going to let them hurt my family."

The rest of the day was spent gathering supplies. I bought a cheap locking briefcase at a second-hand store and stuffed it with bundles of newspaper, topped with layer of hundred dollar bills. The Salvation Army Thrift Store supplied loose fitting, baggy clothes for Aurora. They would make her a bigger target, in case the exchange devolved into a shooting war. It might be enough to draw their aim off the vital zones, giving her a little better chance. A concealment holster for my Glock completed my ensemble, and we were ready.

I would have loved to make reservations at our favorite restaurant. It would have been a nice way to finish the evening, possibly our last together, but an appearance in the public eye was not in our best interest. I suggested we spend the night back at the hot springs, talk about the past and see what came up, but she had other ideas. We drove back to Medford where we upgraded to a forty-dollar room. Aurora was pleased to find a virgin bar of soap and a working door lock. I was pleased to see no human remains on the ceiling. The insect population was also much more civilized—wealth does have its privileges.

CHAPTER FIFTY-EIGHT

We showed up for the rendezvous fashionably late, finding the mafia had arrived in two cars. They must have run out of fresh Crown Vics, as their second ride looked like it came from the airport rental car lot.

"You were supposed to come alone," I mentioned, as I pulled up next to the driver. He was the same one I had seen at George's.

"I lied," he said, catching me completely off guard and drilling my nose with a smashing right. "That's for my brother, asshole. You got him with a lucky shot. Our dad had a heart attack when I told him that some numb-nut doctor had killed him. Sammy was always his favorite. He'll probably kill *me* when I get back."

"Sorry for your loss," I sputtered. "Where's my son?"

He motioned to the other car. A battered and bruised

Zack was pulled out of the backseat by an acne-scarred goon, even bigger than the one who broke my nose, and definitely uglier. The fancy suit did nothing to lessen the effect. He had no neck, and his biceps were the size of telephone poles. Steroids are such a wonder. The gonadal shrinkage probably helps with the ladies, too, possibly explaining the constant bad mood I was picking up from these guys.

"Where's my fucking records, asshole?"

As the tears slowly drained from my eyes, I looked around to see if there were any other obvious threats. Seeing none, I stepped out and dragged the backpack from the passenger seat. Zach's captor had what looked like an Uzi or MP-5. I'm no expert, but I could easily anticipate the result if he let a burst loose in my direction. He kept it centered on my chest as I reached into the bag.

"Whoa, easy, mate! I'm just going for your stuff. Every-thing's there. I'll set it down, and it's yours. My wife is in the backseat with the money and you'll get that, too."

I noted his glimpse up at the lover's lane before he approached the backpack; subtle, but it confirmed my suspi-cions. He backed up and stepped to the side before examining the contents, obviously aware that his colleague's well-placed shot might go right through a puny target like me, and carry on in search of another victim.

"No photocopies or tricks, like you mentioned. Give me my son, you get the cash, and we go our separate ways."

CHAPTER FIFTY-NINE

Just like Jack expected, Brad thought, looking through his scope. *Only one group is going home today.* Unfortunately for the mob, it wouldn't be them. They had seriously underestimated their opponent's resourcefulness. The would-be sharpshooter was sighting down his rifle, ready to fire. He had never checked his backside, though, and hadn't even dressed to take advantage of the concealment offered by the rocks. They had brought an amateur. Thinking that they had the upper hand was a fatal error; there would be no second chances.

Force times mass. Even a light thirty-two grain bullet carries tremendous energy when it leaves the muzzle at over four thousand feet per second. The sound of the slug shattering the sniper's skull was louder than the muted report of Brad's silenced rifle. He slumped down behind his parapet, leaving a glistening red trail.

One for the vultures, Brad thought as he racked a fresh round into the chamber.

Brad immediately shifted his attention to the ransom sight. The ugly soldier with the submachine gun had heard the unnatural exploding sound and had gone on alert, eyes rapidly scanning. He was far more the professional than the late sniper. He would have to be the next target.

Zach unfortunately chose the wrong time to climb back to his feet, standing between Brad and his guard. It left a limited window, far too small for a comfortable shot, Brad thought. There was no way he was going to take that chance.

Satisfied with the ledger, the surviving Berlioni son looked me in the eye with a triumphant smile and pulled a handkerchief from his pocket. Confused at the lack of response, he shook it back and forth, as if he was trying to unfold it before blowing his nose. His 'checkmate' look slowly faded as he looked up once more into the rocks, no subtlety this time. Fighting panic, he dove to the ground, rolling toward the shelter of my car. The thug with Zach brought his sub-gun to a firing position, ready to strafe me into oblivion, when a silenced round punched through the window of his car, distracting him. He moved to the side and looked up, trying to isolate the source—it was the last thing he ever did. A third eye suddenly appeared in his forehead, and he retired from his life of crime.

I pulled my Glock from its ankle holster and found myself engaged in a standoff, stalemated across the car. There was no way Brad would have a shot. Getting us out of this would be purely up to me. Unfortunately, I had no idea how I was going to do that. I couldn't run, my fleeing back would be an easy target, and Aurora was stranded in the back seat. I couldn't leave her, even if I did have a clean escape.

Berlioni would soon realize my predicament. If I didn't figure a way to get Aurora out, he would put her into play as a hostage. I reached around the cover of my wheel, firing blindly under the car, and then lunged for the back door.

Aurora bailed out as soon as soon as she saw the door start opening. It knocked me off balance just as the window exploded in my face. Berlioni had recovered faster than I would have expected, and had taken the opportunity of the few moments it took me to move to the back of the car to get into a firing position. I fired back under the car door as I fell, more out of reflex than not, but it forced him back into cover.

Aurora was doing her best to get the briefcase out of the car. What was she thinking?

"Run to Brad," I yelled. "Leave the damn money and get to the rocks!"

I think she was partially in shock but finally realized the money wasn't worth her life and took off. Grateful for my high-capacity magazine, I fired through the windows to keep Berlioni down while I watched her sprint for the hills.

Peering under the car again, I caught a glimpse of a leg. I fired two shots as rapidly as I could regain my bead. Berlioni howled in pain, collapsing as the first bullet shattered his ankle. I fired twice more before my slide locked back. I heard the sound of one of my rounds hitting flesh, and risked a look. Berlioni was bleeding from his midsection. I had scored a direct, and sure to be fatal hit.

Creeping slowly around the car, I found him still alive. He was gasping for air as he tried to replace his spent magazine with a fresh one. Dropping it from his trembling fingers, he tried placing it one more time and then stopped, his formerly hard eyes squinting in agony as he looked up, confronting his failure.

"Go ahead, and do it," he wheezed. "My dad would kill me anyway. He always said I'd never be as good as Sammy. Guess he was right—just make it quick."

If I waited, there would be no option. He was fading fast, arterial blood rising between the fingers which he now clutched over his wound. I thought of George and his girl-friend, Leesa, and especially Rick, tortured to death in his home, as I sighted down the barrel, preparing myself to deliver the coup de grace. My finger was tightening on the trigger when Zach came around the car.

"Dad, what are you doing?"

There was no way I was going to let my youngest son watch me execute this guy, no matter how much I wanted to do it.

"Just making sure he doesn't go for his gun, son," I said, kicking it away from where Berlioni might be able to reach it if he got a miraculous second wind. "You can't trust these guys. They're all killers."

With his gun out of the picture, I was making a show of tying him up, not terribly gently, when things went to hell, again.

"Dad?" Zach said, pointing, alarmed.

Aurora was being held by a third man. He had a gun pressed to the side of her head and they were doing an awkward two-step towards the rental car. I circled around to cut him off, hoping to give Brad a chance, though I knew he'd never take such a risky shot.

"Take it easy," I said. "We've got you outnumbered. There's no way you're getting out of here with my wife, and if she gets hurt, even a little, you'd better put the next bullet in your brain, or you will be the sorriest dying man this desert has ever seen."

"Listen," he said. "The cops are going to be coming before long. Somebody had to hear all that shooting. We both want to be out of here when that happens."

He waived at the two on the ground. "These guys mean nothing to me. They called up and said they were down a few men for a job. All I had to do was to sit in that hole and then come out when the shooting started. I didn't even want to do it, but my boss said he owed the Berlioni's a favor, you know. It's not like I get much of a choice here."

I had wondered how he got past Brad's attention. The hole was cleverly camouflaged, like a goose blind, except this time I was the goose. This whole scenario could very easily have gone the other way if this guy had been more committed to the cause.

"Drop your gun and let her go," I said. "I'll tell my guys in the hills to stand down. I'm a man of my word, and it's like you pointed out, you didn't have much of a choice here. You can still get out of this alive."

He decided to be smarter than a fifth grader and took the offer without further argument. I waved Brad off and waited until the hired muscle was starting down the road before heading out. I left the stolen car for return to its rightful owners, with a few bucks to repair the bullet holes. The Crown Vic would be faster, and its owners would have no further use for it.

Chapter Sixty

As easy as it seems to be to get into our country, you would think getting out would also be easy. Perhaps that would ordinarily be, but with every law enforcement officer hoping to be the one to track me down, that was not turning out to be the case. Every nightly news show had my picture, and snatches of Harvey Nash's interview were endlessly re-broadcast on network TV, giving him the national exposure he had so longed for.

My e-mail was filled to overflowing. No one dared to say it publicly, but good wishes were coming in from all over the country—mainly from doctors, but a few others, too; a handful even identified themselves as police officers. Over and over, there were variations of the same story. Ruined careers and unfulfilled dreams of homicidal revenge, always reigned in but never forgotten. Physicians across the country offered shelter or to make contributions to my defense, and as I was going through them, responding where I could, I finally got the idea for that book I've always wanted to write.

There were several near misses with the law, not to mention the drama of separating Zach from the only life he had ever known. I was treated to a wallet-size picture of his latest at least ten times a day. "She's the best girlfriend I've ever had, Dad, and you're dragging me out of the country! I'll never find another one like her. You guys suck!"

Between that and the constant nagging of the car's computer, I'd finally had enough. It didn't seem to understand that the routes it chose had to be constantly modified to avoid road blocks and major population centers. We stopped at an Internet café, where I pulled up the official tourism site for our new home. The Maldives don't have an extradition treaty with the United States, and after a few minutes of Zach's viewing their white sand beaches and turquoise waters, resplendent with well-tanned beauties, and what's-her-name, the best girlfriend ever, became a thing of the past.

Finances were becoming a problem. Everything is much more expensive when you're on the run. I had over a million dollars in my Channel Islands account, courtesy of the Berlioni's, but no way of getting it. I was just about to invest our last few dollars on lottery tickets, when I checked my phone messages one last time before throwing out the phone. I was tired of deleting pleas from the sheriff, who kept appealing to our past friendship as a reason to turn myself in. You'd think they'd be happy enough with the UPS delivery I sent. The entire Berlioni family would be taking a long federal vacation, at least the ones who were still alive. I'd done law enforcement a huge favor. Couldn't they look the other way for a bit?

There was a message from Harvey Nash, thanking me for rocketing him to stardom. He was doing *Good Morning, America* next week and was thinking of writing a true crime story, promising to put me in a good light in return for my cooperation—"call me, Jack!"

The call that made my day came from another high school classmate, Dick Newcastle. Dick had changed his last name from Rambotthaum, for obvious reasons. High school hadn't been very nice to him. He had excelled at debate, earning statewide recognition his freshman year, an almost unheard of honor. By his junior year, he had achieved the highest award in the sport. The bleachers almost collapsed when they called Dick Rambotthaum out to get his master debater award.

He graduated near the top of his law school class but stayed on the good side. I respected him tremendously. He had turned down numerous lucrative offers, choosing instead to earn a modest but honest living instead of freeing intoxicated drivers from the consequences of their actions, or defending habitual criminals. The morals of the grandmother who raised him had taken deep roots.

Dick's message said it was vital that I give him a call. Aurora thought it might be a setup, but I trusted him. He'd dated my younger sister for almost a year and had come to several backyard barbeque parties we had thrown. He had remained a good friend and confidant; I couldn't picture him throwing me under the bus.

"Dick? It's Jack. I got your message. What's going on?"

"Hey, Jack. Sorry to hear all your troubles, but I have something for you. First, though, you'll have to hire me as your attorney. That way I have to work in your best interest and keep everything you say confidential— we'll both be protected. Don't worry, though, I work cheap."

"Done, but I've got to tell you, I'm kind of strapped at this point. They froze my accounts, and my cash reserves are going down faster than Ellen Jones at football camp that one summer. Running from the law is really expensive!"

"Problem solved. I represented George, and am in charge of his estate. It's fairly sizable. He came by the office a few weeks ago and changed his will to leave everything to you. He anticipated that there might be trouble and specified that everything be immediately liquidated upon his death. I have a pretty fair sum of cash for you, sitting in my safe. My commission is 15 percent, as he specified, and I have already taken that out."

"How much did he leave me?"

"How big is your suitcase?"

We arranged a meeting in Reno. It had to be close to home, within driving distance, as flying with a bag packed with almost a million dollars would gather all sorts of the wrong kind of attention. Dick mentioned that there would have been more, but with time pressure, he had to sell things at fire-sale prices. There were a few items remaining—his pistol, grips burned off but still functional, and a set of golf clubs that had somehow escaped the fire. I told him to keep them as mementos. The insurance company was balking on the house, as it was an obvious case of arson, but he was working on that and expected a settlement check in the next few months.

Aurora insisted we survey the park where the drop would happen. She was not as trusting as I was. We saw no sign of law enforcement, though, and the handoff went smoothly. Dick asked me to pass his regards on to my sister, which I readily agreed to do.

"He was a good man, wasn't he?" Dick asked.

"Yeah," I answered, "the best."

With a late-model sedan, legitimately purchased for a refreshing change, Aurora, Zach and I set out for Key West. We enjoyed a first-hand view of America's back roads on the way, stopping for a quick photo at the world's largest ball of twine; believe it or not, it's actually real. We resisted the temptation of the Button Museum and the UFO Welcome Center. Each had its proponents in the family, but South Carolina was just a little too far off track.

Key West was beautiful, but with our faces all over the news, we didn't feel it would be safe to enjoy it. A smuggler's ship, arranged at great cost and risk, got us to Cuba in the dead of night, and from there it was a flight to Dubai and then on to our new tropical home in the Maldives.

Chapter Sixty-one

Aurora fell in love with our new life. Her enthusiastic energy and youthful good looks made the steady parade of Zach's new "best ever" girlfriends pale in comparison. She loved her position as the editor in chief for my successful new writing career, under the pen name Ricardo George, and became a terror on the island, driving her restored Jaguar Roadster at breakneck speeds, hair flying in the wind.

The locals welcomed the new restaurateur, raving about his cheesecakes and delighting in his stand-up humor, and how he made every meal a total dining experience. Yesterday, a diner left a Cincinnati newspaper on the bar, thumb-nailed over to the local news section. A well-known malpractice lawyer had been electrocuted. The authorities were wondering how someone smart enough to make it through law school would be stupid enough to try to dry his hair while soaking in the hot tub.

Be careful out there, my friends …

ABOUT THE AUTHOR

Sean Dow is a practicing pulmonary and critical-care physician, living in Las Vegas, Nevada. He was born in Iowa City and raised in Kansas. He graduated from the University of Kansas School of Medicine in Wichita, Kansas, where he also did his residency. He completed his sub-specialty training in Tucson, Arizona, at the University of Arizona College of Medicine.

After graduation, he started a fulfilling solo practice in Klamath Falls, Oregon. When not seeing patients, he fell in love with the endless outdoor opportunities of the Northwest—fly fishing, rock and gemstone hunting, and stalking the wild mushrooms of the Cascades. He also developed a fascination for cooking, often spending days preparing special meals.

Writing has been a lifelong dream for Dr. Dow, and in 2011, he finally started the novel that had been yearning to get out but which had fallen prey to a busy schedule and to the willing trout, so eager to rise to his dry flies. *Debridement* reflects the anguish physicians feel when served with a lawsuit and the dream felt by so many of leveling the tables against an adversary that plays by its own rules.

Many have asked if *Debridement* is an autobiographical novel. That, my friend, is a question best left to the reader's imagination.